DEATH OF
A ROUGHNECK

MURDER, MYSTERY AND
MAYHEM IN SHERWOOD FOREST

LINDA STEVENSON

Dedicated to my darling sister
Glenys Rhonda Castledine
1950-2020

CONTENTS

ACKNOWLEDGEMENTS

Thanks go to family and friends who encouraged me to write this book and read through the various drafts during the Covid-19 lockdown, especially my 'writing buddy' Rachel (Rae) Reynolds who inspired me to follow in her footsteps to put pen to paper.

Thanks also to Samuel Stevenson for the painting used on the front cover.

Although the inhabitants of a small village in Nottinghamshire were far away from the drama unfolding on the world's stage, they were destined to become witnesses to events that would alter the course of the Second World War.

The local land army girls couldn't hide their excitement when the Yanks arrived to make a movie and waited with bated breath for a glimpse of John Wayne. Secrets and lies were fuelling the local gossip, destroying the peace and quiet of the countryside. What were the Americans doing in Dukes Wood and where was John Wayne? When a murder was committed it would need all the ingenuity of the local police force to crack the case; who was lying and why, and was it a domestic crime or something more sinister?

Inspector Green, brought out of retirement to investigate, and hapless PC Hopkins, were on the case, but were they up to the task of sifting through the lies and fantasy to get to the truth?

CHAPTER 1

November 1938, Cambridge

Marcus Johnson sat in his favourite armchair in his rooms at Cambridge University. It had been a long and tiring day; the academic year was underway and he had spent the day marking the undergraduates' papers. He was now relaxing with a well-deserved glass of 10-year-old malt whiskey and listening to his recording of Beethoven's Moonlight Sonata. He sat back in his comfortable armchair and closed his eyes, enjoying the soothing music, but not for long; his peace was disturbed by a knock on his door.

'Are you there, Marcus?' The voice of a fellow Don, Frederick Weber, disturbed his reverie. Reluctantly Marcus rose to answer the door.

'Hello Frederick, what brings you here at this time of night?'

'Have you heard the news from Germany? It's starting. The Nazis have been attacking Jewish businesses, the papers are calling it the Night of the Broken Glass. It looks like there's going to be international reprisals, perhaps it's time to mobilise our contacts. If war breaks out, we need to be prepared.' Frederick, who was usually laid back, was looking animated with an air of excitement about him.

'Calm yourself, Fredrick dear boy, there's no need for us to do anything at the moment, we'll continue to maintain a watching brief for the time being and wait for orders. Our time will come, but at the moment we don't want to risk exposure by acting hastily. Let me get you a glass of whiskey, it will calm your nerves.'

'Thank you, I could do with a drink,' replied Frederick, who had taken a seat by the open fire. 'It's so cold outside, I wouldn't be surprised if we have snow before Christmas.' Dr Frederick Weber was a scholarly looking young man who seemingly had a permanently worried expression on his face. He had poor eyesight and wore spectacles with milk-bottomed lenses which magnified his eyes and he had a habit of regularly pushing them up to the bridge of his nose. He had been at Cambridge for 10 years having started out as an undergraduate, slowly progressing through academia to his current position as a tutor, under the supervision of Marcus, in the Political Science department.

Marcus poured out a generous glass of whiskey. 'I'm glad you've called round tonight, there's something I wanted to talk to you about. One of my undergraduates is a potential recruit. Have a look at this essay I've just been marking. I think you'll agree, there are some radical opinions.'

Frederick put on his reading glasses and absorbed the sentiments expressed in the essay. 'I see what you mean, an undergraduate with a German father and an admirer of Hitler's, it's quite a find. Have you looked at the personnel file?'

'Of course, I always do my research before approaching the student to offer them a place in our organisation. The father was a war hero apparently killed on the Somme in 1916 so it's not surprising the essay is pro-Germany. I like to give my students the opportunity to reveal their political leanings under the guise of a hypothetical scenario about world politics.'

'You crafty old fox, I wondered how you found suitable recruits. I suppose you'll discuss the political situation further during the tutorials.'

Marcus smiled and poured himself another whiskey. 'Already have, dear boy. Can I tempt you to a top-up?'

Frederick assented and the two men settled in for a long night of philosophical discussion. 'Who is the undergraduate? Do I know him?'

'Now Frederick, you know better than that. For your own safety I never reveal the names of recruits to our group of merry men. After all, you wouldn't want your name bandied around the hallow halls of Cambridge, would you? The less anyone knows, the safer it is for us all. I've got 60 students graduating next year and am happy to say two of them will be placed in key positions at Whitehall. After all, being a "loyal" civil servant as well as a member of our group of merry men are not mutually exclusive positions. With my contacts, a word in the right ear, and a little adjusting to the final examination marks they'll be seen as potential high flyers and become assets to our cause.'

He raised his glass. 'Lasst uns einen Toast machen!'

Frederic raised his glass. 'Prost.'

The rest of the evening passed pleasantly with both Dons discussing their respective research projects and swopping university gossip. Marcus had been recruited to the underground group when he himself had been an undergraduate. Although not widely known, there was a thriving community set up following the First World War of pro-Nazi sympathisers who agreed with Hitler's stance against the Jewish influence in Germany. In his current position in the secret organisation he was able to identify potential recruits but the final say was from another colleague at the university who had direct links to the intelligence services in Germany.

Marcus was born in 1887 to a respectable middle-class family in Rickmansworth near London. An excellent scholar, he attended a minor public school before going on to study Classics at Cambridge University. At the outbreak of the First World War he became a conscientious objector, a stance that alienated him from his conservative parents who believed in everyone doing their duty for God and the King. At the time he was completing his Doctorate and he'd gravitated towards like-minded scholars who were also opposed to the war effort. In later years he observed how the allies treated the Germans after their defeat had contributed to the collapse of the German economy. This strengthened his resolve to support Hitler and the rise of the Third Reich and hardened his heart towards the country of his birth.

By 1938 he was working as a respected Cambridge Don, spending much of his time doing research and moulding the minds of impressionable undergraduates. Having been recruited himself when on a field trip to Germany to study the effects of the First World War defeat on their political system, he had become a great admirer of the up-and-coming dictator, Adolf Hitler, and was happy to seek out other admirers of the dictator to join an underground network of spies.

As the evening drew to a close Frederick said his goodbyes and returned to his humble quarters. He was keen to support the cause in any way he could. Walking home, he speculated on the identity of the new recruits. There were a few candidates amongst the students in the Political Science department. After all, it was fashionable for young people to criticise the British establishment but he knew most of them would rush to enlist if the current crisis resulted in war against Germany. Finding those who truly believed in the superiority of the Aryan race was not an easy task but Frederick had faith in the ability of his mentor, Marcus, to find new recruits and build the spy network ready for the inevitability of a second world war. He wanted to be on the winning side.

It was a frosty night, and on his walk home he speculated on the events of earlier and wondered whether he should do more to show his allegiance to the Führer instead of burying himself in books and ideology.

He had recently completed his Doctorate and as a Fellow of the university he was undertaking his own research project. If war did break out, he knew which side he was on and was ready and willing to do his bit to spread the Nazi doctrine, but Marcus was right, he needed to bide his time and take a lead from his mentor.

Frederick's own doctorate thesis was a study of Hitler and his rise to prominence following the Great War. It was Hitler's belief that the Germans lost World War 1 due to the weakening of the pure

German race by intermarriage with dark-skinned people and Jews. He took his ideology of the *"Master Race"* from a 19th-century theorist who claimed that there was a hierarchy of races and the Germans were classified as the elite. Frederick realised his hypothesis would be unpopular and slated by the academic community in England so for now, he was keeping his research secret.

If the British government declared war on Germany, he knew his poor eyesight and weak chest would enable him to avoid conscription but he was ready and willing to contribute to the cause and his loyalty was to Hitler and the Third Reich. At Cambridge he wasn't in a position to become active as a spy. Maybe he should consider applying to the War Office to do civilian work, the lack of suitable candidates due to the rush to enlist may work in his favour.

As Marcus prepared for bed and dampened down the fire in his rooms, he too reflected upon the events of the evening. Was Frederick becoming a liability? His nervous reaction to the news from Germany needed to be dealt with; perhaps he should find him something to do to keep his mind occupied before he exposed himself and put the spy ring in jeopardy. Maybe he could become the handler to the latest recruit, giving him a purpose. The prospect pleased him. Frederick's allegiance hadn't been tested, maybe this was a solution.

CHAPTER 2

February 1943

The early evening rush at the Barleycorn saw farmworkers and land army girls calling in for a welcome drink on their way home after a hard day's labour. It had been a cold day, with frost in the fields and a biting wind, so the welcoming fire in the public bar attracted the weary workers like moths to a flame. Jack looked around the bar with satisfaction; there might be a war on but trade was brisk; he was doing his bit contributing to the war effort by quenching the thirst of the young lads and lasses who were billeting in and around the village.

'Evening Jack,' called out PC Hopkins who made his way to the bar. 'A pint of mild, please.'

Jack turned to the village bobby. 'Hello Herbert, coming right up.'

Herbert Hopkins had been working as the village bobby for 5 years, settling well into the country life after growing up in the backstreets of Nottingham. The fact that nothing much happened in Eakring was a bonus for him and he had no ambition to join up. Being a copper, he was exempt from conscription and he had no plans to visit the recruiting office in Newark any time soon.

Jack put the foaming glass of beer on the counter and took the proffered cash from Herbert. 'Any news on the sheep-stealing from Arkwright's farm?' he asked.

'We reckon it was that gang from Nottingham who've been selling lamb on the black market, but unfortunately, as we haven't got any proof, we can't do 'owt about it at the moment. It's amazing how everyone turns a blind eye, no one saw anything. With all the nosey parkers round here it's unbelievable, you can't sneeze in this village without everyone catching colds,' replied Herbert as he sipped his beer. 'Mind you,' he continued, 'there is a bit of excitement brewing that the gossips haven't heard about yet.' The land army girls standing at the bar strained to hear what was being said. 'Apparently there's a Hollywood film crew coming over, although it's all hush-hush at the moment. Word has it they're coming over here to make a film up at Dukes Wood. Not sure what it's about yet but the sergeant reckons it'll either be a cowboy or another one about Robin Hood.'

'Well that'd be a turn up, actually making a film about Robin Hood in Sherwood Forest,' replied Jack, laughing.

'Ger away wi' ya,' said Deirdre. 'What would they want to come here for? It's the back of beyond.' They all laughed and the rest of the punters in the pub stopped what they were doing to listen in to the conversation.

'I'm telling ya, they'll be arriving sometime next week. I've also been told it might be a film about oil production and how the Yanks are winning the war and saving us from the Nazis, apparently to aid the war effort and boost our morale.' Old Joe, sitting in the corner snug roused himself.

'Typical bloody Yanks, they think they're God's gift. You watch, they'll be swanning around as if they owned the place in no time.'

'Oh, I do hope so,' said Deirdre, 'we could do with a bit of excitement around here, and have some eye candy to look at.' She turned to the lads who were playing darts. 'No offence, boys.'

'If you wanted excitement you should have joined the WRENs, everyone loves a sailor and their uniforms are much nicer than the Army's. A friend of mine tells me all the sailors have a girl in every port, and she's the one for quite a few lonely sailors on shore leave,' replied Celia. The girls laughed.

'Where will the film crew be billeted? There's not many hotels around here,' asked Edith, the third land army girl. She was an attractive blonde with typical peaches-and-cream complexion and a winning smile. With her trim figure and slim waist, she even looked good in her land army uniform of kaki jodhpurs and green jumper.

The three girls had been working together on Arkwright's farm since joining up a few months before, and although they had come from very different social backgrounds, in the short time they had known one another they had formed a firm friendship. Deirdre was the youngest and it was her first time away from her home and family in Liverpool. When she first arrived, she suffered bouts of home sickness but had gradually settled with the support of her friends and the watchful eye of the matron at the Kelham Hall where they were billeted.

Kelham Hall, an opulent building in Gothic Revival style built in 1857, was owned by the Society of the Sacred Mission, an order of Anglican monks who used it as a centre to train missionaries. It had been commandeered by the military for the duration of the war to provide accommodation for the war workers who lived harmoniously side-by-side with the monks.

Arthur Harris, Jack's son who was home from the Army recuperating after being injured on the Western Front, was helping behind the bar. He had taken a fancy to Edith and the two of them had been out a few times to local dances and the cinema in nearby Newark. He had grown fond of her and wanted to get to know her better before returning to his unit in a couple of weeks. He was also hoping that she would write to him whilst he was away.

'From what I've seen of the Yanks they like a drink, so it'll please Dad and increase his profits if they come here. Mind you, he might have to water the beer down a bit more to make sure there's enough to go round,' he said.

'That's enough of your cheek, lad, I pride myself in serving the best beer in Nottinghamshire so it would be sacrilege to water it down, and it'll bankrupt George getting himself inebriated every night before he goes to work,' replied Jack.

'Never mind George's drinking habits, I want to know more about the film stars,' said Deirdre. 'Who's coming?' she asked Herbert.

Herbert had to confess he didn't know the exact arrival date for the film crew, nor who was to be expected or where they would be staying, but promised he would keep his ear to the ground to let them know. He drained his pint, pleased with himself for being the first to know what was about to happen in the village for once, and prepared to leave.

'Well I'd better be off,' he said to no one in particular as he returned his pint pot to the bar.

'Keep us posted, Herbert, and if you need a welcome committee setting up you can count on me,' said Deirdre with a smile. She was excited at the prospect of a Hollywood film crew in the village. Her dad was a docker and the family lived perilously near the docks in Liverpool, and although Deirdre herself felt safe in the countryside she worried about her parents and younger siblings. She was a petite brunette with a lively personality and piercing blue eyes that attracted more than one of the local lads, and although she enjoyed the attention, she had no intentions of settling down. She was fond of Billy Carter, who worked at the local school, but felt his prospects as an unambitious primary school teacher didn't endear him as husband material. However, the prospect of Hollywood actors coming to the village was something else, perhaps she could bag herself an American husband. The idea gave her food for thought and she relished the prospect of meeting famous film stars up close and wondering what it would be like to live in America.

Old Joe, sitting in his usual chair in the corner watched the exchange with interest. Village life was changing and not necessarily for the better. He'd lived in Eakring all his life and had worked at the Dukes Wood oil field before it closed down due to lack of investment. He'd enjoyed working on the rigs and had been well paid for the job, enabling him and his late wife, Joyce, to buy a little cottage in the village. Now the bloody Yanks would be swarming all over the site playing at being roughnecks; they didn't know the half of it. It was a difficult and dangerous job, not at all glamourous but he reckoned the Yanks would gloss over all that with their silly film.

'Hey Joe,' called Jack, 'perhaps you could offer to be their technical adviser, I bet no one knows more about the nodding donkeys down at Dukes Wood than you. You can teach them a few things, I'm sure. If you're lucky they may let you be in the film.' The crowd in the pub laughed good-naturedly. 'After all, you look like a roughneck.'

'Dad's right, Joe.' Arthur joined in. 'You could make yourself a bob or two.' Joe laughed with them, but it had given him some food for thought as well. There were still some old mine shafts in the woods and the remains of dismantled rigs and he could teach the poncey actors a thing or two about the oil industry. He had fond memories of the lads who he had worked with over the years, many of them joined up as soon as the war broke out, and sadly some wouldn't be returning. Some good lads from the village had left with high hopes of fighting for their country and fallen in battle. He asked Arthur for another pint and retreated into his corner, lost in his memories and feeling all of his 57 years.

Gradually the crowd in the bar drifted away. The three land army girls sat together, still chatting about the film stars' imminent arrival and speculating on which of their favourite actors would be coming to the village. As they cycled home, they joked about who it could be.

'I hope Gregory Peck's coming, he's gorgeous,' said Celia as they rode home.

'I prefer John Wayne,' replied Deirdre. 'He's more likely to be in a film about oil workers. Did you see him in Stagecoach? He was great. I'm going to write to me mam tonight to tell her about the film, she'll be dead jealous, she loves John Wayne.'

'Well if John Wayne's coming the film might be about cowboys, or perhaps Errol Flynn is coming to make another movie about Robin Hood. If he is, there'll be plenty of merry women around here,' laughed Celia.

'Why don't you wait until they arrive? It's only a rumour and you know what PC Hopkins is like, he's probably got it all wrong,' Edith replied, the voice of reason.

'Oh Eddie, don't be a spoilsport, it's the best bit of news we've had since we got here. It's got to be right. Just think, we could all end up married to film stars,' said Deirdre.

'Well if we are, I bag Gregory Peck, I certainly wouldn't kick him out of bed,' shouted Celia as she rode off ahead of the others. 'Last one home's a sissy!'

Eakring, a small village in the heart of Sherwood Forest between Ollerton and Southwell in the Nottinghamshire coalfields, consisted of a number of farm cottages, a small shop that doubled up as a post office, St Andrew's Church and the public house. Arkwright's farm was situated on the edge of the village leading up towards Dukes Wood to the east. The wood itself being situated on the top of an escarpment, gave good views over the Trent valley to the east and towards Southwell to the south, and was surrounded by the farmland where most of the local people, who didn't travel to Newark for work, were employed. The farm hands who hadn't been conscripted were elderly and the labour shortages was being filled by the enthusiastic land army girls. Many of whom were city girls and although they were finding the work hard and the hours long, their determination to do a good job had endeared them to the locals. The three friends worked on Arkwright's farm and together they supported the elderly farmer and his wife after the conscription of their two sons left them struggling to cope. They were unlikely friends having coming from different social backgrounds but working and living together had made them realise they had lots in common, mainly because they each wanted to do their bit for the King and country. Having been randomly thrown together they had formed an unlikely and enduring friendship.

The village is within commuting distance of Nottingham where a number of factories, such as the Royal Ordinance factory, were in full production for the war effort. Further to the east there were a number of airfields, including RAF Scampton, the base for the 617 Squadron who carried out the daring raid on the dams in Germany in 1940 using the infamous bouncing bombs. To the south and west of Eakring a number of coal mines were in full production; Bilsthorpe, Clipstone and Thoresby were churning out record levels of coal for the war effort. The shortage of skilled men, due to the fact that many miners had joined up, was made up by the Bevin Boys, conscripted to work in the mines by order of Ernest Bevin, the Minister of Labour and National Service. Thousands of ordinary people pulling together throughout Nottinghamshire for the war effort but largely unaffected by the bombing raids that pounded the major cities in England night after night. In the peaceful village of Eakring there was the feeling that although the war was raging all around them, nothing disturbed their day-to-day lives. Spring was in the air and they were looking forward to a long, hot, and hopefully uneventful summer. Thankfully, the arrival of the film crew with the promise of a patriotic war film was the nearest they would get to the action. No one realised as they all left the pub to go home to their respective beds that night that the events that were to unfold in the ensuing months would change all their lives forever.

CHAPTER 3

London, 1942

By August 1942 the war was going badly for the allies. Oil reserves were at an all-time low; U-boat attacks and the bombing of dockside storage facilities had brought the British admiralty two million barrels below its minimum safety reserves. The oil supply outlook was looking bleak. Meanwhile, German Field Marshal Erwin Rommel's rampaging North African campaign threatened England's access to Middle East oilfield resources and the principal fuel supplies coming by convoy from Trinidad and America were being subjected to relentless Nazi submarine attacks. Something had to be done, so the wartime secretary of petroleum, Geoffrey Lloyd, was called upon to deal with the imminent crisis. Sitting in his office in Whitehall he ordered his secretary to arrange an immediate meeting, bringing together a number of oil company executives and senior civil servants to thrash out a solution.

The meeting was held in his private office and sitting around the table were the men who were best placed to discuss their options. Geoffrey needed some good news to pass on to Winston Churchill who didn't like his Ministers to present him with problems unless they were ready with a solution.

During the meeting, many of the delegates at the Oil Control Board were surprised to learn that England had a productive oil field of its own, first discovered in 1939 by the D'Arcy Exploration Company. The obscure oilfield, situated in Sherwood Forest just outside the village of Eakring in Nottinghamshire, Dukes Wood had previously produced modest supplies of oil from 50 shallow wells. Extreme shortages of drilling equipment and personnel kept Britain from further exploiting the field and it had fallen into disuse. On hearing the possibility of producing a substantial supply of home-produced oil, Lloyd turned to the representative of the D'Arcy Exploration Company, Philip Southwell.

'What do you need to start up production again?' he enquired.

Philip considered the question. 'Well, the main problem we have at the moment is a shortage of suitably qualified men to drill new wells. The previous workforce has all dispersed, many of them joined up at the beginning of the war whilst the others have been conscripted. I could draw up a list of the names from our records but as the team were mostly young men, I'm guessing many of them will be with the Sherwood Foresters and fighting on the Western Front, those who are still alive.'

'Can we train new men? I can have a word with Bevin to see if any of the miners have the necessary skills.'

'The extraction of coal is of equal importance, we don't want to jeopardise our coal reserves,' replied Sir Henry Wadsworth, one of the senior civil servants present at the meeting. 'We can't rob Peter to pay Paul, Winston won't allow it. Bevin is already looking into the possibility of conscripting miners. The production of oil and coal are not mutually exclusive. We have to find a way to do both.'

The discussion continued well into the night as the Oil Control Board looked for a solution.

'What about the Americans? Do you think they would be willing to help?' asked Philip.

'How do you propose that to happen?' replied Lloyd. He was interested in the idea as a possible solution.

Southwell pointed out that the Americans working in the oil fields in Texas had the relevant expertise and the manpower. 'If only we could make contact, we could ask them to send over a crew to open up the oil field.'

'Leave it with me,' said Lloyd. 'I'm sure the old man will be able to pull a few strings.'

A few days later Southwell was on his way to the Petroleum Administration for War in Washington, D.C., on a secret mission to secure American assistance in expanding production from the Eakring field, regarded as an "*unsinkable tanker.*"

Pressing his case in America, he persuaded the widely respected independent oilman Lloyd Noble, president of Tulsa-based Noble Drilling Corporation, to take on the job. Lloyd Noble began his career in the early years of oil drilling in the States, founding the Noble Drilling Company in April 1921 and he was one of the leading experts in the field. Southwell was overjoyed when Noble agreed and he enlisted the Fain-Porter Drilling Company of Oklahoma City on a one-year contract to drill 100 new wells in the Eakring field. What was even more remarkable, Noble agreed to execute the contract for the cost price plus expenses only.

Following the discussions with Southwell, Lloyd Noble invited two experienced oil workers, Gene Rosser and Don Walker, to a meeting in his office on the 24th November 1942, to begin the recruitment of 'The Roughnecks of Sherwood Forest.'

Noble explained to them the nature and scope of the work they would be undertaking. They were to take 4 rigs from America to Eakring for the purpose of drilling 100 shallow wells.

Neither of the two men had any idea where Eakring was but their loyalty to Lloyd Noble and his confidence in their ability to see the job through held their interest.

'If you take the job,' he told them, 'you should get busy right away recruiting the drilling crews because that's going to be tough. Available good men are hard to find, but I want every man who agrees to go to be told the facts of the job. I want them to know exactly what they are getting into. They'll be going into a war zone under severe wartime restrictions. Manpower in the oil fields is getting short, but we must not misrepresent the situation or the potential danger to them in any way.'

Rosser was surprised and somewhat overawed at what he was hearing. Noble told him and Walker that he wanted them by his side to run the operation. 'The whole deal is a highly secret matter,' he went on. 'If the Germans ever found out where the drilling site was, they would, of course give it a hell of a bombing, putting the crew in mortal danger.'

Finally, Rosser said to Noble, 'Mr Noble, let me ask you one more question. Knowing what you know about this deal, and I guess you have told me all that you do know about it, would you take the job if you were me?'

Lloyd Noble's quick response was, 'I certainly would.'

'All right,' said Gene, 'I'll take it then. What's the first thing we're supposed to do?'

'As I said,' Noble replied, 'I think the first thing for you to do is to get started on a recruiting campaign. The US government have given us priority over the military to recruit who we want, and anyone volunteering for our mission will be able to defer their military service, and with any luck, gentlemen, by the time we return home the war will be over.'

By March 1943 a group of 42 volunteers had been selected and briefed and they set sail on the troopship HMS *Queen Elizabeth* bound for the UK. Along with the men, four drilling rigs for "*The English Project*" were transported to England on four different ships. Although one ship was lost to a German submarine, another rig was subsequently shipped safely ready for the work to commence by April.

CHAPTER 4

March 1943, Eakring

The weather was unseasonably warm for March and Edith and Celia were sitting together in the grounds of their billet at Kelham Hall, soaking up the spring sunshine. Kelham Hall was an Anglican monastery situated on the banks of the River Trent. It was being used by the Society of the Sacred Mission as a theological seminary for the education of candidates for the ministry in the Anglican faith. At the beginning of the war, however, the government requisitioned part of the accommodation for essential war workers, which included some land army girls who were working on farms in the area, and, due to the proximity to the oil field at Dukes Wood it was also commissioned to house the American oil field workers.

It was a Saturday afternoon and the start of the weekend after a long and hard week toiling in the fields. Lambing was early this year and it was all hands on the deck at Arkwright's farm. Presently Deirdre came over to them carrying the post.

'Hey girls, the postman's been so I've brought your letters out for you.' She handed two over to Celia and one to Edith. They accepted them gratefully and began to read. Now and again Deirdre laughed out loud at something she read in her letters. They had been sent from her mother and siblings in Liverpool and contained a wealth of local gossip. Edith's letter was from Arthur who had recently returned to his unit in the Sherwood Foresters. She smiled fondly as she read his words; because of wartime regulations he wasn't allowed to reveal information about his posting but he'd written to tell her he was well and looking forward to visiting his Aunty Polly the following week. Like many young couples during the war they had agreed on a code and his mention of Aunty Polly meant that he was being deployed overseas in the near future. Edith had become fond of Arthur and knew she would worry about his welfare over the coming months.

Celia looked upset as she started to read the letter from her mother. 'Oh no,' she cried out, which caught the attention of her two friends.

'What's wrong?' asked Edith. Both friends turned to Celia who had started to cry. Without a word she passed the letter over to Edith who read out "*Missing in action*" and looked towards Celia. 'It only says he's missing in action, I'm sure he'll turn up. Perhaps he's been captured and is a prisoner of war. You won't hear anything for a while but I'm sure the Red Cross will find out what's happened to him and they will be in touch with your mother.'

Deirdre moved to put her arm around her. 'Come on, Celia old girl, Edith's right. I'm sure he'll turn up. I know it's a shock but this happens all the time. You'll be worrying yourself silly whilst all the time he's fit and well. He probably had to ditch his plane in a field somewhere and is being looked after by a beautiful mademoiselle in a French farmhouse. You know your brother can look after himself and he can charm the birds out of the trees.'

Celia looked at the two friends who were trying to comfort her, and she smiled weakly. 'Thank you girls, I'm sure you're right. Mummy has spoken to his CO who said he was seen to be bailing out over Normandy, on the way back from a raid on Berlin, in an area that isn't heavily occupied by the Germans, so they're hoping he'll be able to make his way back to Blighty with the help of the French Resistance. They're active in that region and if they pick him up, he'll be home in no time.'

'I'll pop inside and get us all a cupper. If I tell Matron about your news, I bet she'll let you have some sugar in yours,' said Deirdre. As she ran off she turned to her friend. 'Don't worry, Celia, I'm sure he'll be OK.'

Edith and Celia sat in companionable silence as they continued reading their respective letters. Edith decided she'd write straight back to Arthur; he sounded worried despite his bravado. Suddenly the reality of war and the fragility of life hit her. Arthur was far from home and like many soldiers waiting for deployment he was scared and excited in equal measure. Millions of young men were being sacrificed for a war that they hadn't started and one that many of them didn't understand. Sitting in the sunshine in the peaceful Nottinghamshire countryside was far removed from the bloodshed that was raging overseas. She hoped that Celia was right and that her brother was safe and on his way home.

When Deirdre returned with the tea, she was looking excited. 'You'll never guess what I've just heard. You know they've been getting the quarters ready in the west wing for another intake. Well, the new arrivals are due to arrive later today, and it's been all hush-hush until now but Matron has just told me it's the film crew who are coming here to stay. She said we'll have to keep our distance though. They'll have their own common room and won't want to fraternise with the likes of us but you never know, I'm sure we'll be able to attract their attention. I'm going up to my room to put on something a bit more decent, I want to look my best when John Wayne arrives.'

The two friends laughed as Deirdre ran back into the house. 'What about your tea?' shouted Celia.

'Never mind tea, I bet they'll be bringing champagne with them, and if we're lucky some silk stockings,' replied Deirdre as she disappeared into the Hall.

'What about you, Celia, are you going to change? We may only get a glimpse of them when they arrive but it would be nice for them to see that we local girls scrub up nicely.' Celia folded her letter and returned it to the envelope.

'Why not? Richard can look after himself and the CO did say he'd bailed out safely so I'm sure he's going to pop up again without a scratch on him wondering why we were so worried.' Richard was based at RAF Scampton, the home of bomber command, and had visited his sister at Kelham Hall on a few occasions with his best friend, Aubrey. Edith thought he was a serious and intelligent young man who would be quite capable of looking after himself. Presently they drank their tea and returned to the Hall to spruce themselves up.

Around 5pm a convoy of trucks drew up outside the main entrance to Kelham Hall, and a group of young men started to disembark. By this time the three girls had changed into their Sunday best clothes and were loitering around the entrance, pretending to be engrossed in their own conversation but surreptitiously keeping an eye out to see if they recognised any of the new arrivals. As the men climbed down from the trucks, they noticed some of them were carrying instruments; one carried a banjo whilst another had a fiddle case, and unbeknown to those watching several others had French harps hidden in their pockets. It looked like they were equipped to provide their own entertainment during their stay.

'Hey guys!' shouted an attractive, tall, blond man as he jumped down from the truck and looked towards the girls. 'It looks like we've got a welcoming committee. Hello ladies,' he said, smiling at them.

Deirdre being the boldest, approached him holding out her hand. 'I'm Deirdre and these are my friends Edith and Celia, we thought it only polite to come out to say hello and welcome you to England.'

He shook her hand. 'Well that's mighty nice of you, young lady. I'm James Carmichael, at your service. Perhaps we can get to know each other better after we've settled in.' Deirdre wanted to quiz him about the film crew but deciding not to look or sound too eager, merely smiled in assent.

A British Army captain who had driven up in a Jeep accompanying the convoy stepped forward to addressed the new arrivals. 'I think it's best if you all go in to find your quarters before fraternising with the locals, you don't want to detain the ladies. It looks as though they are on their way out,' he announced as the men began drifting towards the entrance. 'You've had a long journey and I'm sure you'll want to settle in and freshen up before supper is served.'

'Arrogant sod,' whispered Celia to Edith as they watched the exchange. The Army officer approached the girls.

'Good evening, ladies, I'm sure you'll get to know our American friends in due course, but I'm sure you'll understand they've had a long journey so their priority is to get settled in.' He looked at Celia who realised he'd overheard her remarks but seemed to find it amusing. 'I'm Captain Blenkinsop,' he said, 'and who might you be?'

Celia blushed. 'I'm Celia Fenwick,' she replied as she formally shook hands with the captain. 'Of course, you're right but my friend was just being friendly,' she replied, stressing her cut-glass vowels. Blenkinsop noted the Knightsbridge accent with approval.

'I've been assigned to help the Americans settle in and take charge of their security whilst in the country,' he said with the intention of asserting his authority. 'You can expect to be seeing more of me over the next few weeks, and I look forward to getting to know *you* better.' He smiled at Celia and nodded towards the others before walking away to organise the group of men.

'He's rather good looking, don't you think? And it looks like he's taken a fancy to you, Celia,' said Edith.

Celia replied that although he was pretty good looking, he was still an arrogant sod. 'Come on, girls,' she said. 'Seeing as we're all dressed up with nowhere to go let's cycle down to the Barleycorn and we can tell the locals that the film crew have arrived.'

As they rode off towards the village Captain Blenkinsop watched them before entering the building. *This assignment to keep an eye on the "film crew" won't be as boring as I first thought,* he mused.

Although the village was a few miles by road from Kelham Hall, the short-cut across the fields reduced the journey considerably and they arrived at the Barleycorn before the early evening rush. As they entered the public bar, Jack, who was serving behind the bar, welcomed them warmly.

'Have you heard 'owt from our lad?' he asked Edith.

'As a matter of fact, I got a letter from him today. He seems chirpy enough but reading between the lines it looks like his unit will be going overseas soon.'

'No wonder he's chirpy then, he was getting stir crazy hanging about here, he'll be chomping at the bit to see some action. Don't mention it to Vera though, will you? She worries about him.'

He poured the girls their usual tipple, port and lemonades all round, as he was talking. 'There you go, girls, this round's on the house. You look like you need a stiff drink after that ride from the Hall.'

Old Joe sitting in his usual corner perked up when he heard the offer of free drinks. 'Mine's a half, Jack, if the drinks are on the house,' he shouted, more in hope than anticipation.

'Nice try, Joe, you cheeky bogger, but the offer's only extended to the girls here.' The local lads playing darts laughed good-naturedly at the exchange. Deirdre sauntered over to them to watch the match.

'The Yanks have just arrived. They're billeted at Kelham Hall,' she announced to the group. 'We didn't see John Wayne though, I guess he'll be coming later. He's too important to turn up on an Army truck with the rest of the crew, he'll probably arrive after the others have settled in.'

'He'll probably be staying in one of those fancy hotels in Nottingham, such as the Black Boy. A famous man like him won't be expected to bunk up with the plebs,' said Billy Clarke.

Billy was the local school teacher who had been to pictures in Newark with Deirdre a couple of times, and he wasn't happy about the news. He was hoping that Deirdre would become his steady girlfriend and thought she was coming around to the idea but just playing hard to get. After all, he was a teacher with ambitions to become a headteacher one day, surely a girl from the back streets of

Liverpool would be flattered by someone with his standing in the community and would see him as husband material. Although he had been keen to join up when war was declared back in 1939, to his dismay, he was rejected for military service on health grounds. Something that rankled each time one of the local lads left to fight. He was also fed up with getting stares from people when he went to Newark because he wasn't in uniform. Now the Yanks had turned up he was concerned that Deirdre would be swept off her feet by one of them. Nevertheless, faint heart never won the fair lady, he thought he'd try his luck. 'There's a James Cagney film on at the Odeon,' he said to her. 'Do you fancy going to see it on Monday night?'

'Could do, I suppose,' she replied, sounding cool. 'I'll meet you at the bus stop. What time does it start?'

Pleased that she'd agreed to go out with him, '7.30, so we can catch the 6.30 bus. I'll even treat you to a bag of chips on the way home if you don't have time for tea before we go,' he replied, smiling, turning back to continued his game with the lads.

'Ooo, last of the big spenders. You certainly know how to treat a lady, Billy Clarke,' laughed Deirdre.

Celia looked at Deirdre. '...And they say romance is dead! You shouldn't lead him on, you know he really likes you.'

'I'm just having a bit of fun, Celia, and if he's happy to pay why should I complain? You're only young once, you know, or have you forgotten?'

As they finished their drinks they chatted about the new arrivals, speculating on which of the men that had arrived that day were the stars of the film. Deirdre thought the tall blond hunk was bound to be one of the leading actors. Presently Celia went to the bar to get another round in when the door opened and Captain Blenkinsop walked in. He noticed Celia standing at the bar and sidled up to her as Jack was pouring out their drinks. 'Let me pay for those drinks for the ladies,' he said, smiling at her.

'Oh, thank you,' she replied as she scooped up the drinks to return to the others.

'So, the dashing captain has bought the drinks for us. You need to be careful, Celia, you don't want to take advantage of him. You never know what he's after!' remarked Deirdre as the girls raised their glasses in a toast to the captain who returned the gesture, raising his glass of beer.

Captain Blenkinsop turned to Jack to explain the reason for his visit; he told him that the Ministry of Defence had authorised an increase on his rations of beer from the local brewery to cater for the influx of trade expected from the film crew. They were keen to extend the courtesy of hospitality to the Americans after a hard day's filming and, as the Barleycorn was the nearest pub to the site, it had been chosen to receive the extra rations. This not only pleased the landlord but the local lads who were listening in to the conversation were delighted at the prospect of getting beer that hadn't been watered down.

A little later, Herbert Hopkins entered the bar and ordered himself a pint of bitter. Having just finished his shift he was looking forward to a drink before returning to his lodgings. He noticed Blenkinsop standing at the bar. 'Evening Captain Blenkinsop, I hope the Yanks have settled in up at the Hall, I heard they were arriving today. I trust they found their billets comfortable.'

'Yes, thanks old boy. Although their accommodation is far from salubrious, the matron has done a splendid job and I'm sure they'll want for nothing up at the Hall. The three ladies over there even formed a welcoming committee which I dare say was much appreciated by our American friends. I'm sure they will be frequenting this fine hostelry when the filming starts next week to get to know more people, they seem very laid back and happy to mix with the locals, although I guess they'll be working long hours.'

'Well you can rest assured that the locals will give them a fine welcome, I'll make sure they don't get pestered for autographs so they can get their film in the can and be on their way before the end of the year.' Herbert was secretly hoping to see some of the film stars himself. 'Of course, I'll be making a courtesy call up at Dukes Wood in a couple of days to make sure they aren't being disturbed, we don't want the local kids swarming around the place. Their arrival has certainly excited the school kids; Billy will have to keep an eye on them to make sure they don't bunk off school to creep over to the woods to watch the filming.'

'That's good of you, old boy, but my men will be securing the perimeter and I wouldn't want you to neglect your duties to babysit the Yanks. We can manage quite well and I can always let you know if there's any trouble brewing. I'm sure you have lots of other duties to take care of,' he replied with a superior smirk on his aristocratic face.

Herbert felt a bit put out, he wanted to watch some of the filming himself and didn't take kindly to this condescending Army captain telling him he wasn't wanted. This was his patch and he had every right to patrol Dukes Wood. The locals were listening in to the exchange, some of them with wry smiles on their faces. They felt PC Herbert Hopkins needed taking down a peg or two and it looked like he'd met his match in Captain Blenkinsop!

Old Joe watched the exchange with interest and decided to wander up to Dukes Wood himself sometime to see if they'd be interested in his local knowledge of the oil field and his expertise as a roughneck. He'd heard that film crews often appointed local experts to ensure the film was realistic and he thought he could try his luck.

The girls were enjoying their evening and decided to stay for another drink as they didn't want to miss any snippets of information coming from the captain. Celia was despatched to the bar for another round with the explicit instructions to use her considerable charms to engage him in conversation. A task she was only too pleased to accept, and although her mission to elicit information wasn't successful, she did make a favourable impression on the captain.

Celia was the daughter of Sir Stanley Fenwick and his wife Mary who lived in a town house in Knightsbridge. After school she had been to a finishing school in Paris and was expected to marry early and settle down with a wealthy husband in the City. She, however, had been keen to escape the confines of her privileged life when she joined the land army and she really enjoyed working on the land and making new friends in Eakring.

Herbert went over to join the locals to play darts; he prided himself on being a good player and soon won his match against Billy. Deirdre was watching the match with interest, and after his match Herbert joined her and Edith, offering to buy them both another drink, an offer they gratefully accepted.

'I guess you'll be able to get to know the Yanks seeing as they're billeted up at the Hall,' he asked. Deirdre feigned boredom and implied that she for one wasn't interested in fraternising with them, although she was keen to find out if Herbert had any inside information about the crew who'd arrived.

'I don't suppose being a lowly PC you'll know anything we don't about the film crew?' she goaded him.

'I wouldn't say that,' he replied, preening. 'I may be a local bobby at the moment but I'm biding my time. I joined the police force after university so my inspector has high hopes for me, I just need to get some experience of front-line policing before I put in for my sergeant's exams.'

'Oh,' she replied, feigning surprise, 'I didn't know you'd been to university. Why did you join the police?'

'It's a good career and helping people in my community gives me job satisfaction. I could end up as a chief inspector one of these days with my qualifications and experience,' he told her. Not that he had any intentions of working his way up through the ranks, if truth be told he'd chosen the police force because he was fundamentally lazy and it suited him to be working in a rural area where the main crimes involved sheep stealing and poaching.

'Hey Herbert,' shouted Billy across the now crowded bar, 'why don't we challenge the Yanks to a darts match? With you in our team they wouldn't stand a chance.'

'I don't know about that! I think the rest of you need a bit more practice. I may be good but I can't beat them on me own,' replied Herbert, although he was secretly flattered by the idea.

Captain Blenkinsop overhearing the exchange said, 'I think that's a topping idea, boys,' joining in the conversation. 'It would be a good PR exercise. I'm sure the Yanks would agree to a match. I'll have a word with Mr Southwell after they've settled in,' he said, asserting his position as the liaison officer. 'Mind you, you had better field a good team, we don't want to lose, we are British after all!' he said, half joking although secretly hoping they could take the arrogant Yanks down a peg or two. He was still smarting at the posting he'd been given as he felt he was missing out; the rest of his battalion were on standby to ship out to Europe and he didn't want to miss the opportunity for action overseas.

Looking across at Celia, though, he thought, *Maybe this posting will have its compensations!*

CHAPTER 5

1943, Kelham Hall

The group of roughnecks were assembled in the common room at Kelham Hall when Philip Southwell stood up to address them.

'Welcome to England, gentlemen, I trust you had a good journey and have everything you need. I received a message from Mr Churchill, the British Prime Minister, this morning, he's asked me to pass on his personal thanks and says his government are extremely grateful to you for volunteering for this mission. We have a busy time ahead of us if we are to get the oil field up and running before our oil stocks run out, and I am sure you all appreciate the seriousness of the situation. Before I hand over to Lloyd Noble, who is managing this contract, I just wanted to have a few words about the secretive nature of your mission and the cover story that we have been circulating, thanks to one or two well-placed people in the area. As you know, we've let it be known that you are here to make a Hollywood film and although some of you will be quite happy to pose as film stars, we can't all take the glory so some of you will be posing as cameramen, writers, editors and other backroom boys. We want to keep it all as low key as possible so we are hoping you will confine yourselves to the common room here and the local pub near to Dukes Wood. The pub is called the Barleycorn and it's not too busy so the handful of locals you're likely to meet there will be easy to hoodwink if you stick to your cover stories.

'The transport will collect you at 6am each morning, starting tomorrow, and take you straight to the oil field. We've organised a two-shift system so we can cover production 7 days a week, and the rotas will be posted on the noticeboard here in the common room. Lunch will be served out at the oil field and the return transport will pick you up again at 6.30pm. Dinner will be served here in the common room and the bar will be open until 10.30pm. If you do mix with the locals make sure you keep quiet about the real reason for our presence. Any questions?'

There were quite a few ribald comments and laughter from the audience. James Carmichael stood up. 'Just the one,' he said. 'Can I be a film star? I thought I'd call myself Errol Peck.' This brought laughter from the audience and a wry smile from Southwell.

'With your good looks, mate, you'll be beating the local girls back with a stick even if you're not a film star,' shouted someone from the audience.

'I know, what can I say? Some of us have it, Aaron!' he replied good-naturedly.

'OK, gentlemen, settle down. I'm going to pass over to Lloyd who will explain the contract and how we're going to get the job done,' said Southwell.

Lloyd Noble was a well-respected oil man who had started the Noble Oil company in 1921 at the tender age of 26, and by the start of the Second World War he was seen as a leading expert in his field and the obvious choice to take on the challenge at Dukes Wood. He was a smartly dressed man of medium build, and with a shock of curly hair and his youthful, friendly demeanour he was well liked by his team. His philanthropic nature had prompted him to agree to undertake the task on a not-for-profit basis which not only endeared him to his crew but earned him the respect and gratitude of the British government.

'The work we are about to undertake is in a war zone and you will be working under wartime conditions and restrictions,' he began. 'It's going to be a really tough job. The British outfit we're working for are furnishing the drilling equipment which we will buy new for them. We have already purchased the type of equipment we need and 4 rigs have been sent over from the US. As you know you are on the payroll of the Noble Drilling Corporation and as employees you will be subjected to my supervision. My two right-hand men, Gene Rosser and Don Walker, will be responsible for the site management and the day-to-day operation. If you have any problems whilst here don't hesitate to speak to me or my management team.'

Noble went on, 'If the Germans ever found out where the drilling site is, they would, of course give it a hell of a bombing, so we must stick to our cover story. If you are suspicious of anyone hanging around the site acting suspiciously don't hesitate to pass on the information to Captain Blenkinsop who, with his team, is responsible for the site security. Make no mistake, things are going to be tough but rest assured the work that you are doing here is of vital importance to the war effort.

'Our task, gentlemen, is to expand the decommissioned oil field in Dukes Wood. The production closed down due to lack of investment and manpower but after reading the site documents I think there is a rich seam for us to tap into and we could potentially double or even treble the previous production targets. Don't underestimate the importance of this mission, the crude oil from this site is of a very high quality, superior to Middle Eastern oil and after it's refined it is particularly suited to the Rolls-Royce Merlin Engine which is used in high-performance fighters and bombers. Our work here is important and with luck we will be able to help our allies win this war.'

The oilmen were all nodding in agreement; Noble was a popular manager and those who had worked for him before found him to be a charismatic leader who would treat them fairly and would not ask them to do anything that he was not prepared to do himself. His words were met with a round of applause from the audience. 'Can't wait to get started, boss,' said Carmichael and the other volunteers nodded in agreement.

Captain Blenkinsop, who had been loitering at the back of the room, sauntered to the front and held up his hand to get the attention of the men as they were leaving. 'If I may just have a quick word before you leave the room, gentlemen,' he said. 'As Lloyd has explained, my men will be overseeing the security at the site and we will be keeping the locals well away. However, I'm sure you'll be coming into contact with them when you are off duty so I think you'll need to maintain our cover story. It's probably best if you keep mum about your work, and remember, men, *"Careless talk costs lives."* That will be all for now, however I'd just like to ask you to be vigilant and report to me if anyone is seen to be asking too many questions about the operation.'

As the group started to head for the bar Noble called after them, 'The first round is on me, gentlemen, but don't forget you'll all need to be up early tomorrow for our first day at work,' to which they all cheered.

Carmichael sat with his mates and took an appreciative swig of his pint. 'These limeys certainly know how to brew a good pint,' he said as he raised his glass. 'Here's to a successful trip.' His companions joined him to raise their glasses for the toast.

'I can't wait to get started. The sooner we get the job done the sooner we can get the hell outta here,' said Red McCarty, 'and the sooner the allies win the war the better.'

'I'll drink to that,' replied Aaron Long, another seasoned roughneck who had been keen to make the trip. 'When we get home, I'll be able to sign up for the Marines and get into the thick of the fighting. In the meantime, here's to a productive and quiet year.'

The group of men included experienced oil workers who had volunteered not only to have the opportunity to travel, but also to get involved in the war effort. Herman Douthit joined in the toast before turning back to his companion to show him a photograph of his wife who he had left behind in Oklahoma. Already some of the men were feeling homesick and couldn't wait to utilise their skills to resurrect the oilfield and bring it back to life.

Douthit was a derrick hand, whose job it was to sit on top of the derrick on a drilling rig to guide the stands of the drill pipe into the fingers at the top of the derrick. A dangerous but ultimately well-paid job, and one that Douthit was well qualified for. James Carmichael and many others were manual labourers called roughnecks; they were used to hard work and relished the challenge the next 12 months was to bring. Although the job was difficult and dangerous, their spirits were high and for many of them, the prospect of spending the next 12 months in the company of the attractive local girls, held certain compensations. The countryside in England in the spring was beautiful and the trees in Sherwood Forest were coming alive and bursting with colour. They hoped the good weather would hold, enabling them to get started on their mission with few hold-ups. It was a tall order to bore over 100 wells but they were feeling confident.

They had heard about the unpredictable English weather and hoped as the summer approached it would keep fine to enable them to complete the work on time. Carmichael, for one, was looking forward to spending part of the war in the relatively peaceful countryside and getting to know some pretty English girls. He already had his eye on Deirdre, although he decided he wouldn't kick Edith out of bed either given half the chance, and with his looks and personality, he thought his chances were pretty good.

For many of the men it was the first time they had left their homes in America. Some didn't even know where England was on the map, and the sea journey had been long with the ever-present threat of attack by the Germans. Now they had arrived in the peaceful countryside they were able to relax and concentrate on the job in hand. It was the start of an adventure and one that on successful completion they would return home and be subjected to conscription into the US Army, unless the war was over by then.

CHAPTER 6

1943, Dukes Wood Oil Field

Lloyd Noble lit his pipe and ran his expert eye over the site diagram for the oil field. The drawings that had been made back in 1938 showed the layout for the 50 shallow wells that had been sunk prior to the closure. He was joined in the office by his management team, Eugene Rosser and Don Walker.

'Our first task, gentlemen,' he began, 'is to examine the condition of these existing wells. There hasn't been any maintenance work done on them for the past 4 years so I can't vouch for the condition. Unfortunately, this appears to be the only diagram that has survived so we don't have a complete picture of the operation. I've asked the president of the Oil Control Board to contact the D'Arcy Exploration Company to see if they can provide any more information, but if not, it would be useful if we could speak to someone who worked on the wells previously. We could do with some local knowledge of the operation although as this is a young man's game, I guess most of the men will have joined up and left the area by now.'

'I've set the men to work clearing the areas around the nodding donkeys. Once we've cleared out all the vegetation, we'll start to see the lay of the land,' said Rosser, who was keen to get started.

'Good man,' replied Noble. 'I'll take a walk around the site again to have a good look. Perhaps you'd like to join me, Don, I could do with talking over the operation with you.'

Don was flattered by the request and agreed readily. He had been recently appointed as a supervisor and was keen to show Noble that he was capable of the job in hand.

It was a bright morning and the men had made an early start clearing the ground; they were glad to be out in the fresh air after their long and arduous journey from America. Many were keen to get on with the job and they loved the beautiful green surroundings of Sherwood Forest, and on such a lovely day it bode well for the contract. They shared good-natured banter as they set to work and were all keen to make a good impression on their boss, Noble, as he watched the operation. Noble had a reputation of being a hard but fair taskmaster whose primary concern was for the safety of his men. Working in the oil fields was a hard and dangerous job and they all had to be concerned not only for their own safety but also the safety of others in their team as one mishap could prove to be fatal.

Presently one of the areas around an oil well had been cleared for inspection and Noble, with his managers, assessed the situation. 'Well, it looks as though we can get this one up and running in no time, it's in surprisingly good condition in spite of it being mothballed for a few years. Whoever decommissioned it knew what they were doing.' The management team agreed and Noble thanked the workers for their hard work.

One by one the existing bore holes were cleared and Noble divided up the men, setting one group with the task of reactivating the existing wells and the other group to start the process of drilling new wells. The work continued for the rest of the first week and Noble had set out a timeline for the extraction and transportation of the crude oil. At the end of the second week he travelled to London to deliver a progress report to the president of the Oil Control Board, Geoffrey Lloyd.

'Ah, welcome, Mr Noble,' Geoffrey Lloyd began when Noble and his companion Red McCarty entered his office in Whitehall. 'Can I get you some refreshments before we begin the meeting? Travelling by train isn't the most comfortable mode of transport just now and you must be tired after your long journey.'

Lloyd turned to his secretary and ordered tea and refreshments.

'I took the liberty of bringing along one of my team. May I introduce you to Red McCarty. He's one of my more experienced men and will be able to answer any questions you may have about the day-to-day operation,' he said.

'Of course,' replied Lloyd, crossing the room to shake hands with Red. 'You are most welcome as well. I'm sure Mr Noble has passed on the British government's thanks to all of the men who have volunteered for this mission. I trust your accommodation is comfortable?' he said, addressing Red.

'It sure is, sir, we're billeted at a place called Kelham Hall, and when I first saw it, I thought it was an English castle, it's so grand. Me and the boys expected your King George to come out to meet us,' he replied, laughing. 'We've been made very welcome by the locals in the village, although it seems mean to be hoodwinking them into thinking we're a film crew.'

'Can't be helped,' replied Lloyd, 'it is for their own safety.' Turning to Noble, he asked, 'Have you had any problems with maintaining the cover story?'

Noble replied, 'Not really, the locals are pleasant enough and haven't asked too many questions, but we've had a couple of reporters from the local paper in Mansfield hanging around asking for interviews with the film stars.'

'I suppose that was inevitable, I'll get someone to have a word with the editor and warn them off. Now what about the production, how's that proceeding?'

Noble replied, 'Well we've had a lot to do and the first couple of weeks have been quite hectic but we've made a good start.'

'Excellent, we've been keeping in contact with Captain Blenkinsop and he has passed on your request for additional equipment. My secretary is procuring the kit you've asked for and he has assured me the supplies will be delivered early next week. Come, have a seat and we can discuss the progress you've been making in comfort.'

For the next hour the men discussed the situation and projection of progress over the coming weeks. As the meeting was nearing its conclusion, Noble asked, 'There is just one thing I wanted to discuss with you. As you know, the original site drawings for the oil field seem to have been lost and it's hampering our progress a little. I met a local man in the pub one night,' he checked his notes, 'a Joseph Wainwright who told me he'd been the site foreman at the oil field before it was decommissioned in '39. The rumour that has been circulating about us being a film crew had reached his ears and he asked me if there was any possibility of employing him as a "consultant" to help us make the film more realistic. Obviously, I didn't give away anything but if it's true that he was the site foreman he could be a useful addition to our team.'

Lloyd considered the request. 'Umm, you could be right but we can't risk the real reason for our work in the woods getting out. What do you know about this man? Is he trustworthy?'

'Not a lot, he's in his 50s and seems to be quite fit and well and I think he's telling the truth, he's certainly knowledgeable about the oil business. Perhaps you could investigate and if he's got the information we need, he could be useful to us.'

'You could be right. Leave it with me and I'll get Captain Blenkinsop to do some digging. If he is what he says he is, we could do with his help. If we get him to sign the Official Secrets Act it may be alright to employ him. I'll get back to you next week.'

The men shook hands and Noble and McCarty took their leave. They had decided to stay the night in London before travelling back to Nottinghamshire to see some of the sites they'd heard about: Buckingham Palace, the Houses of Parliament, St Paul's Cathedral and Piccadilly Circus.

London was a dangerous place to be and by 1943 the city had suffered extensive bomb damage after the Luftwaffe's raids during the Blitz of 1940 left over 30,000 Londoners dead, with hundreds of thousands more made homeless. The constant threat of attack only served to strengthen the resilience of the locals and as Noble and McCarty walked around the bomb-damaged streets, they were greeted cheerfully by tradesmen who were plying their wares under extremely difficult circumstances. After they left Whitehall they strolled along the Embankment before heading up to Piccadilly Circus where they were disappointed to see that the statue of Eros had been boarded up for safekeeping. The two men then headed towards the back streets of Soho where they found a servicemen's club that was selling a local brew. There they spent a pleasant evening in conversation with some fellow Americans who were on leave from the US Army, and they were happy to accept their invitation to accompany them to their NAAFI to eat a substantial meal. The two men decided it was prudent to keep to their cover story and told those who enquired about their presence in the UK that they had been commissioned to make a documentary film without being too specific. Luckily no one asked too many questions so they were able to relax and enjoy their time in London in the company of fellow countrymen.

Although they already knew about the relentless bombing raids in London from newsreels, they were amazed to see the great City in such a state; everywhere they looked buildings had sustained bomb damage and many of the people looked tired and demoralised. Beautiful buildings were crumbling and in danger of falling into the streets, even Buckingham Palace had been subjected to the attacks from the bombs dropped by the Luftwaffe. During the early years of the war it had been attacked on a number of occasions but managed to escape without too much damage, so the following morning before their return to Eakring the two men strolled through St James' Park to take a look. After all, reasoned Noble, you can't go to London and not see the place where the King and Queen lived and maybe catch a glimpse of them and the two pretty princesses on the balcony.

On the crowded train journey back to Nottingham they agreed that their meeting had been successful; the gratitude they had received from the representatives of the British Government renewed their resolve to help the country and the people who were fighting for their survival and to protect their way of life. McCarthy was pleased to have been given the opportunity to attend the meeting at the Ministry; he couldn't wait to write home to tell his family. Noble had shown once again his democratic leadership, making sure his men recognised the value of their hard labour.

The next day on returning to the oil field, Noble called a meeting with the crew. He passed on the thanks they had been given by the British government and told the men about their trip to London, describing the extent of the destruction they had witnessed in the once beautiful capital city. He praised his team on the work they had done so far and suggested it was time for them to host a social event for the local people. 'After all,' he said, 'all work and no play will make us all dull boys. I'll have a word with Captain Blenkinsop and see if we can organise a dance up at the Hall next weekend.' Rosser agreed to speak to Brother Edgar to get permission. After all, they were guests at the Hall and didn't want to do anything to antagonise their hosts.

'We'll have to stick to our cover stories though, but I'm sure some of you won't mind posing as film stars!' said Noble as the meeting broke up.

'No problem, boss,' shouted Carmichael. 'Anything to oblige.' The crew joined in the laughter.

CHAPTER 7

May 1943, Kelham Hall

The girls were getting ready for the dance organised by Captain Blenkinsop and his men to bring together the film crew with a number of locals. Celia was in a good mood; that morning she'd received a letter from her mother to say her brother, Richard, was safe and well. After his plane had been shot down, he had been taken prisoner by the Germans and sent back to Germany to sit the rest of the war out in a POW camp. The Red Cross had managed to get the message to his mother who was relieved to hear he was safe and unharmed, but she continued to worry about his welfare and was looking forward to receiving a letter from him. As a commissioned officer he would not be required to do hard labour in the camp, and the Red Cross were sending food parcels to supplement the meagre rations in all of the German POW camps. Celia hoped he was coping and that his time in captivity, and the war, would soon be over. Tonight though, she was looking forward to the dance. Captain Blenkinsop would be there and with luck she'd be able to spend some time with him so they could get to know one another better. He had certainly made it obvious during their brief encounters at the Barleycorn that he was interested in her, so she dressed carefully in a new dress her mother had sent to her for her birthday. The dress was in green silk and it complemented her flowing red hair and green eyes. Edith had spent the afternoon helping her to get ready and as she made a twirl in front of the mirror, she had to admit she had scrubbed up pretty well.

Edith, too, was looking forward to the dance; she was feeling weary and felt all work and no play was sapping her spirits and not for the first time she wondered why she had given up an easy office job to work on a farm. Her dress was an old one that she particularly liked, it was in a blue flowery material with a white Peter Pan collar. The two girls shared a room at the hostel and had become firm friends, helping each other to draw straight lines on the back of their legs to give the impression that they were wearing stockings. The myth that all Yanks had silk stockings to give out to the local girls, was just that in Eakring!

A knock on the door heralded the entrance of Deirdre who burst into the room to tell them the dance was about to start and they needed to hurry up. Deirdre was a petite brunette who had a slim figure and the bright red woollen sheathe dress she wore made her look sophisticated as she had pinned up her hair in a victory roll. As always, she seemed larger than life, and although the war had been raging for nearly 4 years, she was determined to stay positive and enjoy the freedom it had brought her. Leaving Liverpool and her large family had been a wrench but she had adapted well to her new surroundings and the new friends she had made.

'Come on, you two, let's not be late. I've got my eye on James and I don't want Brenda to get there first. Not that she's much competition with her buck teeth and BO!' she laughed.

'You are incorrigible,' laughed Edith as she picked up her handbag to follow Deirdre down the corridor. 'Come on, Celia, don't keep the handsome captain waiting.'

The men's common room had been decorated with balloons and streamers in red, white and blue and a trestle table had been set up with bowls of punch and bottles of beer. The star-striped banner and Union Jack were draped above the small stage, proclaiming the friendship between the two countries. Captain Blenkinsop had roped in some of his men to act as bar staff and to deal with any problems if trouble broke out between the Yanks and local men. 'Make sure that punch isn't too strong, Corporal,' Blenkinsop ordered the barman. 'We don't want any of the ladies getting drunk and the locals have been used to watered-down beer so it won't take much to tip them over the edge. We don't want any trouble tonight. I promised Brother Edgar that everyone would be on their best behaviour.'

'That's alright, sir,' replied the barman who had secretly emptied a bottle of vodka one of the Yanks had given him into the punch when no one was looking.

Some of the Yanks had started to arrive and helped themselves to the beer, which had been requisitioned from the Barleycorn earlier in the day. James Carmichael was with a small group of his mates and they put their heads together to embellish their cover stories.

'I'm going to tell the girls that I was in Gone with the Wind, just a small part though in case anyone saw it. I can tell them that Clarke is a mate of mine back home. That should impress them,' said James.

'Don't overdo it, mate,' said Red, 'they may live in the back of beyond but the locals aren't stupid, they weren't born yesterday.'

'It's not the locals I'm out to impress but that pretty brunette who has just walked in,' he replied, pointing towards Deirdre who was hovering expectantly near the door.

The band began warming up as the singer approached the microphone. 'Good evening, ladies and gentlemen,' she announced. 'We'll be playing some of your favourite songs tonight but if anyone has any requests don't be shy, come up and let me know. Anything to oblige our allies.' A few of the men at the back of the room cheered as the band started to play a Glen Miller favourite, *That Old Black Magic*, and one or two started swaying to the beat. Captain Blenkinsop looked around the room as it started to fill up; he was keeping a lookout for Celia who he was hoping to meet again, and as she entered with Edith and Deirdre, he raised his hand in welcome. Deirdre was quick to notice the gesture and turned to Celia. 'I think you've pulled already, Celia,' smiling at her before making a beeline for the drinks table.

Carmichael had also noticed the three girls as they entered the common room and nudged his companion. 'I think my conquest for the night has just arrived. Watch and learn, my friend,' he said to one of the younger members of the crew. He made his way to the drinks table and edged close to Deirdre. 'Hello again,' he said. 'I was hoping you'd be here tonight. I hope you friends won't mind if I lure you away so I can get to know you better before the scary matron catches me.'

Deirdre was over the moon; she had a crush on the handsome yank ever since he arrived and feigned shyness to hide her eagerness to spend the evening with him. 'Well,' she replied, 'seeing as you are so far away from home, it's the least I can do. Hands across the sea and all that.' Together they made their way to the seating area to talk. Edith saw them making their way across the dance floor and smiled to herself. Deirdre really knew how to get her own way. No doubt she would hear everything there was to know about the handsome yank when they were back at work in the morning. Celia having hooked up with the captain was dancing with him to a popular Mills Brothers song, *Paper Doll.*

Edith watched them, pleased that her friend was looking so happy after the worrying time she had when her brother went missing in action. She helped herself to another drink and looked around at the locals and Yanks dancing and laughing together, when she was tapped on the shoulder. 'May I have this dance?'

She turned around and saw PC Hopkins for once wearing civilian clothing. 'Hello Constable, I didn't recognise you out of uniform,' she replied. 'I'm not a great dancer but if you're willing to risk having your toes crushed, I'd be delighted.' So together they joined the throng.

Jack Harris, having supplied the beer had decided to close the pub for the night and join the festivities along with his wife Vera, who was dressed up to the nines with a little too much makeup and hair that was unnaturally black for a woman of her age. She watched Edith dancing with PC Hopkins and sniffed disapprovingly. 'Look at her,' she said to Jack. 'As soon as our Arthur's away she's up to no good.'

'Don't be silly, woman, the lass is just having a good time and Herbert knows the score. He's a mate of our Arthur's and he's not the sort to steal his girl when he's away fighting for his country. Leave the lass alone. Arthur wouldn't want her to miss the fun.' Jack was enjoying a well-deserved night off and Vera appreciated the change of scenery. It was rare for them to go out together since they'd taken on the tenancy of the pub.

The band started to play some slow music and the singer's sultry voice rang out as the dancers welcomed the respite from the more energetic routines. The local girls were delighted that the Yanks were great dancers but pleased with the slower pace so they could get their breath back.

'Come on, Jack,' said Vera. 'Let's have a dance, see if you remember how to do it.'

'What're you talking about, woman?' he replied as he led her onto the dance floor. 'There's life in the old dog yet! Let's show the youngsters how to do the foxtrot.'

'Well, it looks like the dance is a great success,' said Celia to Blenkinsop as they sipped their drinks watching the festivities from the seating area.

'It's all down to planning. If you fail to plan, you plan to fail,' he said in his superior manner. 'I pride myself on my organisational skills. I guess that's why the powers that be posted me to this assignment. You may think that filming is a bit trivial when there's a war on, but I can assure you Churchill is keen for this film to be completed for the morale of the people, and it's a tricky task keeping the Yanks in order. My superior officer was in London the other day speaking to one of the government ministers who told him that Mr Churchill is taking a keen interest in our activities. He mentioned what a splendid job I'm doing to support the crew. I wouldn't be surprised if I was mentioned in despatches. After all, the work we're doing on the home front is just as important for keeping up the morale of the British people.'

'Well I must say, Deirdre's morale is sky high at this very moment, she's certainly doing her bit for King and country,' she laughed as she watched Deirdre and Carmichael slip out of the door together.

'I'm more interested in your morale at this very moment, my dear,' said Blenkinsop as he slid his arm around her shoulder. 'Why don't we go out for some fresh air? It's getting a bit stuffy in here and it's a lovely evening.' Celia agreed it was a great idea and they also weaved their way past the dancers towards the front door.

'Sir?' the corporal intercepted them as they passed the drinks table. 'We're running low on the punch and the beer is running out as well. Are there any more supplies out back?' Blenkinsop, having preened himself about his excellent organisational skills, didn't want to appear a failure in front of Celia, so he despatched the corporal to have a word with Jack Harris to see if he could rustle up some more supplies from the local pub.

It was indeed a lovely night outside and the fresh air was a welcome change after the smoke-filled air in the common room, so Blenkinsop and Celia decided to have a stroll around the grounds where they would have more privacy to talk and get to know one another better. The grounds around the Hall were extensive and a path led down to the banks of the River Trent where they decided to sit and talk for a while.

Celia told him about her family back home and her aristocratic family's disappointment that she had opted to work on the land, explaining that she enjoyed the outdoor life and the friendships she had made during her time in Eakring. She did think her father, Sir Stanley, was secretly pleased about her choice of occupation though. He was proud she had chosen to do something useful for the war effort, unlike some of her chums who were spending the war swanning around London on the arms of various senior officers on the lookout for suitable husband material.

'So Captain Blenkinsop, now you know my life story,' she said as they sat by the river, 'what about you? How come you were chosen for this posting? I would have thought you'd prefer to be in the thick of it instead of babysitting a bunch of actors?'

'Oh, you're quite right, I've seen quite a bit of action overseas in the last few years but I was injured whilst out in Tunisia so they shipped me back to Blighty to recuperate. I was about to return to my regiment when this posting came up and I guess I was in the right place at the right time. It's certainly not my first choice, but,' he replied, looking at her, 'it has got its compensations!'

Celia began to shiver as the night was turning cooler, so Blenkinsop wrapped his jacket around her shoulders. 'Come on, old girl,' he said, 'it's getting a bit parky out here, let's get you back inside.'

As they walked back through the grounds towards the Hall, they overheard a heated argument, and turning the corner to the front of the Hall they saw Deirdre and Carmichael being confronted by a drunken Billy who was berating the yank for trying to take his girl away from him.

Deirdre was angrily shouting at him, telling him to leave them alone – she wasn't his girlfriend and he had no right to behave like that. Blenkinsop decided to wade in to defuse the situation.

'Now then, lads,' he said, 'that's no way to behave in front of these ladies. Have a bit of decorum.' And turning to Billy, he said, 'I think you've had enough to drink for one night, don't you? Now get off home with you before I have my lads put you under armed guard.'

Billy blinked at Blenkinsop who he thought was an arrogant bastard. 'Mind your own business, Captain Blimp, this is between me and the yank. Piss off, you stuck-up sod.'

'I'm making it my business so be off with you before I call on PC Hopkins to arrest you. I'm sure the school board would be interested in one of their teachers being hauled in front of the magistrate accused of common assault.' This seemed to sober him up so he turned to walk away.

'Don't think I've finished with you!' Billy shouted to Carmichael as he left. 'You haven't heard the last of this. You think you're God's gift coming over here,' he threatened as he walked away, 'just watch your back.'

The exchange had upset Deirdre who despite her bravado, was sorry she'd upset Billy, she was fond of him and he had been a good friend to her when she first arrived in the village. Celia went over to comfort her and together they returned to the dance hall. Carmichael brushed off the threat. 'It'll take more than that little squirt to stop me pursuing the lovely ladies around here,' he said with a laugh as he offered Blenkinsop a cigarette before they both returned to the Hall.

'A word to the wise, old man,' said Blenkinsop, 'don't underestimate the locals. They may be inbred and aren't men of the world like you and I but they know how to hold a grudge. Just watch your step.'

Old Joe and Jack Harris overheard the encounter as they stood outside enjoying a cigarette and some local gossip. 'There's bad blood there, you mark my words,' said old Joe. 'I've known Billy since he was knee high to a grasshopper, he's got a temper on him and a long memory.'

'He was also a nifty boxer a few years back, I remember him and our Arthur going to Goose Fair in Nottingham to take on the fighters in the boxing booth. Billy earned himself a few bob knocking the professionals out. I blame that slip of a girl mesen; she's been leading him on for a while now. If he does 'owt stupid it'll be her fault, you mark my words,' replied Jack as he stubbed out his fag and walked towards the Hall. 'I'd better get back, the old gal will be wondering where I am, and I wouldn't put it past her to chat up one of the Yanks. Mind you if she did, I'd probably have to pay him to take her off me hands.'

Blenkinsop intercepted old Joe as he walked towards the Hall. 'I wonder if I can have a quick word with you, old man?' he said.

'Oh aye, and what might that word be?' answered Joe, looking suspiciously towards the officer.

'I was meaning to catch up with you. You used to work at the oil field when it was active before the war. Is that right?'

'That's right,' he replied, 'so what's it got to do wi' you?'

'Mr Noble, the erm… director asked me to sound you out. He'd like to have a chat with you if you can spare the time. Can you come up to the Wood on Monday morning?'

'I daresay I can if I've nowt else on. Tell him I'll be there about 10, and he can put the kettle on. Tell him I take 3 sugars.'

'I'm sure that will be fine, just make sure you're not late, he's a busy man,' replied Blenkinsop in an effort to reassert his authority. 'Enjoy the rest of your evening.'

'Oh, I will, there might be another fight brewing and I wouldn't want to miss that. You know what we inbred are like, we enjoy a good scrap!' he said, grinning, enjoying the look on the captain's face as he realised his comments to Carmichael had been overheard.

Inside the dancing was winding down; the band were playing slow music and couples were shuffling around the dance floor to the rhythm. Edith had enjoyed the evening; she'd danced and flirted with some of the Yanks and made an effort to spend some time talking to Vera when Jack disappeared outside with old Joe. Although she wasn't serious about Arthur, it didn't hurt to keep in with his parents, especially as they owned the local pub. Celia had said goodnight to Blenkinsop and told the girls she was ready for her bed so Deirdre waved to Carmichael and the three girls left together. Matron was talking to Brother Edgar as the girls passed through the hallway on their way to bed and said goodnight to them both. They were pleased that the young people had enjoyed their evening, but both were relieved that life at the hall would be returning to normal the next day.

Deirdre couldn't wait to tell the girls what she had learned about the film crew but thought it was news that could keep until the next day as they said goodnight to one another. Carmichael had told her about his appearance in Gone with the Wind, one of her favourite films, and she couldn't wait to write to her sisters to tell them of her conquest.

Blenkinsop reflected on the success of the evening. As the revellers started to make their way home, he instructed his men to clear up before finishing for the night. His men were in high spirits mainly due to the amount of punch they had all consumed so agreed good-naturedly to leave the room spick and span before heading home to their billets.

CHAPTER 8

Dukes Wood, Eakring

Monday morning, the sun had risen early and it promised to be another warm day for early May. The cherry trees had started to blossom and the countryside was coming alive with new-born lambs romping in the farmers' fields as old Joe cycled by Arkwright's farm towards Dukes Wood for his meeting with the film director. He was wearing his Sunday best suit, which looked slightly incongruous with his bicycle clips and trouser legs tucked into his socks, preventing them from catching in the wheel mechanism. For once he'd shaved and smartened himself up, although he finished off his outfit with his old flat cap. He was excited to be summoned to the oil field and was curious to see what was happening with the filming. He would certainly have something to tell the lads in the pub who had been pulling his leg about becoming an adviser for the film crew. His boast that he knew more about the operations up at the Dukes Wood than anyone else, was actually true and he wondered not for the first time that morning if he was about to be offered a job. They had been good days for him and his wife Mary when he worked at Dukes Wood, and the money he earned as a roughneck had certainly given them a good standard of living. Since the closure and his wife's early death, he had started to feel his age and getting by on a meagre pension had put an end to his previous comfortable lifestyle. The only companionship he enjoyed nowadays was his dog Jan, and the locals down at the Barleycorn. There weren't many of his old mates left now as the youngsters had been called up one by one, and the crew from the oil company had either left the area to find work or died. Still, today he was feeling optimistic; the boss wanted to see him and that had to be a good sign.

As he approached the perimeter gate he called out to George, the night watchman who was packing up for the day. 'Ay-up, George, how're you doing mate?' he shouted, knowing that George was slightly deaf. Especially when it was time for him to buy a round in the pub!

'I'm alreet, Joe, what're you doing up here? It's a bit early for you to be out and about. Couldn't you sleep?'

'I've got important business with the boss up yonder; he's asked to see me,' Joe replied, preening his chest with his own self-importance.

'I didn't realise they were looking for a cleaner. If I'd known I'd have recommended my old gel for the job.'

Joe waved to him as he dismounted his bike to walk up the track to the Nissen hut that had been erected to serve as an office for the managers on site. As he neared the inner fence, he was stopped by the duty guard who asked about his business and after checking the visitor list waved him on with instructions to go straight to the office. Passing by some of the nodding donkeys, he noticed they had been cleaned up and if he wasn't mistaken, they looked as though they had been recommissioned. He couldn't see any cameras but there were a lot of men milling around; it was reminiscent of his time there, hearing the good-natured shouts coming from men who were working. To his trained eye, the site looked like a real oil field rather than a film set.

'Good morning, sir,' the voice breaking into his daydream. 'Thank you for coming. My name is Lloyd Noble. I'm honoured to meet you. This, as you know, is Captain Blenkinsop. Come and join us in the office.' The voice was coming from a smart middle-aged man who walked towards Joe to shake his hand.

'Good morning Mr Noble,' replied Joe as he removed his cloth cap. He was feeling quite confused. The man wasn't dressed as he imagined a Hollywood director would dress, he was wearing blue workman's overalls, hard hat and work boots.

Joe entered the office and was offered coffee or tea. 'Tea please, with plenty of sugar.'

'Coming up,' said Noble. 'I understand you Brits like it strong and sweet.'

'Aye, you're right there, sir, plenty of sugar keeps our energy levels up,' replied Joe, smiling.

'Before we start the meeting, Mr Wainwright,' said Blenkinsop to Joe, 'I would be grateful if you wouldn't mind signing this piece of paper.' Joe put on his reading glasses and after reading the paper he looked up at Blenkinsop.

'Why are you asking me to sign the Official Secrets Act?' he enquired.

'All will be made clear once you've signed the paper,' replied Blenkinsop, passing him a pen. Although still confused about the situation Joe went ahead and signed on the dotted line and passed the pen and paper back to Blenkinsop.

'Thank you, Captain Blenkinsop,' said Noble. 'I think you can leave us now. I would like to speak to Mr Wainwright alone, if you don't mind.' Blenkinsop hesitated before leaving, but thought better of insisting to remain.

'Come and sit over here, Joe,' Noble said to Joe, pointing to two old armchairs that had been scavenged by one of the workmen from Kelham Hall. 'Is it alright for me to call you Joe?'

'Aye, it is,' he replied.

'Good, and you can call me Lloyd. I'm afraid the captain is a little bit stuffy for my liking. Between you and me, he's full of his own importance. We Americans don't like to stand on ceremony.'

Joe warmed to Lloyd who had put him at ease. 'Neither do I. It never does any harm calling a spade a spade. I'm a bit confused though, why did you ask me to come here, and what's all this about signing the Official Secrets Act?'

'Well, I've been asking around and I was told you used to work here. In fact I've spoken to your old employers, the D'Arcy Exploration Company, who gave you an excellent reference. I understand you were the site foreman when they were drilling for oil here back in '39.'

'That's right, it was a pity the money ran out, there's a rich seam of good quality crude oil underground here. Much better than that stuff they've been importing. We had a good team of men as well who knew the job. Not many of us are left now, much the pity,' he said, supping his tea. 'Well for a yank you know how to mash a good cuppa.'

'I'll take that as a compliment, Joe, I think the two of us are going to get on well. Let me explain what's happening and the reason why you've been asked to sign the Official Secrets Act. Last year my company in Oklahoma was approached by a member of your government who is the chair of the Oil Control Board here in the UK. He told me the British oil supplies were running low and if something wasn't done to rectify the situation it may jeopardise the war effort. Philip Southwell of D'Arcy's, who you may know, told the government about the operation here that had to be closed down even though there's a wealth of oil underground that can be exploited given the right level of investment and resources, and that's where me and my men come in.'

'So, you're not making a film then,' said Joe. His confusion was starting to clear up as he took in what was being said.

'We had to concoct a cover story about making a film to satisfy the curiosity of the locals, and I have to admit they have fallen for it hook, line and sinker which has been good for us. As long as we can maintain the cover it will assure the safety of the people living in the area. If the information got into the wrong hands it would be dangerous for everyone concerned, so I'm sure you can understand why we did it.'

Joe chuckled. 'Well it'll disappoint one or two of the lasses round here if they found out their film star boyfriends were really roughnecks.'

'Exactly, and I must admit some of our lads have relished the idea of posing as film stars,' concurred Lloyd, laughing along with him.

'So where do I come into all this?' asked Joe, who was beginning to get excited about the prospect of working with the Yanks and getting his hands dirty doing the job he'd always loved.

'Some of the drawings and paperwork for the site seem to have got lost or were destroyed so a man with your local knowledge of the site and previous operation here is invaluable. What I'm proposing is for you to join us. We can employ you on your previous terms and conditions and I don't expect you to get your hands dirty. I'd like you to work with me in the office to help me identify areas where we can start to drill up to another 50 wells. So, what do you say, are you willing to join me?'

Joe smiled. 'I'm certainly willing and I'm bloody able. I may be a bit long in the tooth but I'm still fit and I've got all me marbles,' he replied.

'I can take that as a yes then?' laughed Noble.

'You certainly can, sir,' said Joe.

'Well that's settled then, I'll arrange for a contract to be drawn, and don't go calling me "sir", I haven't been knighted yet! There is one thing though. It is imperative that we maintain our cover story so we will have to decide on a role for you. Have you any ideas?'

'Funny you should ask. I certainly do,' said Joe with a grin. 'I realise casting me as the leading man might be a bit far-fetched but we could tell people I'm a technical adviser. They've been joking about that down at the Barleycorn, so it'd be one in the eye for that leery lot.'

'You know, Joe, I think we're going to get along just fine. Welcome to the team, now let me show you around the site.' They shook hands to seal the deal.

The two men spent the rest of the morning walking around the site and talking about the plans for expansion. One or two of the roughnecks recognised Joe from the pub and shouted greetings to him as he watched the production. Joe was impressed by the progress they had made in the few short weeks they had been there. He was happy to be working again doing a job he loved and feeling proud that his skills were needed for the war effort. It put a spring in his step and he looked ten years younger already as he felt his life had purpose again; he hadn't felt this good since before Mary died last year. On his way home he reflected on the events of the day and not for the first time wished that Mary was at home for him to share his good fortune.

Lloyd Noble was also reflecting on the events of the day and was congratulating himself on persuading Joe to join the team; his expertise would certainly be an advantage. He dismissed Blenkinsop's concerns that the local wouldn't be able to keep his mouth shut and not for the first time he wished they had assigned a less pompous ass as liaison officer. Blenkinsop was the epitome of the stereotypical British Army officer and Noble couldn't help himself calling him Colonel Blimp in his head whenever he saw him. He just prayed that he wouldn't say it out loud one of these days but speculated that if he did, it would go down well with his men, as well as the soldiers who were stationed with him.

That evening Joe decided to frequent his local hostelry, to spread the news about his good fortune. He was relishing the chance to tell them about the cover story and big up his part in the "Hollywood Film". He was fed up of the locals laughing at him and calling him a has been. *This'll show em*, he thought. They'd be all over him from now on, hoping to find out titbits of gossip from the site. He sure was going to enjoy himself over the next few months.

Joe was disappointed to see the pub empty when he arrived with his dog, Jan. Jack was setting up the bar.

'You're early, Joe, usual?' he asked. Joe nodded his assent.

'Well it's been such a nice day I thought I'd have a walk before the sun goes down,' he replied. 'I guess the lads and lasses from Arkwright's will be in soon though, I saw them packing up as I passed.

Has there been any news of the sheep stealing? It's been the second time in a few months, old man Arkwright'll be spitting feathers!'

'No, and I don't suppose Herbert will be putting hissen out to find out who dunnit. He'd rather spend his evenings supping in the pub than keeping a watch on the fields. I reckon the gang from Nottingham know that and keep a lookout to see when he comes in.'

'Well they'll have easy pickings when the Yanks start coming into the pub more, it'll be good for your profits and leave the coast clear as all the local farm hands will be spending more time in the public bar cadging drinks off them. Perhaps there's somebody in the village tipping them off. I wouldn't put it past some of 'um. I reckon I smelt lamb cooking when I passed the Urnshaws' place last Sunday when they were up at the church. Can't trust those Bible bashers, they probably asked for forgiveness before they tucked in to their Sunday roast.'

'You could be right there; I don't trust anyone from that end of the village either. They think they're too good to slum it down here, you never know what they get up to.' The two men enjoyed the banter.

'Any road up, I hear you were summoned to the oil field this morning.'

'Oh, aye, let me guess, George.'

'Spot on, you know you can't keep a secret around here. George called in at lunchtime, he reckoned you were up there asking about a cleaning job.'

Joe laughed. 'He's a barmy bogger. As a matter of fact, I have been offered a job up at Dukes Wood. You, my good man,' he paused for effect and enjoying the moment, 'are looking at the Technical Adviser to the Director of the Hollywood Blockbuster film the Roughnecks of Sherwood Forest.'

'Well I never, the lads were joking about that but I'd no idea the Yanks would employ locals. Mind you, if anyone knows about oil production around here it's got to be you.'

'You're right about that, the Yanks don't know their arse from their elbows but that Director chap, his name's Lloyd Noble, seems to be a good bloke and he's employed me to put them straight on a thing or two.'

Jack raised an eyebrow. 'Well I hope they're paying you.'

'They certainly are, I'll be rolling in it soon.'

As he spoke the door opened and Billy entered with his mate Fred.

'What's this, Joe, have you gone and got yourself a job? We've just seen George and he reckons that lot up at the wood have employed you as a cleaner,' he said, laughing at his own wit.

'As a matter of fact, smart arse, I have got a job but not as a cleaner.' He supped his pint before continuing to impart his news. 'You are looking at the Technical Director for the filming that's being made up there.'

'I thought you said Technical Adviser, not Director,' interrupted Jack.

'So I did, I think I'll have a word with my mate Lloyd and ask him to put Director on me contract. That's more in keeping with what I'll be doing.'

'Well congratulations, old timer, I guess the drinks are on you tonight. I'd be happy to drink to your good fortune,' he said, winking at Jack. 'We'll have two pints of your best bitter, mine host, and none of that massy watter you served at the dance last night. I'd downed 8 pints of it and went home as sober as a judge.'

'You cheeky young bogger. I could bar you for libel spreading rumours like that. My beer is the best you'll get in the county.'

'Actually, it's slander, not libel, and you can't sue someone for slander if it happens to be true,' he laughed.

'You can't win, mate,' chimed in Fred. 'You can't argue with a man who's been to university.'

'Less of your bloody cheek, the pair of you, if you want serving tonight. Any roads up, I hear you got yourself into a bit of bother up at the Hall. What was that all about?' asked Jack.

'It was nowt, just that bloody big-headed yank throwing his weight around and showing off in front of Deirdre,' replied Billy.

'Now then, I won't have you name calling my work mates if you don't mind. I won't have a word said against that fine body of men,' said Joe.

'You've changed your tune. Fine body of men, you were calling them blind last week. I think you've finally lost your marbles, Joe, if you think that lot are gentlemen. They're all out for trouble, you mark my words! They'll take what they want and leave the lasses behind when they go back to Hollywood. They've got no respect for our girls,' said Billy, getting hot under the collar.

'Come on now, lad, that's enough, calm down. The girls know the score and it's all just a bit of fun. You can't deny them that, there's a war on and they need to let their hair down now and again,' replied Jack.

'You wouldn't say that if you saw what I did up at the Hall,' went on Billy mysteriously. 'Your Arthur's gel, Edith, was lurking around the Yanks' living quarters during the dance. I bet she was just having a bit of fun as well.'

Jack looked annoyed at the thought of Edith taking up with one of the Yanks. 'You better keep your mouth shut about that, lad, our Vera'll have a dicky fit if she thinks Edith is two timing our Arthur.'

'Don't let him wind you up, Jack, the state he was in last night he couldn't bloody well see straight. I'll have a top-up and whilst you're at it pour one for yourself and these two reprobates, we might as well drink to my good fortune,' said Joe, trying to defuse the situation. Billy was out of order. Since Deirdre had started to two-time him with one of the Yanks, he was becoming a loose cannon.

As Jack poured the drinks the bar started to fill up and the exchange was forgotten for the time being but he decided to ask Vera to have a quiet word with Edith. The last thing he wanted was for Edith to go off with one of the Yanks and send his lad Arthur a Dear John letter whilst he was fighting overseas.

After the pub closed Joe walked home speculating about his day and congratulated himself on his ability to stick to the cover story. Mr Noble would be proud of him and he was looking forward to working with the Yanks. 'Come on, Jan,' he said to his collie dog. 'Let's get home and we can share that bit of the fish that George brought round at lunchtime.'

CHAPTER 9

May 1943, Cambridge

Frederick was enjoying the spring sunshine as he walked along the banks of the River Cam watching some undergraduates having fun punting inexpertly on the river. He was wearing a striped blazer and a straw boater, looking every inch the English gentleman of his time and as he was reflecting on the peace and tranquillity of his surroundings a voice disturbed his musing.

'Oh, what it is to be young and foolish,' Marcus said as he approached.

Frederick turned to meet his mentor. 'Hello Marcus, I got your message. Is there a problem?'

'Problem? Of course not, old man, I just wanted to catch up with you to see how things are going your end and what better place to meet than on the quintessential English riverside.' He indicated towards the students on the river. 'And you never know, we may be fortunate to see one of those fools fall in. It never fails to amuse me to see undergraduates fooling around with not a care in the world. When I was their age, I was far more serious and concerned about the state of the world but this lot seem to be in denial, living it up on Daddy's money and avoiding their patriotic duty at all cost.'

'I thought you were a conscientious objector during the last war?' ventured Frederick timidly.

'Too true, old boy, I was,' replied Marcus airily. 'That's not to say I wasn't being patriotic to the cause though. I believed the war in 1914 was a travesty and as you can see from what is happening now, it didn't solve a thing. All they managed to achieve was over 5 million deaths and economic disaster. The Führer has the right idea, we need to purge the world of the substandard species who think tribal warfare is the answer to the world's problems.'

The two men fell into step as they continued their walk along the towpath. Now and again one of the students passing by on a punt would shout a greeting and they waved back. It was late afternoon and lectures had finished for the day as the two men walked in companionable silence.

Eventually Marcus spoke. 'So, what news of our latest recruit?' he asked.

'Not a lot at the moment. I was mindful about your instructions for maintaining a watching brief. I've had regular reports and things are beginning to happen so I'm expecting some intelligence in the not so distant future. Things are pretty quiet on the whole and I don't want my agent to do anything at the moment to risk exposure.'

'Very wise, but you will keep me posted as soon as you have some useful intelligence to report. I'm in regular contact with my opposite number and we don't want to miss anything. The war should have been over before now, it beats me sometimes how Churchill has managed to counter some of the brilliant strategies of our leader. Pure luck, I'd say. Look at what happened at Dunkirk, total disaster but old Winnie somehow managed to turn the heroic failure into a patriotic victory. He had everyone cheering when the little ships limped into port with the bedraggled survivors. He couldn't do it again though so soon after when the Germans sank the *Lancastria*. They estimated over 9,000 died on that day but there's been a total blackout from the British press.'

Frederick nodded in assent; the war seemed to be dragging on with heavy losses of life on both sides.

'You'll be the first to know as soon as we uncover something. I have a feeling what we are on to may just be of vital importance to our war effort. My only regret is that I can't be there in person when the balloon goes up.'

'Now Frederick I've told you before, we can't all be glory seekers. Those also serve who watch and wait. You are a vital cog in the wheel; between us we've recruited a number of agents who are beavering away for the cause in strategic places. Our network is growing by the day and we need to make sure to keep our agents safe, that's just as important as working on the front line. You can rest assured we will be amply rewarded when the time comes.'

'You're right, and I agree wholeheartedly. It just seems that life is passing me by being stuck here.'

'Don't worry, old boy, you shouldn't be too impatient, I'm sure your time will come. You will have to be ready when that day comes and not lose your nerve.'

As the sun began to set the air turned chilly and the two men turned to retrace their steps. The river was quiet by the time they walked up the steps towards their rooms in the grounds of the university.

'Would you like to join me for a snifter before we go to dinner, old boy?' asked Marcus.

'Thank you but no, I have some papers to mark and a seminar to prepare for by tomorrow so it's going to be a long night for me,' Frederick replied before taking his leave.

Marcus watched him as he walked away towards his rooms. Frederick was becoming restless with his watching brief. He hoped he didn't do anything rash that might jeopardise the cause. Of all the agents he had recruited over the past few years he worried about Frederick; a weak link in the chain may have to be removed if it was in danger of breaking. Maybe he should take a trip to the Midlands himself, posing perhaps as an uncle of the agent who was stationed there. He was sure he could pull it off and a face-to-face meeting might reassure the agent, who hadn't sent any useful information so far about the operation in Sherwood Forest.

CHAPTER 10

Summer 1943, Eakring

Summer on Arkwright's farm yielded no let-up to the hard work for the land girls. The weather was improving by the day and the lighter nights meant an extension to the working day. Even so, the girls still had free time to spend up at the Hall sunbathing and flirting with the film crew. Deirdre was continuing her romance with Carmichael, much to the annoyance of Billy who was still suspicious of the yank's intentions towards her and wasn't afraid to vent his anger during his frequent trips to the Barleycorn.

Much to the delight of Jack, however, the film crew had adopted the pub as their regular haunt after long days filming and to an extent they mixed well with the regulars, mainly due to the generosity of the visitors who had money to burn so were happy to buy rounds. Carmichael and Deirdre met often during the summer months and she had started to hope that their romance would continue long after the end of the war despite the warnings of her friends who didn't share her optimism. She, along with the rest of the locals, was still blissfully unaware of the real reason for the presence of the Yanks in Dukes Wood.

Edith continued to write to Arthur although wasn't opposed to flirting and enjoying the company of the men who were more accessible, much to the disgust of Vera at the pub who cast a disapproving eye on her behaviour when she frequented the pub. Jack, however, was more pragmatic about it just as long as Edith continued to write affectionately to Arthur. His son's regiment were stationed overseas but there was little information about his exact whereabouts which in some ways was a blessing but it didn't stop his parents worrying. Although Eakring was a small village, a number of the local lads had joined up and occasionally news of someone killed or missing in action always brought home to those left behind the sacrifice they were making. Arkwright's two sons were fighting alongside Arthur and when news arrived in July that the elder brother, George, was listed as missing in action the locals spent a sombre night at the pub, discussing the brutal reality of war.

During the First World War a total of 44 young men left the village to fight, only for 12 of them never to return. Those who did return, including Joe, had fond memories of their brothers-in-arms. He had been one of the lucky ones, having survived without a scratch and when war broke out in 1939, he was more than willing to join up, but was rejected as being too old. He still had nightmares about the carnage on the Somme in 1916 when over 60,000 men were killed or injured and he still couldn't believe his luck as one by one his comrades had fallen, but even those bad memories failed to crush his enthusiasm to do his bit for King and country. He was happy now to be working hard alongside the Yanks at Dukes Wood and had become an invaluable member of the team. Lloyd Noble had even mooted the idea that there would be a job for him in back in Oklahoma if he had a mind to emigrate, a notion that frightened and excited him in equal measures.

In Cambridge the academic year had ended and the two Dons, Marcus and Frederick, decided to spend a fortnight on a walking holiday in Sherwood Forest. Marcus contacted Jack at the Barleycorn to enquire if he had rooms to rent at the pub for two weeks and had been delighted when Jack replied in the affirmative. They duly arrived in Marcus' car at the beginning of July having agreed to stay for their two-week break and were greeted by Vera. She was overjoyed at the prospect of having two distinguished gentlemen staying on the premises, and had spent the previous week preparing the rooms, getting out her best linen and giving the bedrooms a thorough spring clean. Vera badgered Jack to make sure there was plenty of food and asked him to use his black-market contacts to ensure they could feed the visitors. A table had been set up for their exclusive use in the snug bar and Jack hung a sign on the door to indicate the room was for resident guests only.

When Joe arrived in the evening for his usual pint, he noticed the sign and nodded to Jack.

'Ay-up lad, it looks like you're going up in the world, bet that was lady Vera's idea,' he said.

'Tell me about it, you'd think we'd got the King himself staying,' he said and leant towards Joe. 'Between you and me, we got a couple of poncey blokes from Cambridge here. They're on holiday and want to do some bird watching and walking around Sherwood Forest.'

'I always thought it was a strange hobby for grown men, but don't knock it. A couple of paying guests isn't to be sniffed at, I'm sure the extra money will come in handy. Mind you, why grown men want to spend their time looking at feathered birds beats me.'

Carmichael and Aaron Long entered the bar after a day of graft in search of a welcoming pint before trudging back to the Hall.

'Who does that posh car out front belong to? Don't tell me you've bought that out of your profits, Jack?' said Carmichael.

'I couldn't afford a bicycle with the profits I get from you lot, let alone a fancy car like that one,' he replied.

The car was a 1939 Riley Kestrel, one of only a few manufactured prior to the outbreak of the war by Lord Nuffield after he took over the Riley works in 1938. It was in immaculate condition having been garaged for a time by its first owner, who couldn't drive it due to the petrol rationing when the war broke out. Marcus had acquired it early in 1943 and had managed to get enough petrol to last for the trip to the Midlands.

As the bar started to fill up with the usual crowd on their way home from working in the fields, they were joined by the two academics who, after changing and freshening up, were ready for their evening meal. Vera escorted them through to the Snug and took their drinks order. Both men opted for whiskey, much to the dismay of Jack who was keeping a bottle behind the counter for himself.

'Something smells good, Jack, what's on the menu for the paying guests tonight? Don't tell me you've purloined a leg of lamb?' asked Billy with a smirk on his face.

'None of your bloody business, that's between me and them. When you book a room, you'll be able to join them. Until then, keep your nose out of other people's business,' replied Jack. He had managed to buy some joints of lamb on the black market but didn't want the news bandying about in case the coppers found out and started asking awkward questions. Vera on the other hand had no such scruples, she had begun to have delusions of grandeur and thought the experience of running a small "guest house" would be useful if they wanted to open a hotel when the war was over. She was even badgering Jack to take on extra staff and had considered offering a job to Edith, thinking she could keep an eye on her if she was working at the Barleycorn, and a bit of extra cash for the lass wouldn't go amiss. Jack, however, with an eye on his profits felt it best to give the extra work to Vera who he thought had too much time on her hands.

As they finished their meal, Marcus commented to Frederick that their trip to Eakring was a good idea. They could spend their days walking in the forest and make contact with their agent who was one of the locals at the pub, and was above suspicion. Perhaps, thought Marcus, the time was right now to mobilise the agent. Vera entered the snug to clear their plates.

'That was an excellent meal, thank you Mrs Harris. My compliments to the chef,' said Marcus.

'Oh, thank you sir, I'll pass that on,' she replied, pleased with the compliment but reluctant to let them know that she was the cook, preferring the illusion that as the landlady she employed staff to help with the running of the establishment. 'Can I get you both another drink?'

'You certainly can, we'll have another round of your exceptionally good whiskey if you don't mind and then I think we'll retire to our rooms. We want to make an early start tomorrow to explore the area, I've been told that Sherwood Forest is an area of outstanding beauty and we'd like to visit the major oak and see Robin Hood's old haunts.'

'Oh, I think you'll be impressed by the countryside around here. Jack and I took on the tenancy of the pub about 10 years ago now and we've been so happy here. The locals are friendly once you get to know them and I'm not one to gossip but we have an American film crew staying nearby. They're making a film up at Dukes Wood and this has become their local so you will be rubbing shoulders with real-life film stars. We don't make a fuss though and they are very well behaved on the whole, for Yanks.'

'My word, Marcus, I didn't realise we'd be mixing with film stars, how exciting. I can't wait to tell the others when we get back to Cambridge,' said Frederick who was enjoying the gossip. 'Perhaps we can take our drinks into the public bar and see if we recognise anyone.'

'Now then, old man, we don't want to be thought of as star struck, and as the lady says they prefer to keep low key. After all, they come here for a quiet drink like the rest of us,' replied Marcus with a glint in his eye. 'Maybe tomorrow night we'll join them in the public bar after our evening meal, and I promise not to bring my autograph book. Tell me, Mrs Harris, will there be anyone we recognise?'

Vera laughed. 'To tell you the truth, sir, I don't recognise any of 'em. I think all the big stars like Jimmy Stewart have joined up. Still, you never know, when all this is over and the film's out people will be flocking to the pub to see where the stars used to hang out,' she said with a laugh.

'Perhaps you should take their photographs to hang up around the bar, it would certainly draw the crowds,' replied Frederick who was enjoying the banter.

'Well, that's for another day. As for now we will enjoy their company and have something to tell others when we dine out after the war,' said Marcus, raising his glass.

Frederick agreed and the two men made a toast to their good fortune having found such comfortable accommodation with the added advantage of spending two weeks in the company of "American film stars".

Meanwhile in the public bar, the locals were intrigued to see the two Dons from Cambridge, who had arrived in their sleepy village: first the Americans and now posh blokes from Cambridge. The village was certainly attracting some distinguished visitors these days. There was one of the locals, however, who knew the real reason for the Dons' visit and resolved to find an opportunity to approach them for a quiet word.

As closing time approached the locals drifted off home to their respective beds having enjoyed the hospitality of the landlord and the opportunity to catch up on local gossip. The news on the war front that filtered through was beginning to sound more optimistic and the speculation that it would soon be over was discussed at length. Towards the end of the evening as the two academics passed through the public bar, they enquired about local walks they could do whilst staying in the area. Joe told them that Dukes Wood was out of bounds but if they ventured to the west of the village there was a wealth of footpaths and they could walk to Edwinstowe where the local inn sold a good pint so they could quench their thirst before returning to Eakring.

Gerald Blenkinsop was also in the bar enjoying a quiet pint. Recognising the two academics from earlier in the day, he intercepted Marcus on his way to his room.

'I say, old man,' he began, 'that's a splendid car you have outside. I tried to get my hands on one of the new Riley models after Lord Nuffield took over the company in '38 but they were snapped up quickly, and I have to admit they were a bit out of my price range. It's certainly a handsome-looking beast you've got though.'

'Too true, but with a 16 horsepower engine it's a bit thirsty on the juice and as you know, petrol is pretty scarce at the moment for us mere mortals,' replied Marcus. 'My friend and I are staying here for a couple of weeks so if you fancy a quick spin, I daresay we'll be able to oblige.'

Blenkinsop replied to the affirmative, saying he'd certainly look forward to that particular treat, before saying goodnight to one and all in the bar.

The following morning the sky was overcast although warm enough for walking, and after the two academics had eaten a hearty breakfast, Vera produced a packed lunch for them both to take with them. They wrapped up warm in thick jumpers under their waterproof jackets and were wearing sturdy walking shoes, ready to face the elements. They were determined to see the countryside despite the English unpredictable weather conditions.

'Will you be taking up Joe's recommendation to walk to Edwinstowe today?' Vera asked as they were preparing to leave.

Frederick replied, having spread out his Ordinance Survey map on the breakfast table and traced the route, 'It looks about 6 miles to Edwinstowe from here and judging by the map we would be passing by a place called Rufford Abbey. Is that worth a look?' he asked.

'Oh, it certainly is,' Vera replied. 'The actual abbey is derelict of course but the grounds are splendid. It's a wonder we don't get more visitors to the area. A little further to the north there is Thorseby Hall and to the south there's Newstead Abbey – that was Lord Byron's family seat.' She was quite enjoying her role as a hostess to visitors and pleased to be able to share her knowledge of the local tourist attractions. Marcus found the information interesting and decided to visit some of the places she mentioned. He for one was more than happy to mix business with pleasure and felt it would divert suspicion if they travelled around the local beauty spots.

'We are also fortunate that the Germans aren't bombing around here, we hear such awful stories about the attacks on the cities. Of course, there are a number of airfields in Lincolnshire and heavy industries in Nottingham and some nights the sky is lit up when the raids are on, but thank God we haven't been affected. Not that there's anything to bomb around here,' she said. 'Listen to me rabbiting on, you'll want to be on your way. Have a good day. I'm cooking rabbit stew for supper tonight; I dare say you'll be ready for it after all that walking.'

She started to clear the breakfast things and carried them into the kitchen, leaving the two men to finish getting ready for their day out.

Walking through the village they met Billy on his way to the school house and stopped to pass the time of day with him before passing the church and waving to the vicar who was tidying up the graveyard.

They passed by Arkwright's farm where the land army girls were clearing up the mess the cows had left in the farm yard. Edith recognised the two men from the night before and waved to them as she watched them walk by.

'Hello, hello,' said Deirdre to Edith. 'Don't tell me you've got your eye on one of the posh Dons from Cambridge.'

'You're joking, the tall one's old enough to be my father and the little skinny one's no match for my Arthur,' she replied.

'Well, beggars can't be choosey during war time and when the cat's away and all that,' laughed Deirdre. 'Not everyone can have a film star boyfriend like my James!' Edith rolled her eyes.

'Is she bragging about the love of her life again?' said Celia who came out from the farm house. 'Mrs Arkwright's sent me out to tell you to come in. She's mashed the tea if you want a cuppa.'

'No need to ask twice,' said Edith who put down her broom and headed inside.

Celia paused to watch as the two men walked up the road away from the village. She wondered what the attraction was in the area for two academics. As they turned the corner they caught her watching them and Marcus raised his hand in a mock salute.

The walk to Edwinstowe took longer than they thought; the roads meandered around the countryside, although they both enjoyed the peace and quiet after the hustle and bustle of Cambridge. Rufford Abbey was a spectacular sight. Even though it was partly derelict the proportions of the building were magnificent, and just as Vera said, the grounds were beautiful. They walked to the lake and stopped to look at the ford where one or two vehicles splashed through much to the delight of local children who were hanging around hoping someone would get stuck.

On arriving in Edwinstowe, they spent a pleasant hour resting at the pub, the White Swan (or Mucky Duck to the locals), where the beer was every bit as good as Joe had promised. The real reason for their trip wasn't discussed by mutual consent, both men finding solace in the relaxing countryside after a hectic term at the university.

They had made contact, albeit briefly, with their local agent, and there was no doubt in their minds that an opportunity would soon present itself for them to find out more about the secrets in Dukes Wood. Even if their agent took time to provide a report there were plenty of locals who knew a thing or two and as they had observed last night, alcohol loosened their tongues.

On their return walk they took a more direct route as they were both beginning to tire by the afternoon. They decided to stroll in the vicinity of Dukes Wood another day, after all, despite the overt friendliness there was a deep-seated suspicion of strangers in the countryside and a word in the wrong ear may just become their downfall.

They had spoken to the village bobby the night before and thought he posed no threat. Marcus had commented to Frederick as they left the bar, 'He had perfected the look of someone who was a sandwich short of a picnic, and certainly wouldn't be uncovering any clandestine activities.' They had both laughed at the joke. They certainly knew that appearances could be deceptive.

'Still, waters sometimes run deep, my friend, as we saw up at the ford today,' said Marcus ominously.

Entering the public bar at the end of the day, Marcus was amused to see the usual crowd. Many of the farmhands, including the land army girls, called in every night on their way home to relax and socialise and to listen to the latest news on the radio in the bar. It was a time when they could also pick up the local gossip and if they were lucky some of the crew from Dukes Wood would be there to regale them with titbits of information about the progress of the filming. James Carmichael was a frequent visitor although the attraction was the land army girls rather than the watered-down beer. He was propping up the bar laughing at something Deirdre had just said when he noticed the two Dons.

'Good evening, gentlemen,' he shouted to them across the crowded bar. 'I hear you've come down from Cambridge for a few days. Hope you're enjoying the peace and quiet of the countryside.'

'Thank you,' replied Frederick, who despite himself was feeling a bit overawed as he admired the handsome yank. 'We've just been to see the major oak. I guess you Yanks have heard about Robin Hood and his merry men. I saw the Hollywood film with Errol Flynn in the title role a few years ago.'

'That's right, it was filmed just before the war, I remember it well,' replied Carmichael.

'Oh James, were you in Hollywood when it was being made?' asked Deirdre who had been trying to find out which films James had been in so she could show off to her family and friends back home.

'As a matter of fact,' he said, 'I was one of the merry men. Of course, it was when I was just starting out in Hollywood so it wasn't a speaking part but the director did say I showed a lot of promise.'

'So, this film,' interjected Marcus, who was pleased to get around to talking about the "activities" in Dukes Wood, 'is going well, is it? I bet you are one of the leading men.'

'Well, I don't like to brag but I do have quite a major part in this one.' He smiled at Deirdre who was looking at him in admiration.

'Oh God,' Celia whispered to Edith on hearing about Carmichael's exploits. 'You do realise we won't hear the last of this.' Edith laughed out loud, enjoying the good-natured camaraderie in the bar. She caught Frederick looking admiringly in Carmichael's direction and catching his eye she raised her glass to him. He was looking suitably impressed with the "film stars", and had certainly found the tall blond yank to his liking.

The two-week holiday passed quickly for the two academics and on their last morning after eating yet another hearty breakfast they bid their farewells to Vera and Jack.

'Thank you, we have had an excellent holiday; in many ways it is a shame we have to return to the hurley-burley of life back at the university but needs must. Perhaps we can prevail upon your hospitality again next year, when with any luck this dreadful war will be over.'

Vera preened at the praise and assured them they would be very welcome.

CHAPTER 11

Eakring, November 1943

The work at the oil field carried on throughout the summer and autumn, and despite working under wartime restrictions and continuing to maintain secrecy of the operation the roughnecks did a sterling job. The number of oil wells recommissioned and additional ones being dug continued to increase the production. On the morning of the 13th November Rosser set off for the supply depot at Burton-on-Trent to pick up the weekly American food rations. The day was heavily overcast with thick fog that hung close to the ground, impeding their progress as they drove along the A38. Finally, the truck pulled up outside the guardhouse and Rosser was told that there had been an emergency telephone call from Kelham Hall for him. It turned out to be Don Walker with some bad news. Tragedy had struck; he told Rosser that Herman Douthit had fallen from the double board of the drilling mast at location 148 in Dukes Wood. At 11:30am that morning Douthit had climbed up to the derrick for the purpose of attaching a rope to the platform. As he was coming back down to take the cat line off, he fell about 55 feet and died of head injuries.

The sad news of the tragic accident spread like wildfire amongst the locals at the Barleycorn by the afternoon as the farmhands called in on their way home. By this time the locals and Yanks had gained a mutual respect for one another and life in the sleepy village had so far passed by without major incident. Together they had kept themselves informed of the progress of the war and celebrated minor victories for the allies. Farmer Arkwright's son who had been listed as missing in action early in the year had been located and was a prisoner of war. The news came as a relief to the farmer and his wife, although they continued to worry about the fate of their second son who was fighting in Belgium. The land army girls had become fond of the elderly farmer and his wife and they tried to keep the Arkwright family's spirits up by working hard and spending some of their spare time at the farm helping around the house.

Arrangements were made with Chaplain Carlsen at the American General Hospital in Mansfield for Herman's funeral to take place a few days later and it was attended by both his American mates and the British friends he had made since arriving in England. The locals were still in the dark about the true reason for the work at Dukes Wood and speculated on the reasons for the tragedy, but out of respect for their loss they didn't question the oil men when they called in for drinks in the evenings. On returning to the village after the funeral the locals and friends of Douthat's from the oil field gathered together in the Barleycorn to drink to his memory. Some of the men brought along musical instruments and they played late into the night and although the mood became more subdued as the evening wore on, it was a fitting tribute to their fallen comrade. Although he hadn't died fighting on the front line, he had lost his life doing vital war work far from his home and family. He was later laid to rest at the American War Cemetery in Cambridge, the only civilian to be buried there, but one who had given his life for the war effort.

The sombre mood of the men continued as Christmas approached, and one day in early December Noble visited the pub to discuss ways in which the locals could help the Yanks celebrate the forthcoming holiday and to alleviate their homesickness and sadness over the death of their colleague and friend, Herman.

Jack suggested a social get-together and resurrected the suggestion of a darts match, an idea that appealed to Noble, so together they began making plans. Jack persuaded Vera to make up some sandwiches and Noble agreed to pay for a barrel of beer to ensure the evening would go with a swing.

Two nights later the locals and Yanks arrived at the bar in anticipation of a pre-Christmas celebration to raise their spirits and help them come to terms with the sad demise of Herman.

By now the work at the oil field had been going for 9 months and most of the crew were looking forward to returning home to their wives and families. The locals were still blissfully unaware of the true nature of the operation in Dukes Wood, although some of them had suspicions as they heard the rumble of heavy lorries passing through the village on a regular basis in the early hours. There was a tacit agreement to keep quiet about the possibility of some sort of top-secret war work taking place in the vicinity. The headquarters for British Petroleum was sited not too far away and many mistakenly believed that the lorries were bound for there.

One of the Yanks brought along his banjo and he got the evening off to a great start by playing some popular songs for the locals to sing along to. Deirdre was uncharacteristically in a pensive mood as she sat close to Carmichael who was joining in the singing with gusto and ignoring her when she tried to talk to him. Celia and Blenkinsop were chatting amicably, sitting together near the window, whilst Edith had agreed to help behind the bar and was busy serving drinks. She was enjoying the banter with the customers and was happy to give Vera a hand in the kitchen. Vera was pleased with the extra help as it gave her more time to chat to the boys and prepare the sandwiches to serve up once the darts match finished.

The village team was captained by Billy Clark, who had spent many hours practicing and was determined to help his side win the match against the Yanks. During the evening he kept glaring at Carmichael, still smarting at the thought that Carmichael had stolen his girl but held on to the belief that he would win her back once the Yanks embarked on their return journey to the States. Looking at Deirdre's sad face that night he wanted to punch the smug yank who was making her unhappy by treating her with contempt.

Joe Wainwright, who by this time had divided loyalties, was enjoying the evening and would be pleased with the results whichever side won. He was sharing a table with Noble in the snug bar and the two men were in deep conversation about the safety measures they had reviewed after the tragic accident a few weeks before.

'We've completed the safety checks,' said Noble, 'and there was no breach in the safety measures. The only conclusion we can make is that Herman was momentarily distracted and slipped. Such a waste of a good man, he'll be missed, good derrick hands are few and far between. I've written to his widow and the company will be paying her a pension; under the circumstances it's the least we can do. The lads also had a whip round and we've raised some money for her which I've sent on. I know the men volunteered for this assignment and they all knew the risks but nothing can compensate the lady for the loss of her husband.'

'Aye, it's a dangerous occupation and no mistake, but the safety measures up at Dukes Wood are as good as any I've seen. You've nothing to reproach yourself for, Lloyd, accidents do happen in this business and it's always a shock to the system when someone dies. If anything, the rest of the crew will take extra care from now on, we don't want to lose anyone else. It won't be long now before they'll be going back home. It's amazing how the past few months have flown by and you have all done an incredible job,' replied Joe.

'This time last year we thought the war would be over before we'd sunk the first well but look at us now, another year nearly over with no end in sight. When the lads do get home, they'll be drafted into the Army. It doesn't seem fair somehow,' said Noble, draining his pint.

'Come on,' said Joe, 'the darts match will be starting soon, let me get you another beer and we can join the others in the public bar.'

'That's kind, thanks Joe. I'm not sure if we should be sitting together though, what with you cheering on our rivals,' laughed Noble.

'Not me, Lloyd, tonight I'll be sitting firmly on the fence.'

Celia was talking about her day to Blenkinsop who appeared to be slightly distracted, having been excluded from the arrangements for the darts match and as an outsider, he was not co-opted onto either team. He was feeling bored already and kept looking at his watch. However, Celia appeared to be having fun and had spent the afternoon getting ready for the evening. She was wearing a new jumper and cardigan in soft cashmere with a string of pearls around her neck. The soft peach colour of the twin-set suited her complexion and she had pinned her hair up in a sophisticated style. Before leaving the Hall, Deirdre had remarked at her appearance.

'Blimey, Celia, you're dressed to kill tonight. Don't tell me the gallant captain is on a promise.'

Celia had blushed. Her relationship with Blenkinsop had become close in the few months they had known each other and although Celia had invited him to stay with her family in London when they had some time off together, the opportunity hadn't arisen so far.

After a few drinks the banjo player put away his instrument and they were ready to begin the darts match. Although on the surface it was a friendly match, all of the players were taking it seriously and the local reputation was at stake.

Presently Billy stepped up to the dart board to announce the start of the match. They tossed a coin which the Yanks won and they opted to throw first. Aaron Long, being the captain of their team, stepped up to the board and scored a treble 20 with his first arrow, much to the consternation of Billy Clark who had underestimated the skill of the opposing team. Unbeknown to him the Yanks had been preparing for the match up at the Hall using an old dart board one of the monks had produced for them. Life at Kelham had been running smoothly with the Yanks and resident monks billeted together; "rogues and robes" got along fine as the roughnecks adhered to the monastery rules and were getting used to the quirky ways of their hosts.

The handful of land army girls who were also billeted at the Hall were kept separate in the East Wing under the watchful eye of the matron, who ensured they kept a respectful distance from the monks (and Yanks). There would be no shenanigans under her watch!

When Billy stepped up to take his turn at the dart board the pressure was on after the excellent opening gambit from the Yanks' team. Above all, he didn't want to let his teammates down, nor did he want to show himself up in front of Deirdre who was sitting next to Carmichael and cheering on the opposition. Uncharacteristically his first performance left a lot to be desired, much to the consternation of his teammates, but as the match progressed, he regained his form and the locals were able to secure a victory. The Yanks accepted defeat gracefully, some of them secretly pleased about the loss as they knew how seriously the locals took the game, and didn't want the night to end in an unpleasant fracas.

Blenkinsop characteristically claimed the credit for the success of the evening, magnanimously thanking Vera for providing sandwiches and Jack for hosting the match. Standing next to him at the bar he overheard Carmichael making sarcastic remarks to his mates about the Army captain's exclusion from the local team and suggested that he was in Eakring babysitting the visiting Yanks because of his equal lack of prowess on the battlefield. The roughnecks sharing the joke laughed, although they had warmed to the locals, they found Blenkinsop patronising and disliked his superior attitude towards his men and his contempt for the local farm hands. Old Joe overheard the remarks, thinking to himself that Carmichael would do well not to antagonise the Army officer who was known to bear grudges.

Vera passed around the sandwiches that she had prepared earlier in the day and spent a pleasant evening playing the hostess, lapping up the attention of the Yanks who flirted with her. She was also somewhat starstruck and had taken a particular liking to Carmichael who seemed to be the star of the movie. He, having initially enjoyed her ribald comments and unladylike suggestions, had tired of her advances and had started to ridicule her in front of his peers, pointing out that she was old enough to be his mother, but the last thing on her mind was motherly concern. Comments that hadn't gone unnoticed by Jack who saw how they had upset his wife.

After the darts match the Yanks brought out their musical instruments and began to play some popular tunes before joining in with the locals to sing ballads and country music. The evening entertainment continued well after closing time, although some of the revellers and the land army girls left after the darts match because they had to be up early for work the following day. After saying goodnight to Edith, Jack locked the door and produced a bottle of whiskey to share with the stragglers. The illegal lock-in went on until just after midnight and only finished when Vera threw them out as they had kept her awake when she was trying to sleep. Old Joe and PC Hopkins were the last to leave and thanked Jack for a great evening. As they unsteadily weaved their way towards their respective homes Joe remarked on the hospitality of the landlord.

'Well, that were a right good evening. Where do you think Jack disappeared to after the lock-in? I thought he'd gone to make some more sandwiches but they never materialised.'

'Perhaps he was saying goodnight to his lovely wife,' replied Herbert with a smirk.

'Aye, you could be right. There's no accounting for taste,' laughed Joe as they parted company at the end of the street.

As Jack switched off the lights in the bar he reflected on the success of the evening. The takings had been excellent, although he had to admit they had drunk away a substantial amount of the profits during the lock-in, and having done a bit of business on the side had added to the coffers. All in all, he thought this war had some advantages.

CHAPTER 12

Dukes Wood

The following morning the roughnecks gathered outside the Hall to wait for their transport to work, many of them nursing thick heads after the excessive drinking the night before. Noble, however, had been up with a lark having taken a walk around the grounds before breakfast. He was hopeful that the oil men were in a better frame of mind as he listened to the cheerful banter whilst they were waiting for the trucks to arrive. It was a cool autumnal morning with a clear blue sky.

'It looks like we're in for a good day,' said Don Walker. 'We had to shut down one of the rigs yesterday for a couple of hours due to an electrical failure, boss. I'll check it over when we get there, it should be up and running again today and if the weather stays good we should be able to make up the shortfall in production and, if the light holds we should be able to get a couple of hours' overtime in.'

'Thanks Don,' replied Noble. 'Let me know if the problem persists and I'll contact the national grid to see if there's been any bomb damage on the lines.' Just then the trucks arrived and the men clambered aboard.

When they arrived at the site, George, the night watchman, was preparing to leave and he opened the gates and waved them in. 'Joe's just arrived,' he shouted to Noble.

Joe was standing in the doorway of the site office with a worried look on his face, and as Noble climbed down from the truck Joe ran over to meet him. 'Is everything OK?' asked Noble as he noticed the look on Joe's face.

'No, you'd better take a look inside,' replied Joe quietly.

The Nissen hut that served as an office was a prefabricated steel structure designed in the First World War by the engineer and inventor, Major Peter Norman Nissen. It was made from a half-cylindrical skin of corrugated steel and his unique design made it a popular choice for housing men living around airfields and military installations, due to the fact that it was capable of withstanding bombing raids and could easily be camouflaged from the air. The one in Dukes Wood had stood there since the first war and although having seen better days, it served as a site office for the oil field director and his team. Inside the 16 by 24 feet structure there was a desk and chair at one end with a Bakelite telephone, flanked by two metal filing cabinets. Nearer to the door, in the centre of the room, stood a large wooden table that was used to spread out the site maps for the team to plot the progress of the drilling operation whilst more filing cabinets flanked the side walls. Towards the back of the room a noticeboard held information about delivery of supplies, the daily output targets and staffing rotas and under the window next to two armchairs that had seen better days, the table used for mashing the tea, with a kettle, Bunsen burner and a selection of tin mugs, had been overturned.

Noble peered inside and to his amazement saw a body lying on the floor. Not wanting to cause alarm he beckoned Don Walker over and gave him instructions to get the men to work and away from the office.

Laying on his back in a pool of blood was James Carmichael with a gaping wound in his chest. 'Oh my God,' cried Walker as he approached the office following the dispersal of the men. 'It's Carmichael. What on earth is he doing here?' One or two of the men, sensing a problem had lingered around the site office to see what had happened.

'Where's Captain Blenkinsop?' asked Noble to no one in

particular, being unsure of what to do.

Joe sized up the situation and spoke quietly to Noble. 'It looks like he's been shot. I'll call the police and we'd better wait outside.'

'Blenkinsop should be here to take charge. Where on earth is he?' replied Noble in a shaky voice.

Just then Blenkinsop arrived in his MG, driving up to the site office. Having seen the look on the faces of the men who were milling around he strode up to Noble and Joe to ask what was happening. Noble explained the situation and told him that Joe was calling the police.

'I don't think there's any need for the local plod to be informed. I shall be taking charge here,' he said in his superior tone. 'I'm sure we'll be able to clear up this matter before the police arrive.' He went inside the office to view the body and ordered Joe to step outside and wait. After a few minutes he re-emerged and addressed the group. 'It looks to me like the poor chap came here last night to commit suicide. Tragic, really, but these things happen in war time. Now I think you should all be getting on with your work whilst I deal with the situation.'

Joe stepped forward. 'I think you're wrong, it looks like James has been murdered. If he committed suicide the gun would still be in his hand but there's no evidence of a weapon in the room at all. The room's also been ransacked so it looks to me like he was shot after disturbing an intruder.'

Lowering his voice, Blenkinsop took Joe to one side. 'If I wanted your opinion, I'd ask for it,' he said dismissively. 'If you've forgotten, there's a war on and a murder investigation will only bring us unwanted publicity, and given the circumstances of the Yanks' presence here that's something we can do without. There's nothing we can do for the poor chap and so we need to keep the situation hush-hush as far as possible. I'll get my men to cordon off the area and I'll be conducting the investigation on behalf of the MOD.' Just then PC Hopkins rode up on his bicycle. He removed his bicycle clips and approached Blenkinsop, taking out his notebook.

'Good morning, gentlemen,' he began. 'I understand a crime has been committed so I'll need to take some preliminary statements. Inspector Green from Newark is on his way and will be taking charge of the investigation but in the meantime, I've been asked to secure the crime scene and find out what's happened.'

Blenkinsop, fearing his authority was being undermined, approached Hopkins. 'Now look here, old boy, there is no need for police interference, this is a military site and I have conducted a preliminary investigation so I'd be obliged if you will put away your notebook and toddle off. The man has committed suicide and we don't want any fuss.'

PC Hopkins pulled himself up to his full height and puffed out his chest. 'I don't think you're qualified to draw a conclusion at the moment. The police doctor will be arriving shortly and I think we will let him decide on the manner in which the unfortunate victim has met his end. Now I must ask you to stand back as you are contaminating a potential crime scene.'

The small group of roughnecks were watching the stand-off between the two men with interest when a police car drew up and a grey-haired man in his late 50s stepped out. He was of medium height and was wearing a light brown mackintosh, double-breasted pin-striped suit and a trilby hat. Hopkins was relieved to see his senior officer and stepped over to meet him.

'Good morning, sir, the victim is in the office. It looks as though he's been shot in the chest. I haven't disturbed anything and I've secured the scene for you. The Army officer over there,' he pointed at Blenkinsop who was getting agitated, 'says he has the authority to deal with the matter and doesn't want us to interfere.'

'Oh, does he now?' replied Inspector Green. 'I'll deal with him first and then we can get on with *our* investigation.'

Walking over to Blenkinsop, Green introduced himself and shook hands with the captain. 'Could I have a quiet word?' he asked. The two men moved away from the listening ears of the oil crew. 'Now, I am fully conversant with the situation you have here and I'd be pleased to get your take on things later on, but for now I'd be grateful if you will get your men to clear the area and arrange for the workers to be transported off-site once my constable has taken all the names and addresses.'

'I don't think you need to spend much time here,' replied Blenkinsop, 'it's fairly obvious to me that the poor chap has committed suicide. I don't think we need to make too much fuss; the MOD will want things to be swept under the carpet, so to speak. It's important for national security for us to get things cleared up quickly so that production can resume ASAP.'

'Now look here, old chap,' said Green, 'that's not how we do things in the police. If a crime has been committed, there will be a thorough investigation to uncover the culprit. The British Police Force are not in the game of sweeping murder under the carpet and I am sure our American visitors would not want the perpetrator to go unpunished.'

Blenkinsop had met his match and decided to go along with the orders he had been given. He went over to brief his men who were huddled together in a group. He tried to ignore the smirks on their faces as they followed his instructions. PC Hopkins joined them and proceeded to take down their particulars in his notebook before rounding up the oil-field workers.

Meanwhile, the inspector entered the site office to view the body. Noble and Joe stood outside awaiting instructions. They were both feeling numb and couldn't quite believe that one of their men had been murdered. As they stood waiting another car arrived and the police doctor alighted with his medical bag. He made his way into the office and greeted the inspector.

'Good morning, Inspector, so what have we got here?' asked the doctor, looking down at the body.

'We haven't moved anything, sir,' said Inspector Green who was keeping a discreet distance, standing by the entrance. 'It looks like a chest wound and the corpse is cold,' he added, 'so there's a possibility that he was killed sometime during the night. He was found this morning as the crew arrived for work.'

'What about the weapon?'

'It looks like a gunshot wound although there's no sign of a gun in the office. The constable has had a preliminary look around but we'll need to do a more thorough search. As you can see there are signs of a struggle but until we speak to everyone who knew the deceased we won't know when he came to the site or what he was doing here last night. There's a possibility the weapon may have been thrown into the undergrowth so I'll get some men over to take a good look.'

The doctor knelt down to examine the body as Green left the room to have a word with Noble and Joe who had been asked to wait outside. The police inspector was aware of the true reason for the presence of the crew in Dukes Wood, although this intelligence had not as yet been passed on to PC Hopkins for reasons of national security. He was acutely aware of the likelihood of the murder being more than a domestic crime but he needed to keep an open mind and conduct a thorough investigation.

PC Hopkins had listed the names and contact details for all the men leaving the site, most of whom he was acquainted with, and took the opportunity to begin questioning them about their movements after the darts match finished last night. They confirmed that their transport back to the Hall had arrived just after closing time and the crew, with the exception of Carmichael, went back together. On arrival at the Hall they went to the common room for a nightcap.

After he'd finished questioning the Yanks, Hopkins decided to use his own initiative and ventured down to the security gate to question George.

'What's happening up at the site office?' asked George as he approached.

'There's been a murder, George,' replied Hopkins who was

excited to be part of his first major investigation, 'so I need to ask about your movements since last night.'

'Who's been murdered?' enquired the night watchman, looking worried.

'Can't tell you at the moment, but you'll find out all in good time. I need to find out what you have been doing since last night.'

'You know what my movements were last night, you saw me on my way to work at the usual time. I always clock on when everyone else is clocking off. I arrived about 7 and locked the gates when the boss left the site about half an hour later.'

'And then what did you do?' asked Hopkins, licking his pencil to write down his answer word for word as he thought it was important evidence.

'What do you think I did, you silly bogger, I sat in the hut and read my paper for an hour before going on me rounds.'

'Did you see anything suspicious?'

'Of course not, if I had I'd have said something before now. It was as quiet as the grave as usual. After me rounds I came back to the hut and settled down for the night. Nowt 'appened out of the ordinary.'

'Did you do a patrol of the perimeter fence later in the evening?' questioned Hopkins.

'Don't be daft, it was bloody cold and I don't get paid enough to catch pneumonia,' he replied sarcastically.

Satisfied that George had nothing of importance to report, Hopkins put away his notebook and told him he was free to go for now, but cautioned him that he may have to be questioned again later.

Meanwhile, Inspector Green was walking around the site with Noble and Joe gathering some background information about Carmichael and speculating on the reason for his presence in the office. He had known Joe since they were at school together many years ago and their paths had crossed from time to time so they were on friendly terms. He knew Joe to be a shrewd judge of character and thought he would be of use during the investigation. He also gained a favourable impression of Lloyd Noble, who was keen to do all he could to help the investigation. Presently he told them they were free to leave the site and expressed his condolences for their loss. He was aware of the tragic accident a few weeks before and felt sympathy for the crew who had now lost another work mate, this time in suspicious circumstances.

Returning to the site office he met up with the doctor who was leaving the office having just finished his examination.

'I've completed my initial examination,' he told the inspector. 'When there's a violent sudden death, we have to start by asking four questions. What sort of weapon has inflicted the wound? Here, as you already suspected, it is a gunshot wound. At what range was the gun fired? From what direction? And could the wound have been self-inflicted? As you can see, it is obvious that the poor fellow was murdered. It looks like he was shot from around 6-8 feet away and it is likely the perpetrator was standing near the window, although that will need to be verified. There's no powder burns around the entry wound so I can confirm that there is no way in which he could have committed suicide, even if he had been found with a gun in his hand. The lack of power burns around the entry site puts paid to that theory. We'll take the body to the morgue for an autopsy but judging by the temperature and the condition of the body this morning a rough estimate for the time of death would be between 10.30pm and 2.30am last night. Can't be any more specific than that at the moment, but it gives you something to work with and I'll complete a full report for you by tomorrow night at the latest. The undertakers are outside so I'll get then to remove the body now.'

'Thank you,' replied Green. 'Now the site's been cleared I'll be able to have a good look around.'

After the body had been removed and the doctor had left, Green cast an experienced eye around the room. The filing cabinet had been ransacked and papers strewn across the floor, the top drawer of the desk in the corner had been forced open and some papers were spilling out. The body had been lying near the doorway. It looked like he'd been shot in the chest as he entered and judging by the angle of the entry wound, the killer may have been standing on the right side of the room. On further examination though, he noticed a nick in the steel girder holding up the roof where the bullet had ricocheted. That would indicate that the killer had been standing next to the filing cabinet facing the door when he was disturbed. It was possible the shot had been aimed at the ceiling, perhaps to scare off James as he entered, but instead of passing through the roof it bounced off the girder and hit him in the chest.

So, it could have been a robbery gone wrong; the intruder may have been looking for money or other valuables when disturbed by James, fired off a shot randomly to scare him but it ricocheted and hit him in the chest, possibly killing him instantly. This was not, then, a deliberate murder, but there were so many questions to answer. What was James doing at the site at that time of night, and had he gone alone? If James had a companion with him when he went to the site, that person could be a vital witness. Or if the perpetrator chased him or her outside there could be another body hidden in the woods.

PC Hopkins, seeing the doctor leave with the body returned to the site office to speak to the inspector and to ask for instructions on what to do next. Inspector Green had been given authority to brief the local police officer about the true nature of the activities in the wood, so took him aside and told him, stressing that the information was strictly confidential. Hopkins was amazed, and more than a little upset that he had been kept in the dark up until now.

As he was digesting the information Blenkinsop returned. He and his men had checked out the perimeter fence and discovered a section where the wire had been cut to create a small opening big enough for someone to crawl through. Feeling this was a significant find, and wanting to assist with the investigation, he offered to show the inspector where it was.

'Good work, Captain,' said Green and turned to address Hopkins. 'Before we go and have a look round, have all the workers left the site? We don't want anyone milling around and getting in the way whilst we're conducting our investigation.'

'They have, sir,' he replied, 'and I've collected all their contact details. They're billeting up at Kelham Hall and I've asked them to stay there for the rest of the day in case you want to interview any of them when you've finished here. I've also checked their movements last night when the pub closed. From what I've been told they left the pub together, with the exception of James Carmichael, to drive back to Kelham Hall in the Army truck not long after the darts match ended.'

'I can verify that,' added Blenkinsop. 'Corporal Brown told me he drove them all back to the Hall just after 10.30. As PC Hopkins has said, Mr Carmichael wasn't with them as he was seen to leave earlier in the evening.'

Hopkins continued his report. 'One of the Yanks told me it wasn't unusual for Carmichael to spend the night away from the digs. He had a couple of girlfriends in the village, one of whom had a warm bed to offer.'

'I take it then that the deceased was a bit of a lad. Well, that gives us a lead to follow up. Well done, Herbert. Did you get the names of the lady friends by any chance?' replied the Inspector.

Hopkins preened at the praise from his superior and went on. 'I have. One is called Brenda, she lives in the village, and the other is Deirdre, one of the land girls who's billeted up at the hall. I've also interviewed the night watchman who said he saw nothing suspicious overnight.'

'Well the man must be blind as well as stupid,' cut in Blenkinsop. 'My men just found where the killer entered the site. If it was done last night, surely the man would have heard something.'

'Good work, both of you,' said Green. 'Let's go and have a look before we go over the crime scene in the office. The police doctor has confirmed it was murder and will be giving us a full report later.

We need to search the whole area with a fine-tooth comb to see if the killer has left any clues, and if Mr Carmichael had a companion with him there may be a second body somewhere. Let's get started with the point of entry and work our way back towards the Nissen hut from there.'

The three men retraced the captain's steps towards the perimeter fence. The point of entry was around a slight bend in the road, obscured from the main entrance by a row of trees. Hopkins reported George's movements after starting work the night before. He had walked around the perimeter around 8.30pm before settling down for the night. If the damage had been done before then, he would have noticed. George the night watchman had made no further checks as it was a cold night with rain in the early hours, so remained in his hut to keep warm.

On examination of the fence Green found a small fragment of green wool caught on the barbed wire and put it in an evidence bag. Any footprints had been washed away during a storm but they did find the remains of a tyre track in the mud from a bicycle. Hopkins noted the finds in his notebook and told the inspector he would write up his report the moment he returned to the station. Inspector Green was impressed by his enthusiasm. PC Hopkins had a reputation on the force for being lazy and turning a blind eye to the poaching that was rife in his patch up at Thoresby Hall. Green was amused; maybe the constable wasn't so lazy after all! Perhaps being given some responsibility in a major investigation would be good for the lad.

'The next thing I want you to do,' he said to him, 'is to set up an incident room for us in the village. Do you have any idea where we can go?'

'As a matter of fact, I do, sir,' he replied. 'I'm sure we could use the snug bar at the Barleycorn. It's a quiet room away from the main bar and they can pull the shutters on the bar down so we wouldn't be disturbed. It's in the middle of the village, not far from the site and we can interview all the witnesses there. Most of them spend a lot of their spare time drinking in the bar so it will save us rushing around the village looking for them.'

Green agreed to the suggestion and sent Hopkins off to speak to the landlord. He emphasised that they needed the room to be private and to make sure that neither the landlord nor any of his customers could listen in to any confidential interviews that would be taking place. Hopkins also suggested that the inspector could book a room at the pub if he wanted to stay in the village during the investigation but that idea was dismissed as a step too far.

The team of roughnecks had been sent back to Kelham Hall with specific instructions not the discuss the morning's events with anyone else. Hopkins knew the local gossip mongers would be out in force as soon as the news got out about the murder and speculation would be rife. A murderer was in their midst and everyone would have an opinion about the culprit; this was the most excitement some people had experienced in their lives and they would be pestering him for all the gory details.

As Hopkins made his way to the Barleycorn to secure an incident room, Blenkinsop and his men, under the direction of Inspector Green, remained at the site to continue the search for a possible second body or murder weapon.

It was lunchtime by the time Hopkins arrived at the pub and news of the death had reached the public bar where a few of the locals had gathered to gossip and speculate. When he arrived, they gathered around him in search of news.

'Can I get you a pint, Herbert? Hair of the dog and all that,' asked Jack.

'Not at the moment, Jack, I'm on duty. Can I have a quiet word?'

Jack moved to the end of the bar. 'What can I do for you, mate?' he enquired, lowering his voice.

'There's been an incident up at Dukes Wood and the inspector has asked if we can set up our incident room in the snug bar. It's not used much by the locals and seeing as you haven't had any paying guests since those couple of poncey blokes in the summer I thought it'd be a good place as any for us to conduct our enquiries. Mind you, we can't have any one listening in, this is possibly a murder enquiry.'

Jack was pleased that the pub would become a hub of police activity and agreed willingly. The prospect of more custom was always welcome and he could charge them rent whilst they were there. He would have to watch his step though, and perhaps curb some of his racketeering activities for the time being.

Hopkins had registered the effect his presence had made on the assembled customers who clambered to find out juicy gossip but for once he was keeping his counsel. The revelation about the true nature of the Yanks' presence in the village had taken him by surprise and he needed to process the information; life was certainly getting interesting for the village bobby. As soon as Jack had given his agreement to the use of the snug, Hopkins wasted no time in setting up the incident room. He rearranged the chairs and tables to replicate an interview room and by the time Inspector Green arrived he'd purloined a filing cabinet and a supply of stationery from the police headquarters in Newark. As Inspector Green entered the room, he was arranging pens, paperclips and notepaper on table ready for use.

'Nice work, Herbert,' said Green on entering the snug. 'You've done a grand job. There's just one thing that you've overlooked.'

Hopkins looked crestfallen; he was keen to make a good impression on his senior officer. 'I'm sorry, sir, what's missing?'

'Well lad, seeing as these are licenced premises, I'm assuming the landlord's got a nice bottle of scotch behind the bar that he could spare. Investigation is a thirsty business and we need to oil the grey matter somehow,' he replied.

Hopkins laughed and told Green he would see to it straight away.

CHAPTER 13

December 1943, incident room at the Barleycorn

The two police officers spent the afternoon after the grisly discovery discussing the events leading up to the murder the night before. The woods had been thoroughly searched by the Army lads and additional coppers from Newark but no body, nor a murder weapon had been found, the former coming as a relief and the latter disappointment.

Hopkins, who had not previously been privy to the real reason for the presence of the Yanks in the village before today, was given the opportunity to ask questions if he needed clarification, but was told it was imperative he kept the information to himself. It was vital for the war effort to keep the production of oil secret, not only for national security but also the safety of the local people. The oil production could have a bearing on the murder although it was imperative for them to explore all options. Hopkins was thrilled that he was now part of an important investigation but found his loyalties divided. He knew the locals would be badgering him for information and his credibility with the police would be compromised if they found out that he had participated in the lock-in at the pub the previous evening.

Inspector Green began by asking him to run through what happened the previous night, especially what happened when the darts match finished and Carmichael left the pub. It was important to get a clear picture of his movements. Hopkins thought carefully as he needed to make sure he recalled the events accurately. He realised he was an important witness, one who was a trained observer.

He began by recalling the events that took place during the darts match; James Carmichael had spent the evening propping up the bar, chatting to Deirdre and flirting with the other girls, in particular Brenda, a local farmer's daughter. This seemed to upset Deirdre who appeared to be unusually quiet and withdrawn. There was a lot of good-natured banter flying around, although at one point in the evening there was an altercation between Carmichael and Billy Clark. Hopkins was sitting too far away to hear what was actually said but he reported that things appeared to calm down quickly. Green made a note to ask Billy about it. The rest of the evening passed uneventfully and Carmichael was observed leaving with Deirdre after the match had finished around 9.45pm.

When the inspector finished his interview with the hapless PC, he gave him instructions to put together a list of all those present at the darts match and begin the process of interviewing the locals to see if they had anything more to add about the activities during the match and if they saw or heard anything that may have a bearing on the case. Green wanted to interview Billy Clark himself the following day and left to attend the post mortem in Newark, a task he would willingly delegate given half the chance.

Hopkins stayed behind to draw up a list of witnesses, some of whom had already drifted into the bar in the late afternoon to find out the latest news. Old Joe was in demand as he had been the one to find the body but uncharacteristically, he refused to discuss the morning's events. He was relieved to be summoned to the snug interview room and sat facing Hopkins.

'Ay-up, Herbert. It's a rum do, all this,' said Joe as he took a seat facing the PC.

'You're not wrong there, Joe,' he replied. 'I just need to check with everyone their whereabouts last night between the hours of 10pm and 2.30am.'

Joe laughed. 'Well if you weren't too drunk after the lock-in you'll be able to vouch for most of us. I think it was after midnight when I left with you so you can cross me off your list of suspects. I was a bit worse for wear and certainly in no state to climb over the fence up at the woods as you well know.'

'I know all that, Joe, but the problem is I can't tell the boss about the lock-in. He'd have my guts for garters and Jack would lose his licence so we'll have to think of some way round it without dropping the landlord in it.'

'You're right there, we'll have to get our heads together and come up with something,' said Joe. 'I'll just top up me pint while we're thinking about it.' He patted his dog, Jan, who was making himself comfortable near the fire, and went to the bar.

The two men discussed their predicament and agreed the way forward. Herbert took Joe's statement and as agreed they said the pub closed at the usual time of 10.30pm, after which Joe went straight home to bed. As he lived alone, he had no alibi after 10.45pm but didn't think he would be a suspect as he had liked James and had no quarrel with him leading up to his demise. The others who stayed for the lock-in all agreed to the "cover story" that after the pub closed for the night, they all retired to their respective homes.

Billy Clark was called in for an interview next and was warned that the inspector wanted to see him again the next day.

'Now then Billy,' said Hopkins, 'this is just routine but we need to establish everyone's whereabouts after the pub closed. What time did you leave?' asked the police officer, licking his pencil and preparing to write out the statement.

'As you know I left just before 10.30 after last orders was called and went straight home to my digs.'

'Did you see anyone on your way home?'

'Aye, the rest of you boggers who left at closing time, seeing as there was no lock-in.'

Hopkins didn't write down the last statement. Feeling embarrassed, he nodded. 'Now I'm just asking you about your movements, let's just stick to that if you don't mind. Did you see your aunty when you got in? Can she verify the time you arrived home?'

'Nay, she goes to bed early so I try and keep as quiet as possible so as not to disturb her. She gets fed up wi' me getting home drunk and said if I disturbed her again, she'd send me packing so I was extra careful and went straight to bed like a good boy.'

'Did you see anyone on the road going into Dukes Wood? You'll have passed by George's hut at the entrance on your way home.'

'I didn't even see George. I looked into the hut as I passed by to say goodnight, but he wasn't there. I just assumed he'd gone on one of his patrols, not that he does that very often. He is more likely to be sleeping on the job but he wasn't there. Perhaps he done it!'

'Now there's no need for speculation and spreading rumours like that, there's probably a simple explanation for his absence, perhaps he had a call of nature.'

'More likely his call came from the widow that lives at Rose Cottage, but I don't suppose he'll own up to that as his old lady'll be on the warpath again.'

Hopkins made a note to ask George about his nocturnal wanderings. If he had been absent from his post anyone could have just walked into the site without being seen.

One thing puzzled Hopkins about the statement though; it was unusual for Billy to miss a lock-in. He was well known for his drinking habits and wasn't one to pass up the offer of free drinks. Having questioned him about it, Billy merely shrugged and said he'd had enough to drink and fancied an early night.

'Did you see Carmichael outside when you left?' he asked.

'No, I didn't, he and Deirdre left a while before me and were long gone. There wasn't anyone outside when I left.'

Realising he wouldn't get any further information out of the school teacher, he thanked him for his time and sent him back to the bar.

Hopkins was finishing his notes when Inspector Green entered the pub and ordered a pint of bitter before joining the PC in the snug.

'Well lad, how's it going?' he asked.

'Not bad, sir,' replied Hopkins. 'I've taken a few statements already and most of the locals I've spoken to left the pub at closing time and went straight home.' He told the inspector about the allegations made by Billy about the missing night watchman. Green smiled and decided to have a word with George in the morning. If it were true that he'd deserted his post for any length of time it would explain why the perpetrator had left the scene of the crime without being noticed. It also raised the possibility that the night watchman could have been the killer so he also resolved to find out if there was any bad blood between the two men. But that could wait, it had been a long day and the inspector was ready for home. He bid Hopkins goodnight and arranged to meet him again in the morning for a briefing.

Hopkins was also ready for home and wanted to avoid being questioned by the locals so called it a night and returned to his cottage to reflect on the events during the day. Like many of the locals, he had got to know Carmichael and knew about his relationship with Deirdre but didn't think anyone would go to such extreme lengths to get rid of the yank. After all, he was going back to America in the new year so it was likely that the romance would have fizzled out by then. Carmichael hadn't been averse to chatting up other girls, even when Deirdre was around, so even if she had been keen to go back to the States with him, Hopkins thought it was unlikely that Carmichael felt the same. Writing in his notebook, he decided to have a word with Deirdre in the morning. He had a soft spot for the girl and didn't want to think she'd resort to such drastic action, but it needed to be checked out.

CHAPTER 14

December 1943, the Barleycorn

The following morning as Hopkins rode his bicycle down to the Barleycorn, he was passed by the truck taking the Yanks to Dukes Wood for another day's work. The crime scene had been cleared out by the forensic boys overnight and the Army had tightened up the security on the site. George, having resumed his duties overnight was on his way home. Seeing Hopkins approach he quickened his step but was intercepted before he could disappear into his cottage.

'George,' said Hopkins, 'the inspector would like a word with you, can you come over to the incident room this afternoon?'

'I've told you all I know, Herbert, what's more to say?'

'We have a witness who said you weren't in the hut around 10.30 the other night so you'd better have a good excuse for lying to me yesterday.'

'I didn't lie to you. I might have been attending to the call of nature around that time. There aren't any facilities in the hut so I have to go in the woods behind the fence. That's right, that's where I would have been.'

'Well I suggest you have a good think about it before you see the inspector. Lying to the police is a serious business and can get you into a lot more trouble than you think. What you tell us won't go any further if it's the truth, so long as it has no bearing on the murder. See you this afternoon.'

With that, he left George and rode on to the pub, smiling to himself. He wasn't 100% sure that the trouble George would get from the police would be worse that the wrath of his old lady when she found out he'd by cosying up to the widow from Rose Cottage. He even felt a bit sorry for George's dilemma but he only had himself to blame.

When he arrived at the pub, he found that Jack had lit a fire in the snug and a pot of tea was waiting for him on the table. Hopkins was beginning to enjoy this investigating lark and speculated that a career in the constabulary wasn't such a bad option. Perhaps he'd think about taking his sergeant's exams after all.

'I suppose you'll be wanting to interview me, will you Herbert?' asked Jack, coming into the snug from the bar.

'That's right, Jack, you were busy yesterday with all the comings and goings, this murder seems to be good for business.'

'I've had a reporter on the blower this morning from the Mansfield Chad wanting the low down, the cheeky bogger offered to pay me if I can give him some inside information, would you believe it?' he said.

As he was speaking Inspector Green arrived having overheard the last remark. 'There had better not be any leaks in the investigation, Jack, and if any reporters ring again tell them to contact the Newark Police Station for more information. Now if you'll excuse us, we'd like a bit of privacy.'

Hopkins offered the inspector a cup of tea and the two men settled down to review the case so far.

Green had received a report following the post mortem. James had died after being shot in the chest from an estimated 6-8 feet away. The bullet had pierced his heart which resulted in sudden death. On examination of the scene of the crime, as he had already surmised, the bullet that hit Carmichael had ricocheted from the ceiling post after the intruder panicked after being disturbed. It didn't, therefore, appear to be a premeditated murder, nor did it rule out local kids who may have broken in to see what they could steal. It was important to trace the gun and so Green had asked for the team of PCs to continuing searching the undergrowth in the woods. Depending upon the type of weapon used, it may point to a possible culprit and that would be another avenue to follow so he rang the ballistics team to hurry up with their findings. The first task, however, would be to rule out the people who were at the darts match.

'Now then, lad,' Green said to Hopkins, 'take me through the events on Friday night so we can get a feel of the situation leading up to the murder.'

Hopkins took out his notebook and began plotting the whereabouts of the people who attended the darts match. He felt nervous, realising he was about to lie to a superior officer but realised he was compromised as one of the guilty parties who remained in the bar after closing time for the illegal lock-in.

The match was set to begin about 8pm and by that time most of the locals had assembled at the bar. The locals drifted in between 7 and 8pm and the Yanks had arrived around 7.45pm in the Army truck driven by Corporal Brown. In the days leading up to the match there had been some good-humoured banter between the Yanks and locals and most were looking forward to the evening. Billy and his mate Fred arrived earlier so they could get in some practice and had already started drinking along with some of the farm hands. Joe and Noble arrived together and before the match started, they sat talking in the snug. The two of them had been working late at Dukes Wood and George saw them leave the site just after 7.30pm when he locked the main gate. Noble and Joe walked down to the Barleycorn, a short journey which was to take them about 10 minutes. Captain Blenkinsop also entered the bar around the same time as the Yanks and shortly afterwards the three land girls arrived on their bicycles having cycled together from the Hall.

The evening was a success, although there was a slight altercation between Carmichael and Billy but that feud had been simmering for some time as Billy resented the yank who had taken up with Deirdre.

The darts match went well and for most of the regulars, honour had been restored when they won the match and as far as Hopkins was aware no one seemed to be bearing a grudge. Vera, the landlady, brought out sandwiches as the match ended and Lloyd Noble offered to buy a round of drinks to prove they weren't sore losers, which had been met with a round of applause. At closing time Hopkins tried to recall the sequence of events but as the bar was packed it was difficult to say who left with whom. He stuck to the story that everyone left at 10.30 more or less together. He was confident that the Yanks were picked up by the truck and as far as he knew the land girls cycled home. They had all left before Hopkins himself so he couldn't be too specific of the exact sequence of events. Jack had commented the day before that one of the bicycles had been left overnight at the pub, but he wasn't sure which of the girls had left it so Inspector Green decided to visit Arkwright's farm to interview the three girls, leaving Hopkins to speak to Jack.

It was an overcast day and the morning frost was still patchy as he walked towards the farm. The air was crisp and the three girls working in the farm yard were wrapped up warmly to keep out the cold. He was introducing himself to Celia when the farmer came out of the barn.

'I hope you've come to tell me you've found the boggers who've been stealing my sheep,' he said as he approached the inspector.

Taken aback, Green explained the reason for his visit and assured the farmer that the investigation into the sheep rustling was on-going. He told Arkwright he needed to interview everyone who was at the darts match on the night of the murder and wanted to speak to the land army girls. Arkwright was annoyed by the disruption to his day and reluctantly led the way to the farmhouse kitchen and introduced him to his wife. They had been at the darts match but left early and went straight home to the farmhouse. They saw nothing out of the ordinary at the pub nor did they see anyone as they walked home. He did hear noises later in the evening, around 11pm, and went to investigate, finding the gate open in the far field and on further inspection in the morning found that two sheep were missing. He told the inspector that he'd phoned the police station and was expecting Hopkins to turn up to take the detail.

'It's that bloody gang from Nottingham again, you mark my words. I don't know why you don't just go and arrest the boggers. They're laughing at you. If you go down to Sneinton Market you'll catch 'em red handed selling it off.'

Green assured the farmer that the police would be investigating and someone would be checking all the markets in Nottingham. As for him, he needed to get on with the murder investigation, so asked to speak to the land girls who had been at the pub. The farmer agreed to fetch them but said Deirdre was still upset and was being looked after by his wife.

Whilst the inspector was talking to Arkwright, Celia went over to Edith in the barn.

'Edith, I wonder if you can do me a favour,' she began. 'If you're asked could you say I was in bed when you got home?'

'But you weren't there when I got back, what happened?'

'I was with Gerald, but he doesn't want anyone to know. It's a bit complicated but believe me, we had nothing to do with the murder. Please, I need your help, but I'll understand if you can't.'

Edith looked concerned but readily agreed to stick to the story; she knew that Celia and Gerald Blenkinsop had no reason to attack James but couldn't help wondering where they had got to on that night. Celia was reluctant to say more, so Edith reassured her that she would stick to the story.

In the meantime, the farmer had fetched Deirdre who was being interviewed in the kitchen and being supported by Mrs Arkwright.

'If you could just confirm your name and address for me and in your own words tell me what you were doing on the night of the murder.'

Deirdre took out a handkerchief and started to cry quietly. 'Take your time,' he encouraged as Mrs Arkwright patted her hand.

'I met James at the pub as arranged. We've been going out for a few weeks and were planning to get married before he returned to the States next year. We enjoyed the evening and when the match finished, I wanted to go straight home as I had a headache. I had ridden to the pub with the other girls so my bicycle was outside. I didn't want spoil James's fun just because I had a headache and after we'd said goodnight, he said he was going back into the pub for another drink.'

'And did he?' asked Green.

'Did he what?'

'Go back into the bar?'

'I think so, but as I rode off, he was waiting outside to wave to me. I didn't actually see him go in but he must have.'

'Was there anything different about him that night? Did he seem excited or worried about anything?'

'No, he was fine. We sat at the bar and had a few drinks and he was in high spirits chatting to people as we watched the match.'

'What about the argument he had with Billy Clark?'

Deirdre looked uncomfortable. 'It wasn't an argument as such. Just a bit of a spat. I'd been out with Billy a few times before I met James but it wasn't anything serious. Billy took it hard when I dumped him and he thought that James was leading me on. But it wasn't like that at all, James and I are in love.'

'Did you see anyone as your rode home?'

'No, I didn't, I rode along the footpath and when I got home, I went straight to my room. I have my own room so there wasn't anyone around who can give me an alibi if that's what you are asking.'

Green thanked her but said he may need to speak to her again, although for the time being she was free to go. He felt sorry for the girl who was obviously in love with the late roughneck.

He asked to speak to Celia next, and she entered the kitchen looking anxious. Green invited her to sit and, to put her at ease, he assured her he was only there to ask some routine questions. As an experienced copper he knew how concerned people became when faced with authority figures and even those who were completely innocent acted guilty when under pressure. He started by asking her contact details and then asked her to talk through her movements on the evening of the murder.

'I rode to the pub along with Edith and Deirdre and we arrived just before the darts match started. Deirdre went off to speak to James and Edith was asked to help behind the bar as it was going to be a busy night. I sat with Captain Blenkinsop whilst the match took place and we had a couple of drinks. Deirdre left early as she had a headache. I offered to go with her but she said she'd be OK. When the match ended the captain offered to give me a lift home in his car so I left my bicycle in the pub yard to pick up the next morning.'

'Why didn't you wait for Edith?'

'She was helping out behind the bar so I wasn't sure how long she'd be and thought she'd be cadging a lift home with the Yanks. Captain Blenkinsop drives an MG and there's only two seats so we couldn't take her as well,' she replied.

Inspector Green made a note to ask Edith if she rode home alone or joined the Yanks in the truck. 'What did you do when you got back to the Hall, did anyone see you arrive?'

'I don't think so and I was asleep by the time Edith arrived home. I don't think there is anything else I can add.'

The inspector filled in the details of the interview in his notebook. He had a feeling that Celia was holding something back but wasn't sure if it had a bearing on the case. He decided to ask Blenkinsop his version of events to see if it tallied with Celia's.

Edith had offered to take Deirdre home after her interview with the inspector; talking about that night had upset her as it reminded her of the last time she had spoken to James. She was still trying to come to terms with the fact that she would never see him again.

Edith told the farmer's wife she'd return straight away, after leaving Deirdre in the care of the matron, to speak to the inspector. He was content to wait and was drinking tea and eating a piece of homemade cake in the warm farmhouse kitchen when she entered.

'I'm sorry I'm late, sir, Deirdre was so upset Mrs Arkwright didn't want her to go back to the Hall on her own. I've left her with Matron who will look after her. I'm afraid Deirdre's overreacting slightly. I don't want to speak out of turn but she's convinced James was about to propose. He was much too fond of playing the field to settle down and in recent weeks he's not been as attentive towards her.'

'I see, and was he playing the field with you?'

'Good Lord, no,' said Edith, alarmed at the idea. 'I didn't know him very well at all but he did flirt with some of the local girls. Deirdre is a bit of a dreamer and I think she was in for a big disappointment when the Yanks leave. She's very young and James was leading her on a bit. Celia and I did try to warn her but she's really fallen for him.'

The inspector looked at his notes and cleared his throat. 'Now, for my records, can I just have your full name and contact details?'

Edith gave her details and seemed to relax; she told the inspector about working behind the bar after they'd arrived, and said she was busy all night serving the customers. She went into the back room during the darts match to help Vera prepare the sandwiches and when last orders were called, she decided to go straight home. She was tired and both her friends had already left.

'And what time did you arrive at the Hall?'

'Oh, it must have been about 11pm. I did stop at the phone box to make a quick call to my mother after I left the pub. I'd received a letter from her to say she wasn't feeling well so I thought I'd give her a ring to see if she was any better.'

'It was late to be making a social call,' queried Green.

'My mother doesn't go to bed very early; she has a flat in London and often stays up late in case there's an air raid.'

'I see, go on…'

'I rode home along the footpath, it takes about 25 minutes, and didn't see anyone as I rode by Dukes Wood. When I arrived, Celia was already in bed. I didn't want to disturb her as I thought she was asleep, but she may have heard me moving around. We share a room and the door squeaks so she may have noticed the time when I got back.'

The inspector gained a good impression of the young woman. She seemed happy to co-operate and gave a straight forward account of the time between leaving the pub and arriving back at the Hall. Her recall of the events during the darts match seemed accurate and also tallied with other statements. It occurred to him that she may have noticed some unusual activity at Arkwright's farm on her route to Kelham Hall as the sheep stealing was going on that night, so he asked her if she passed any vehicles on the road.

She thought about it before answering. 'As a matter of fact I did, a black van passed me when I reached the crossroads on the 617. You don't think it was the sheep rustlers, do you? I never thought, I was a bit preoccupied thinking about my mother.'

'It could be, the timing's about right. What sort of van was it?'

'Well, as I said it was black and quite big. I think it was an old model as I remember the engine was struggling a bit and it could have been a Ford. Is that any use?'

'I'm sure it will be, you seem to be a credible witness and it did happen on the same night. I'll pass the information on to the officer dealing with the case and he may be in touch with you to get a written statement.'

A thought occurred to her. 'You don't think there's a connection between the murder and the sheep stealing, do you?'

'We're keeping an open mind at this stage; two crimes being committed on the same night may be linked or it could just be a coincidence. Now if you think of anything else that may be useful you can contact me or PC Hopkins, we've set up an incident room at the Barleycorn. I don't have any more questions at the moment, thank you for your time.'

'I'm more than happy to help, Inspector,' she replied. 'It's a terrible business. I do hope you'll be able to find the culprit. It's all very unsettling thinking there could be a murderer in the village.'

'Rest assured, my dear,' he spoke kindly, 'we are doing everything we can to apprehend the killer.'

'Do you have any idea why he was killed?'

'We have a number of leads to follow up so I'm fairly confident that we'll be able to close the case soon,' he replied, sounding more confident than he actually felt.

After Edith had left the kitchen the farmer's wife returned and offered Green another cup of tea, which he was only too pleased to accept whilst he thought about the statements from the girls. Mrs Arkwright busied herself mashing the tea and wasn't averse to imparting a bit of gossip whilst she was working. She was fond of the girls but felt that girls in general had too much freedom these days, gadding about the countryside on their own late at night. It was different in her day. While she was talking a thought occurred to Green.

'Did you see any of the girls that night after you and Mr Arkwright arrived home?' Looking at his notebook, he continued, 'I understand your husband went out about 11pm when he heard the noise. That was about the same time as Edith would have been riding by.'

'No, when Harry returned, he said there was no one around. He must have just missed her, if she was out then. If I had a daughter, I wouldn't be letting her ride around these dark lanes at that time of night.'

As the inspector was interviewing the land army girls, Herbert was finishing off a bowl of lamb stew prepared by Vera at the Barleycorn. He had finished the interview with Jack and had assured him the illegal lock-in at the pub on the night of the murder wouldn't be recorded, which put the landlord's mind at rest. Jack had given a full account of his movements during that evening; it had been a busy night and he was serving customers until closing time. After the lock-in he set up the drinks for the lads before leaving the bar for a short while to change a barrel in the cellar where he admitted to having a rest and a fag before throwing the lads out around midnight when, all the worse for drink, they made their way home.

Herbert realised that there would have been time for any of the participants of the lock-in to take the bicycle left at the pub by Celia and meet up with Carmichael at the oil field but seeing the state most of them were in, he doubted that they could ride a bike without falling off. This thought eased his conscience for lying about the lock-in and for the life of him he couldn't think of any of them having a motive for killing the roughneck. He decided to have a word with the inspector to suggest they widen their search. Surely no one from the village was capable of murder!

CHAPTER 15

December 1943, Cambridge

The Faculty dinner to celebrate the end of the Michaelmas term was in full swing. University staff from the different departments were mingling and flirting outrageously. Marcus watched with interest as the Dean who, normally so strait-laced, was backing one of the young secretaries into a corner, making improper advances. As Frederick approached him Marcus laughingly commented, 'Someone will have a thick head tomorrow and if his wife finds that lipstick on his collar, I doubt he'll survive until Christmas.'

'I think he'll have some explaining to do to the Christian Society as well in the new year if the gossip mongers get busy. It's the same every year, must be something in the punch, the respectable professors will be returning in the new year with red faces and unconvincing excuses for their behaviour at the end-of-term bash. Thank goodness I haven't overdone the alcohol intake; I have to be up early tomorrow to catch a train. I'm off to spend Christmas with my uncle. He lives in the Midlands and is in his dotage so I reckon if I play my cards right, I'll come into a substantial inheritance when he kicks the bucket.'

A momentary look of distaste crossed Marcus' face but Frederick failed to notice. 'Unfortunately, we have a bit of business to attend to first, old boy, so if you don't mind delaying your departure for a few days I'd be obliged if you can call on me tomorrow, we have something important to discuss.'

Frederick looked concerned. 'Oh, is there a problem?'

'Don't worry, old man, it's nothing we can't sort out before Christmas. It may be best though, if you don't tell anyone of your change of plan. Just leave to catch your train as arranged and I'll pick you up at the station. We can drive to my house in the country and you can stay with me until we can get things sorted out. My housekeeper will be there to look after us, she can be trusted, and I will drive you up to the Midlands by Christmas Eve at the latest.'

Although Frederick wasn't happy about changing his plans, he was intrigued to find out what the problem might be and if he admitted it to himself, he was quite looking forward to doing something to further their cause. Perhaps he would be embarking on a secret mission. He had been getting disillusioned about the undercover activities at the university and his "agent" in the field hadn't reported anything significant so he'd begun to wonder if it was all part of an elaborate fantasy thought up by Marcus, his mentor. He dismissed his doubts about the importance of their activities and decided to have a glass of punch after all. He'd been admiring one of the librarians from afar all term and thought if he had enough to drink, he might pluck up the courage to speak to him.

Marcus, on the other hand, had no such misgivings about the undercover activities and thought it would only take a couple of days to sort out the problem. He wondered whether it had been a mistake to trust Frederick to be a handler, and not for the first time doubted his loyalty. If, as he suspected, Frederick was becoming a liability, he could kill two birds with one stone.

CHAPTER 16

December 1943, Kelham Hall

It was the Saturday before Christmas and the girls had decided to catch the bus to Newark to do some Christmas shopping. Edith had persuaded Deirdre to join them, saying it would take her mind off the murder investigation that was continuing to dominate the conversations in and around the village. People were speculating and the theories were getting more and more outlandish with the police getting no nearer to apprehending the culprit.

They set out early so they could visit their favourite teashop for refreshments before spending the rest of the day shopping and watching a new film in the afternoon at the picture house. They had plenty of time to browse around the marketplace for Christmas presents and soak up the festive atmosphere. Celia was unusually quiet and seemed to have something playing on her mind, matching Deirdre's sombre mood, who was also preoccupied and not her talkative self. Although Edith had tried to make conversation during the bus journey, she had little success. Instead all three girls fell silent, and passed the journey watching the changing views of the countryside as the bus meandered through the small villages and hamlets. It was a dark overcast day, with the threat of rain in the air and a cold north wind blowing. On arrival in the market town, they alighted from the bus near the imposing derelict castle walls standing majestically on the banks of the River Trent. Their first stop was at their favourite café for a warming cup of tea before Edith and Celia walked through the Butter market towards the town hall and market square where colourful stalls had been erected selling Christmas wares.

Deirdre had decided to go for a walk along the riverside footpath instead of shopping, saying she had bought all her Christmas gifts and wanted to be alone for a while. After assuring her friends that she was fine, she agreed to meet them outside the picture house later in the afternoon. Although they were reluctant to let her go, Edith and Celia agreed and walked to the marketplace together, arm in arm.

'Celia, I know you said you asked me to cover for you on the night of the murder but I'm worried. You didn't come home all night. I know you didn't have anything to do with what happened but where were you? You've not been yourself since then. You can tell me, I won't say anything, you know you can trust me.'

Celia seemed to struggle before coming to a decision. 'Oh Edith, I've been such a fool,' she said. 'I wanted to tell you ages ago, I hated lying to you and I know I could get into trouble with the police but Gerald insisted. I was with him all night; he didn't run me home like he told the inspector.'

'Go on,' encouraged Edith.

'We came here to Newark and stayed in a friend of Gerald's flat. We were there all night and he drove me to the village to collect my bicycle then next day,' she laughed nervously. 'He's worried in case his CO finds out as it isn't proper behaviour for an officer and a gentleman, so he sworn me to secrecy. Honestly, I can't see why but he is a bit old fashioned that way. He says he doesn't want to ruin my reputation! Not that I care a jot, but he insisted. I can't help thinking though that he has something to hide. After all, his lying could get us both into trouble.'

'But that's silly, it that gives you both an alibi. I'm sure if you told the inspector it wouldn't go any further, they're only interested in finding out who did the murder and this puts both of you in the clear,' said Edith.

'Yes, I know that but I thought they would have found the killer by now. If I tell the inspector the truth, I'll also get you into trouble for lying as well. I feel so bad about that.'

'Look, don't worry about me,' said Edith. 'I'm a big girl and it was the least I could do to help a friend out. I knew you had nothing to do with the murder, the very idea is ridiculous, why would any of us want to kill James?'

Celia hesitated. 'Do you think Deirdre is hiding something?'

'Of course not, she's just upset, anyone in her position would be in the circumstance,' replied Edith. 'She's taken it so hard. I worry about her. She's not been herself since James died.'

'No, I think it's more than that, she was really star struck over James but I don't think he was as keen on her as she made out. He was always flirting with other girls, even when she was around and I've heard some talk about him and Brenda.'

'I know,' said Edith. 'I saw him with her the week before he died, they were going into the woods together. I didn't say anything to Deirdre though but it didn't look like they were going for a picnic and you know Brenda's reputation.'

'Do you think Deirdre found out and tackled him about it that night? After all, he wasn't being discreet when he was flirting with Brenda. I got the feeling he was getting bored with our Deirdre, and her obsession about going back to the States with him as a war bride. I know it's a horrible thing to say but they did leave together on the night of the murder and James wasn't seen again. You don't think that they went up to the oil field together and had an argument?' speculated Celia.

'I think you're letting your imagination run away with you,' said Edith. 'He was shot, remember. Deirdre hasn't got a gun and she wouldn't know where to get one from. I can imagine them having an argument but why would they have gone to Dukes Wood at that time of night? Look, why don't we have a chat with her tonight after the pictures and get her side of the story? I'm sure she lied to the police but that may be just to save face. Perhaps James finished with her and went off with Brenda to Dukes Wood. It's more likely that she'd be the one to go with him for a bit of *how's your father*.' Celia laughed at Edith's turn of phrase.

'Maybe, they went to the site office for sex and James refused to pay her. I wouldn't be surprised if Brenda had a gun, she's been with enough soldiers in her time and could have been given one as a souvenir,' Celia replied.

The two girls continued to speculate on the walk to the marketplace and they decided to have a word with Deirdre on the way home to see if they were correct about their theory. It would, they agreed, explain why Deirdre was behaving the way she was. It wasn't simply grief at losing her boyfriend, but there was more to it and they wanted to get to the bottom of it to help their friend.

'It's a pity no one saw Deirdre arrive back at the Hall. Surely Matron was around and could have heard her arrive, and I guess the same for you, Edith.'

'I tried to be quiet and I guess Deirdre was the same. You know what Matron's like if we disturb her when she's off duty. Anyway, I suspect the police inspector will have questioned her already by now.'

Celia sighed. 'Oh, this is such a beastly business. It's horrible, with people suspecting one another. I really hope the police will find the culprit soon so we can just get on with our lives and put all this behind us. I'm going home on Christmas Eve to spend some time with my parents, Mummy insisted, she's been so down since hearing about Richard. She worries about him being a prisoner of war and I know it will be difficult for her over the holiday. Goodness knows what sort of Christmas he'll be having. I really wanted to stay here with you all but I need to see how the old girl's managing and letting her fuss over me will give her something to do. Daddy's busy with war work and has never been one to wear his heart on his sleeve which makes it more difficult for Mummy. What about you, have you made any plans to see your folks?'

'No, I won't be going home, there's nothing there for me. I

thought I'd stay here and spend Christmas Day with the Arkwrights. They're missing their boys so at least I'll be company for them.'

'You don't talk much about your family. Is it just you and your mother or do you have any brothers or sisters?' enquired Celia.

'There's just Mum and I, and we don't really get on that well. She'll be spending Christmas socialising with her friends and I'd only get in the way.'

'But I thought you said she hasn't been well.' Celia looked confused.

'She's a lot better now, thanks, and Mum has never been one to allow a bout of illness to stand in the way of her social whirl. I'll be better off here with the Arkwrights. I've become very fond of them in the last few months. They're kind people and it is so hard for them keeping the farm going at their age. Anyway, I would have thought you'd rather be staying here as well to spend some time with Gerald over the holidays?'

'No, he's got a few days off and has decided to go home. He said his father is an invalid, apparently, he was wounded in the last war, and his mother is finding it difficult to cope. He would like to take me to meet them but as he'll be helping to care for his father, to give his mother a bit of a break, it wouldn't be much fun for me, or so he says. We're going to book into the B&B in in the new year and have our own celebration.'

After reached the marketplace they spent a couple of hours browsing and enjoying the camaraderie of the stall holders who were calling out cheerfully to one another and persuading customers to buy their wares. The hot chestnut man was standing next to his brazier handing out bags of piping hot chestnuts and around the Christmas tree near the town hall a choir of local children were singing carols. Celia bought a scarf for her mother and found a second-hand silver cigarette case for Gerald. She also bought some lacey-edged handkerchiefs for Edith and Deirdre and decided to invite them both for a pre-Christmas celebration at the Barleycorn.

She wondered why Edith was so reluctant to go home for Christmas, and realised how little she knew of her background. Edith had told her that her father had been killed during the last war but she rarely mentioned her mother.

Before the murder Deirdre had made plans to go back to Liverpool to spend Christmas with her extended family. She had asked James to go with her, promising him a warm welcome from her parents. She said he'd declined because he would have to work over the holiday period as they were behind schedule with the filming. Celia knew that Deirdre was disappointed, but she had tried to cover it up with a joke, saying it was probably for the best as her mother would talk him to death and her father would grill him about his intentions towards his eldest daughter.

Farmer Arkwright had promised to give each of the girls a box of vegetables to take to their respective homes for the holidays; fresh produce was hard to come by during the dark days of the war and in short supply in the cities so they all gratefully accepted the offer. As Edith had been invited to spend the day at the farm, she offered to pass on her box to the matron to supplement the turkeys from the Army supplies.

The day out in Newark was a pleasant change for the girls and they talked animatedly on the way home about the film they had seen. The *Pathé* news reels at the cinema were encouraging, highlighting successful battles that suggested the tide was turning and an end to the war was in sight. Celia didn't want to spoil the mood but was keen to find out more about the night of the murder from Deirdre and gently questioned her as they began the walk home from the bus stop. Deirdre had been uncharacteristically secretive about her final moments with James and her movements that night and refused to confide in her two friends. When Celia persevered, Deirdre became upset and started to cry so Edith changed the subject.

'You know where we are, Deirdre, if you want to talk to us. You can trust us,' assured Celia.

As they entered the Hall, Deirdre ran straight up to her room, passing the matron who was in the reception area. Matron looked concernedly towards Edith and Celia, asking if there was anything she could do to help.

'We've tried to help her, Matron, we thought a day out would do her good but she's so grief stricken at the moment. It will take a while for her to get over losing James. I think it will be good for her to go home to her family for a while,' replied Edith.

CHAPTER 17

December 1943, Police Incident Room

Herbert Hopkins was getting used to and enjoying the rhythm of his days. He arrived at the incident room at his usual time and settled down in front of the open fire with his cup of tea. Inspector Green arrived a few minutes later and together they reviewed the evidence collected the previous day and made plans for the rest of the day. It seemed like the investigation was grinding to a halt and going nowhere, no one saw anything and everyone apparently had an alibi with no reason to do away with James Carmichael.

'Someone is lying, we just need to find out who and why,' said Hopkins.

'If you ask me, I think more than one of our suspects is lying,' agreed Green. 'Sooner or later though, someone will make a mistake. What we need to do is go over all the statements and look for discrepancies. I'm going to speak to Captain Blenkinsop later today.'

'There's something fishy about that man,' said Hopkins. 'I can't put my finger on why but I think he's hiding something.'

'Now Herbert, don't let your personal feelings about the man cloud your judgement. He's a professional Army man and has a natural arrogance. He seems to think he's a peg above the rest of us but that doesn't mean he's our man. What's more, I can't think what his motive would be. He's as upset about the murder as we are. After all, it was committed on his patch and he seems to think it's a personal insult. I can see he wants to catch the culprit as much as we do. I agree though, I think there's something fishy about his statement so it won't harm ruffling his feathers a bit.'

'Maybe he was jealous of Carmichael's success with the women. Blenkinsop has a soft spot for Celia, one of the land army girls, and she was also getting some attention from the yank even though he was courting one of the other girls. Maybe it was all about the yank chatting up one of our girls,' said Hopkins.

'Well from what I can see you'd better put yourself on the suspect list, I thought you'd got your eye on young Deirdre for yourself,' commented the inspector.

Hopkins felt himself beginning to blush; it was true he liked Deirdre but wasn't intending to do anything about it as she was too young for him and although she was a lovely girl, she wasn't the sort to be happy to settle down with a village bobby. He was about to protest the inspector's suggestion but was saved by doing so when Green started to laugh. 'It's all right, lad, don't get yourself into a tizzy, I was only joking. After all, you were tucked up in bed when the murder was taking place.'

Hopkins continued to feel awkward at the turn in the conversation and thought it best to change the subject before he gave himself away. He was still worried about the lock-in and hoped the lads who stayed behind could be trusted to keep their mouths shut. Whilst they had been drinking and making merry at the landlord's expense a murder had been committed, the sheep rustlers had been running amok in the village, and even George's nocturnal wandering had been happening. It had been quite an eventful night whilst the local police officer had been drinking himself into a stupor. Something he was keen to cover up; it wouldn't do his promotion prospects any good if news of the lock-in got out.

'We need to widen our investigations, lad,' Green went on. 'You and I know that the Yanks are here to open up the oil field and although there's been an elaborate cover story to fool the locals, we have to remember this is war time. There is always the possibility that someone in the village got wise to it and that sort of information would be invaluable if it leaked out. Have there been any strangers lurking around the village recently? You know we're forever being told to keep on our guard. Have you seen any unusual activity?'

'Apart from the sheep stealing, I don't think there's been any strangers hanging around. There's been a couple of new lads up at the top farm who were drafted in a couple of months ago but it's been pretty quiet since the Yanks arrived. There was a couple of chaps up from Cambridge over the summer but they were teachers or something coming for a walking holiday and a new couple moved into one of the old cottages on the main street at the beginning of September. He says he is recuperating after contracting TB and they've leased the cottage for a few months so he can get fresh air away from the polluted air in the city. He comes into the pub a couple of nights a week but tends to keep himself to himself. Do you want me to pay them a visit and check them out?'

'Can't do any harm, find out where they came from and check the story of the TB with the local doctor to see if he's been called out to see him. In the meantime, I'm going to pay another visit to Captain Blenkinsop to see if I can work out what he's got to hide.'

Captain Blenkinsop was found at the oil field briefing his men to set up red alert security measures to ensure there was no future breach in the security. George, the night watchman, had been dismissed and the soldiers in the unit were directed to cover the perimeter fence in a shift system to cover the site 24 hours a day. It had been a mistake to leave the overnight security to a local night watchman although at the time it was decided to keep it low key to avert suspicion about the real purpose of the activities taking place in the woods. Blenkinsop had been disciplined following the breach in security leading to the murder on site and he was concerned about the effect it would have on his career. He was also concerned about the enquiry into his own whereabouts on that night and at all costs he needed to keep his indiscretions quiet. When he saw Inspector Green approaching, he resolved to stick to the cover story he and Celia had concocted.

'Captain Blenkinsop, could I have a quick word with you?' asked the inspector.

'Of course. If you give me a minute to finish my briefing, I'll meet you in the site office. Mr Noble is up in London today so we shouldn't be disturbed.' Presently he dismissed his men and took his time walking over to the office, rehearsing his response to the inevitable questions and hoping that Celia was as good as her word and would do the same.

On entry he saw the inspector examining the site maps displayed on the wall and couldn't help but assert his own authority.

'Strictly speaking, old man, you shouldn't be looking at those drawings. The operation here is top secret still despite the events that have taken place. You need to have security clearance.'

'Don't worry, sir, I think you'll find I have the authority to conduct my investigations here at the crime scene. Perhaps if the site security hadn't been so lax in the first place there wouldn't be any need for my presence as the murderer couldn't have gained access to the site,' countered the inspector.

Blenkinsop had antagonised the inspector and realised he needed to build bridges.

'I'm sorry, I'm sure you'll appreciate my concerns. We thought we could rely on the local night watchman but I've tightened up security now. I realise the buck stops with me and I've taken the criticism on the chin, so to speak. Now, I'm sure you're not here to discuss my security arrangements. What can I do to help you? I am just as keen as you are to find the culprit so am putting myself at your disposal.'

'Thank you, Captain…'

'Oh, please, call me Gerald.'

'…Right, Gerald. I just need to revisit the events of the night of the murder and would be grateful if you can run through your own movements.'

'Certainly,' replied Gerald. 'I arrived at the darts match around 7.30pm. I drove there in my MG from my digs in Mansfield. I'm staying there during this assignment and will be re-joining my regiment in the new year. My landlady will be able to confirm the time I left as she saw me leaving. During the night I spoke to some of the regulars as I watched the match. I left as the landlord called time at the same time as one of the land army girls, her name is Celia. I don't want to speak out of turn but I think the young lady had drunk a little too much and wasn't too steady on her pins so I was a little concerned about her safety. She intended to cycle which wasn't such a good idea in her state so, as Kelham Hall isn't much out of my way, I offered her a lift home.'

'Did you drive straight to the Hall?'

'Of course, it only took a few minutes so I dropped her off at the end of the driveway. She didn't want me to drive up to the front door so as not to disturb the matron. It's quite amusing really but the girls are quite frightened of Matron. You wouldn't think they were grown women but there you are. After I'd dropped her off, I drove straight home. I didn't disturb my landlady so I doubt that she will be able to verify my arrival. You can ask Celia; she will be able to confirm the time I dropped her off.'

'Where do you leave your car overnight? There may be someone who saw it parked up that night, it's a beautiful car and maybe someone noticed it when you arrived in Mansfield.'

Blenkinsop looked a bit nervous. 'It's a pity you didn't think to ask straight away. If I had realised that I was a suspect, I would have checked with the others in my lodgings. It's too late now, I doubt whether anyone will be able to confirm that it was there on that particular night.'

'Please don't get upset, I'm sure you'll understand that we have to cover all bases in a murder enquiry. We just need to rule out as many people as possible. We'll be able to verify the account of your movements with Miss Fenwick and then we won't need to speak to you again. Thank you, for your cooperation. Now if I can just ask you about the following morning. I understand from Mr Noble's statement that you were late for work that day. I understand that wasn't a regular occurrence. Is there any reason why you were late on that particular day?'

'I had a flat tyre on my way to work so had to stop and put on the spare. Bit of a nuisance really, I must have picked up a nail in the tyre the night before.'

'I see, thank you. There's just one more question. Did you see anyone on the road as you drove towards Kelham Hall?'

'No. Oh, wait a moment, now I come to think of it I think I saw a Ford lorry driving along the A617 in the direction of the village. I noticed it because it was being driven a tad erratically and I had to swerve to avoid it. That would have been around 10.45pm.'

'Thank you. There were some sheep stolen from Arkwright's farm on that night and you may have seen the vehicle that was used to take them away. I'll pass on your statement to the officers dealing with that investigation. All in all, it was quite an eventful night.'

'Perhaps the people responsible for stealing the sheep chose that night because of the darts match. They may have been given inside information, perhaps some of the locals know more than they're saying,' said Blenkinsop, relieved at the change of topic and keen to be seen to be helping the police enquiry. The inspector closed his notebook to denote the interview was over and thanked Blenkinsop for his assistance. The two men left the site office together and Green returned to the incident room mulling over the information he had collected. He still had the niggling feeling that the captain was lying; his responses sounded rehearsed and he wondered what he was covering up. It would be interesting to see if Celia Fenwick's recollection of the evenings events matched word for word the statement given by the gallant captain.

Hopkins was making notes in the incident room when the inspector arrived, and he offered to fetch him a cup of tea to warm him up after his walk back from Dukes Wood. An offer that was gratefully accepted and the two men spent the next hour sharing information and speculating on the progress of the enquiry.

CHAPTER 18

Sunday before Christmas, 1943

The sky was overcast with a threat of snow hanging in the air as Reverend Sykes made his way from the vicarage to the parish church for the carol service. It was the last Sunday before Christmas and although the locals were looking forward to the festivities, they were concerned about their loved ones who were fighting overseas. St Andrew's Church dated from the 13th century and was a fine example of early English style with perpendicular turrets and stained-glass windows. It had been restored in the early 1670s after becoming dangerously dilapidated and the present organ, installed in 1886 had been carefully maintained and was still in good working order. As the vicar approached the chancel door, he could hear the organist warming up for the carol service and on entering the church he was met by Mrs Arkwright who had just finished cleaning the pews. The ladies of the village had pulled out all the stops to create a wonderful flower display and had decorated the church with holly boughs and winter flowers collected from the hedgerows. On the altar the candles were burning brightly, and candles had been lit at the end of each pew, giving the church a warm glow.

Mrs Arkwright was a devout Christian and prayed regularly for the safe return of her two sons, George and Albert, as well as the rest of the boys from the village who had joined up. Seeing the vicar enter, she rushed to meet him, eager for his approval of the flower displays.

'Thank you, Mrs Arkwright, as always you have done a brilliant job making the church look wonderful for the service,' he said. 'It's been a difficult year with one thing and another and I'm hoping we'll be able to spread some good cheer today to help raise the spirits of our parishioners. The carol service is always the highlight of the year for many in the village. As you know we always get a good turnout and Billy tells me the children have been practicing hard all week. He's been a God send, I'm very fond of that young man, he's a good lad. He was disappointed not to be called up along with his mates and I fear he's been drinking a little too much over the past few weeks. He took it hard when your lad was feared missing in action. I guess he feels guilty that he can't be with his mates doing his bit. Oh well, let's hope the war will be over next year.'

'When Billy first came to the village to live with his auntie, he was always up at our farm playing with my lads and it hit him hard when he was rejected for the Army. It's a shame but we have to be thankful that he's being kept safe here. One less lad for us to worry about, Vicar.'

'That's true, Mrs Arkwright. By the way, have they caught the people responsible for stealing your sheep yet? Times are hard enough without losing some of your livelihood.'

'No, the police are still investigating but as no one saw anything the police think it's unlikely they'll be caught. We're struggling as it is and can't afford to lose any more sheep but we have to thank God for what we have and for keeping our boys safe. I shudder to think how those poor folks in London are managing spending night after night in the air raid shelters. At least we can rest easy in our beds.'

'You're a true Christian, Mrs Arkwright, always thinking of others. If only there were more people like you, the world would be a better place. I don't suppose you've heard if they've found the person who murdered Mr Carmichael. It's such a sorry business. I'll never understand what could possess someone to take a life; it seems so pointless when millions of others are losing their lives in this war. I pray it will end soon. Here we are celebrating the birth of Christ and spreading his teachings of love thy neighbour. Sometimes I feel no one is listening. I'm sure the ordinary people in Germany are as keen as we are for it to be all over.'

The vicar walked towards the altar to prepare for the service as parishioners began to fill the pews. As usual many of the villages joined the regular churchgoers for the carol service, and amongst them was Billy Clarke who had brought the school children to sing carols. He was busy organising them into a ragged choir as their proud parents joined the throng of people squeezing into the pews. There was something magical about the carol service as it brought together the villagers to escape their worries about loved ones overseas, even if it was only for a short time.

Reverend Sykes was a tall man of middle years who loved his calling and worked tirelessly to provide spiritual as well as practical support to his parishioners. He was acutely aware that a murderer was hiding in plain sight in his village and during his sermon he urged anyone who felt the need to seek his guidance to come to him. He assured them that he was there for all his parishioners at this sad time. Inspector Green and PC Hopkins stood together at the rear of the church alongside Captain Blenkinsop and his men, a sombre reminder that a murderer was at large.

By the time the service drew to a close it had started to snow heavily and the congregation said goodbye to one another and drifted off home for their Sunday dinners. One or two of the men decided to make a stop at the Barleycorn on their way, leaving the food preparation to wives and mothers. Billy Clarke, having returned the children to the care of their parents, was one of them. As he left the church yard, he caught up with Deirdre who was getting on her bike to ride back to Kelham Hall.

'Deirdre, have you got a mo'?' he enquired.

Deirdre turned to speak to him, waving on the other girls and saying she'd catch up with them. 'Hi Billy, I haven't seen much of you since... well, you know.'

'I just wanted to make sure you're alright. It must have been a shock to you, I know how fond you were of Carmichael. I know I didn't get on with him, but I wouldn't wish that fate on him. Look, if there's anything I can do for you...' He looked slightly embarrassed to be asking but felt he needed of offer his support.

'At the moment, Billy, no one can help me. I just have to come to terms with what's happened. We were going to get engaged at Christmas, you know, he wanted me to go back to the States with him. Not straight away of course but when the war ends.'

Billy looked at her with a sad smile on his face. 'You know I'm here if you need me. You can confide in me; I won't judge you. You must know how I feel about you.'

'I know, you're very sweet. I'm alright though.' She tried to look confident but failed miserably. 'I'll be going home for Christmas and am looking forward to seeing my family. I've missed them so much especially over the last few weeks.'

'You are coming back, aren't you?' Billy asked, feeling quite alarmed at the prospect that she might leave for good.

'Of course, silly. I've got a job to do and a lot of good friends here. I just need to be with my family for a few days.'

'I'll miss you. Perhaps when you get back, we can go to the pictures or something,' he asked hopefully.

'That would be nice and perhaps they'll catch the murderer whilst I'm away and we can all get on with our lives. I've got to come to terms with the fact that he's gone and being with my family will help.'

'Deirdre,' he said, 'are you sure there's nothing you want to tell me? Sharing a secret can help you know. I do want to help you.'

'Don't be silly,' she said as she mounted her bike. 'I've nothing to hide. All will be fine in the new year. Have a good Christmas, Billy, and take care of yourself.' She turned to wave to him as she rode off the catch up with the other two girls. Billy stared after her, feeling at a loss on what to do. He knew she was trying to keep upbeat but underneath he knew she was struggling with something.

Standing in the graveyard a few feet away, Inspector Green had watched the encounter with interest. *I wonder what Billy thinks he knows about her*, he mused.

CHAPTER 19

Incident room, 1943

Monday morning, the start of the week leading up to Christmas, saw Inspector Green in a pensive mood. Little progress had been made on finding the culprit and the chief inspector had summoned him to a meeting. Before leaving for Newark he decided to discuss the investigation with Hopkins.

'Now then, lad, it's about time we reviewed all the evidence we've collected so far. It's been a couple of weeks since the murder and as far as I can see we're no nearer to making an arrest than we were on that first day. Let's make a list of the suspects, you start,' said Inspector Green as they settled down with their cups of tea.

'Well sir, as I see it there are a number of people locally who had a grudge against Carmichael but most seem to have an alibi for the time of the murder,' replied Hopkins.

'OK, let's list the suspects first and consider possible motives, we can examine the alibis later. The time of death is estimated between 10.30pm when he left the pub and 2.30am the following morning. Most of our suspects would have us believe they were tucked up in bed by then and that's an alibi that can be challenged.'

'OK, well as far as I can see there are a number of people he'd upset over the last few months; top of the list has to be Billy Clarke, the school teacher. They had an argument on the night of dance up at the Hall, and there's been bad blood between them ever since. It's pretty obvious that Billy is very fond of Deirdre and he thinks she was being badly treated by Carmichael. Then there's Deirdre herself, although I don't think a woman would have shot him at close range.'

'Well you can dispel that notion straight away, Constable; I've seen one or two vicious women in my time and a woman scorned and all that. She left at the same time as Carmichael and they may have gone to the woods together. We only have her word for it that she went straight home to bed; no one saw her as she rode home and she didn't disturb the matron at the Hall. Make a note to speak to the matron again to see if we can jog her memory, it seems like she slept through without hearing any of the inhabitants returning from the pub and that seems a bit strange to me. I don't know if Deidre's hiding anything but if she is, we need to get to the bottom of it. Now, let's move on, who else could have done it?'

Hopkins looked down at his notebook and hesitated a bit before continuing. 'Blenkinsop seems a bit suspicious to me. I know you think my dislike of the man is clouding my judgement but I don't think he was telling us the truth about his movements. He claims to have given Celia a lift to the Hall but stopped outside so as not to disturb the matron. I'm wondering why he did that. The pathway up to the Hall from the road is quite long and secluded and if Celia was as drunk as he made out, would he really have left her there?'

'Now, I think you've made an excellent point there, it's not exactly the actions of an officer and a gentleman. You can ask him why he did that when you see him next. No need to arrange a formal interview, it may be best to have a quick word with him next time you see him in the pub. I agree with you though, I think he's lying about something. I'll speak to Celia again to see if the stories match, and if they match too well, we know there's something fishy going on. I can't see the two of them being involved in the murder though, it depends on their relationship and if one of them is covering up for the other. Do you think Celia has a motive?'

'Not that I can think of, sir, she was friendly with Carmichael and he liked to flirt with her, and the other land army girl, Edith, but I don't think either of them took it too seriously. They are both fond of Deirdre and I don't think they would have anything to do with her boyfriend.'

'I agree. So as far as we know Celia went straight to bed and Edith arrived under an hour later. What about Edith, does she have a motive?'

'Not that I can think of. She's courting Arthur Harris, the landlord's son. On the night of the murder she was busy behind the bar helping out. When Jack called last orders, he sent her home. I have to admit though, she was looking a bit tired and on edge that night but it could be because Vera was giving her a hard time. She doesn't like it when Edith flirts with the punters. She was also worried about her mother's illness. Now, according to her statement, when she left the pub, she cycled to the phone box to call her mother and then rode straight back to the Hall. On route she heard the lorry heading towards Arkwright's farm and arrived at the Hall about 11.30pm.'

'One thing that's just occurred to me, what time did the transport pick up the Yanks to take them back to the Hall? I wonder if they passed Edith on the road or Celia as she walked down the driveway. I'll have a word with Mr Noble, he's quite an observant chap.'

'It's alright, sir, if you don't mind, I can follow that up. If Edith rode along the footpath, they wouldn't have seen her as they drove along the road and both Deirdre and Edith passed the perimeter fence on their way home. They would have passed the part of the fence where the killer got into the site. I'll check to see if either of them had seen anyone hanging around. I'll also go up to the woods later this morning to have another look around. It's possible that the bicycle used by the culprit was the one Celia had left behind at the pub and we know it was still there when she left with Blenkinsop. If that was the case both Deirdre and Edith will have passed the site before then.'

'OK, I'll leave it to you. I need to drive back to HQ later to give my progress report to the chief inspector this afternoon. Now, where are we?'

'I guess we should include George the night watchman in the list of suspects. After all, we haven't been able to verify his alibi. We were more concerned about where he wasn't rather than where he was, if you get my meaning.'

'That's an interesting point. What do we know about him?' The inspector made a note in his notebook.

'Well, George was in the last war and was injured on the Somme when there was a terrible battle. He suffered with his nerves when he got home and has never really settled down to a job since then. His poor wife has had a lot to put up with over the years; he drinks too much and is quite lazy. I have to admit I was a bit surprised when he got the job as the night watchman at the site, but we didn't think anything of it as we were kept in the dark about the activities up there at the time. I think he was appointed by Captain Blenkinsop who as far as I can see isn't such a good judge of character.'

'Unless we are underestimating Captain Blenkinsop. Maybe it was a deliberate act to appoint a lazy night watchman so he could cover up some illegal activities at the site,' speculated the inspector.

Hopkins smiled. At last, he thought, the inspector was coming round to his opinion about the smarmy captain.

'So, you think Blenkinsop and George were up to something? Blenkinsop could have dropped off Celia at the Hall, saving time by leaving her at the gate, and doubled back to the oil field to meet up with George. Perhaps they were stealing oil and Carmichael went to investigate and they killed him.'

'That's one theory but they wouldn't be able to get many barrels of oil in his fancy MG,' said Green, thinking out loud. 'Unless the lorry that was heard was on its way to the site to load up the barrels. Perhaps there is a link to the sheep stealing at Arkwright's farm after all. It would be a good night's work taking a couple of sheep as well as oil. Let's keep this theory in mind for now. Who else has a motive?'

Hopkins was feeling proud of himself and his powers of detection and was beginning to suspect everyone in the village.

'What about the chap that's staying in the cottage near the woods? He's been here since the Yanks arrived and the cottage has a good view of the oilfield. Maybe he's a German spy?'

'Did you get round to seeing him last week? If not, have a word with him sometime today, but tread carefully, don't let him know you suspect he has anything to do with it. What do you know about him so far?'

'I think he comes from the Radford area in Nottingham and was in the sanatorium for a few months before coming here. He failed his medical when he tried to join up, or so he says, and as far as I know he was sent to the countryside to help with his recovery. He keeps himself to himself and goes to the pub a couple of times a week but sits in a corner all night reading. His wife's a pretty young thing but doesn't seem to be too bright. She chats to the women in the local shop and is pleasant enough but I think it would be easy to pull the wool over her eyes if he's spying for the Germans.'

'OK, let's explore that idea a bit more. If the motive for the murder has something to do with a German spy in our midst who else is a suspect?'

'That's a tricky one, sir.' Hopkins thought about it for a while. 'I don't think any of the Yanks would be a spy. They all seemed to get on well with Carmichael and I haven't heard about any disagreements amongst them or Joe would have said something. He's quite a gossip when he's had a drink.'

'What about strangers in the village? Has anyone seen anybody lurking around in the last few weeks?'

'No, the only strangers that have been around were those two teachers from Cambridge who came for a walking holiday in the summer. They were a bit posh but pleasant enough and were out walking the footpaths around here most days. Vera will know more about their trips out as she gave them the third degree over breakfast each day. They did mix with the locals in the bar a few times but I didn't get the impression they were overly interested in the activities up at Dukes Wood. Nor have they been seen since the summer so it's unlikely they had anything to do with the murder. I think if anyone is suspicious it's that chap in the cottage. I'll have a good look round when I go to see him.'

'Maybe we should go together,' said Green. 'I don't want you to take any risks.'

'It would look a lot better if I called in on my own just to ask if he saw anything. He'll probably be expecting a routine visit but if we both go he may get wind that we suspect him and do a runner.'

'True, but be careful and don't underestimate the wife either, she could be in on it. Well, I think we've covered everything for now. Do you want to rustle up another cup of tea? This is thirsty business, and I need fortifying before facing the chief inspector.'

'I'll ask Jack to bring one in for us.'

'Now there's someone we haven't thought of, what about Jack?'

'Oh sir, you'll be suspecting the vicar next!' laughed Hopkins as he went in search of the landlord.

CHAPTER 20

December 1943, Thistle Cottage

It had snowed heavily the night before and as Hopkins walked towards Thistle Cottage, he was enjoying the warmth of the weak morning sunlight and thinking about the interview ahead. This was his chance to crack the case and earn himself some recognition from the Nottinghamshire constabulary. He was excited, but mindful of the fact that although they could be totally innocent, they could be dangerous German spies and his life could be at risk.

The cottage was situated near Dukes Wood with the site entrance visible from the upstairs windows, strategically placed to observe the comings and goings at the oilfield. Frank was in his middle forties and his wife a few years younger. He had served in Staffordshire Regiment during the First World War and moved to Nottingham after his demob for him to take up employment at the Raleigh factory in Nottingham as an engineer. He met his wife, Dorothy, at the factory where she worked as a bookkeeper. He had been affected following a mustard gas attack whilst fighting overseas and had suffered with a weak chest ever since, and was deemed unfit to join up when war broke out in 1939. They moved into Thistle Cottage in September and kept themselves to themselves most of the time; he frequented the Barleycorn a couple of nights a week and Dorothy collected her groceries from the local shop and eggs from the Arkwright farm. They were polite and friendly when out and about but didn't encourage intimacy from any of the locals. Frank was recovering from TB after spending 6 months in the Ransom Hall sanatorium near Mansfield and on discharge was advised to move out of Nottingham to the countryside for fresh air to aid his recovery. Hopkins knocked on the door and waited; presently it was opened by Dorothy. At first, she looked surprised to see a visitor but it soon turned to alarm as she noted the police uniform.

'Oh, my goodness,' she cried, thinking he was bringing bad news, 'is everything alright, Officer?'

'Everything is fine,' he assured her, 'this is just a courtesy call. I wonder if I might come in and have a word with you and your husband.'

'Of course.' She let him in and led him to the cosy sitting room where her husband was seated by the fire with a blanket covering his legs.

'Forgive me for not standing up,' said Frank, offering to shake hands with the constable, 'but I'm afraid I'm having a bad day today and feeling a little weak.'

Hopkins crossed the room to shake hands and took a seat opposite the man and Dorothy left the room to make some tea as Frank enquired about the reason for the visit. 'As you know, there was a murder a couple of weeks ago across the road in Dukes Wood. I'm just visiting people who live in the area to see if they heard anything strange on that night.'

'I know, we heard about it. It's all anyone in the village can talk about. It's so insular here, the locals carry on as if nothing else is happening in the world. There are millions dying a bloody death overseas and all they have to talk about is that leery lot over the road. It may sound callous but they get what they deserve running around the village showing off. They should be fighting alongside our lads instead of making a silly movie.' Hopkins was taken aback by the vicious outburst. Dorothy reappeared with the tea tray.

'Now Frank,' she said, 'don't go upsetting yourself. You know what the doctor told you.' And turning to Hopkins, 'Please don't mind him. He takes life too seriously; he's on medication for his nerves.'

Hopkins decided he needed to tread carefully in the face of the apparent hostility of the man. He found Dorothy on the other hand pleasant and welcoming.

'Would you like a scone with your tea?' she enquired. 'I made them this morning so they're quite fresh.'

'Thank you, I'd love one. I haven't enjoyed home cooking since I left home after joining the police force. My landlady's cooking leaves a lot to be desired!' She laughed with him and even Frank seemed to relax.

'What were you asking?' she enquired.

'I was just asking if you or your husband saw anything or anyone suspicious on the night of the murder. You have a good view of the site entrance from your front windows and may have seen or heard something.'

'What time did the murder happen? We go to bed early most nights and our bedroom is at the back of the house so it's unlikely if it was during the night,' replied Frank.

'The doctor estimated the time of death between 10.30pm and 2.30am the following morning. We haven't been able to narrow it down and there are no witnesses. It occurred in the site office which is quite a way from the road.'

Frank was thinking back to the night and asked, 'Was he shot?'

'Yes, why, did you hear anything?'

'I'm not sure, but as I said, we go to bed early. There are some nights when I find difficulty in sleeping and get up for a glass of water. I can't be sure, but I remember hearing a car backfire one night and thought it was late for someone to be driving along the back roads. We'd heard about the sheep stealing a few weeks before and I wondered if they were at it again. That may have been the night of the murder.'

Hopkins was feeling excited. 'And what time would it have been?'

'I remember it was around midnight. I looked at the clock on the mantlepiece on my way into the kitchen. I can't be certain though that it was that night. We didn't hear about the murder until a few days afterwards when Dorothy went to the local shop to pick up some groceries.'

'Thank you, Mr Stevenson, you've been very helpful. If you're right it'll certainly help the investigation. I don't mind admitting that it has us foxed; the night watchman neither saw nor heard nothing and without witnesses we haven't been able to catch the culprit.'

'I don't want to get him into trouble, but quite often the night watchman isn't there all night. Sometimes I see him walking away from the gatehouse when I'm putting the milk bottles out before going to bed,' said Dorothy.

'You're right, he's been sacked now and the Army have taken the responsibility for the night-time security.'

'That seems a bit excessive,' said Frank. 'I'm sure our Army lads have plenty to do rather than babysit a few Yanks who are running around pretending to be roughnecks.'

'I'm sure you're right, sir,' replied Hopkins, mindful to keep the cover story going without raising suspicion regarding the activities across the road. He took his leave of the couple and Dorothy accompanied him to the gate.

'I'm sorry about my husband's behaviour when you first arrived, he's not feeling very well today. Some days are better than others and he's been listening to the news on the wireless this morning which hasn't helped. He wanted to join up at the beginning of the war and do his bit, but was turned down on health grounds which makes him feel useless, especially after he was diagnosed with TB last year. He is on the mend now with all this fresh air, and I know I shouldn't complain but he's not an easy man to live with. I try to help him but he's suffered with his nerves for years now and can't help it when he's feeling down. Since coming here though things have improved, he's been able to walk to the pub for a drink a couple of nights a week for a bit of company and change of scenery. The local people have been so friendly, and we are settling down nicely. I never thought I'd enjoying living in the countryside but there you are.'

'You ought to go with him to the pub one night. They're a friendly crowd and some of the land army girls go in on their way home around tea time so you'd have someone to talk to. It must be lonely for you out here.'

'Thank you, I'll think about it. Frank has suggested I go with him but I guess I'm a bit old fashioned. I think of a pub as a place where men go to get away from the women folk,' she said, smiling.

'It'll be Christmas Eve in a few days so why don't you come down then? You can be assured of a warm welcome and there will be plenty of people to natter to. It'll help Frank as well if you're with him.'

Hopkins took his leave and, on the way back to the incident room, he stopped by at the oil field and walked up to the site office where he bumped into Joe. 'Morning Joe, how's things going up here?' he asked.

'Not bad, production's up this week and the lads are getting on with the job. They're still upset about James though and can't understand why anyone would want to kill him, but all in all they're coping. Mr Nobel wrote to his widow this week to offer his condolence; that's the second letter he's written in the last few weeks. Because of the wartime regulations they can't ship the body home so he'll be laid to rest alongside Douthit in the Brookwood Military Cemetery when they release his body.'

'Was Carmichael married?' asked the police officer.

'You wouldn't think so the way he was carrying on with the local lasses but he was,' replied Joe.

'I don't think Deirdre was aware of that,' said Hopkins thoughtfully. 'I wonder if he told her that night?'

'I guess that would explain why she seems to be so upset,' agreed Joe.

'I don't know, it's a rum business. Let's hope we can clear it up soon. People are getting jumpy and the longer it goes on the more they'll be speculating. I think I've been able to narrow down the time when he was shot though to around midnight. It's a relief as it puts all of us in the clear who were drinking at the pub, but I can't let on to the inspector. That Frank's a queer fella but his wife's a nice woman.'

'Oh aye,' said Joe. 'I feel sorry for her, it can't be much fun for her living with him, he's a bit of a misery guts. What did they have to say for themselves?'

'Well, he said he heard a car backfire around midnight although it could have been a gun shot, and if so, it will narrow down the actual time of the murder for us. It's a pity he didn't come forward with the information before now.'

'Could the sound have carried that far? James was inside the site office when it happened so I guess the sound would be muffled. Still, if the door was wide open it's possible. Perhaps you could test it out. It'll be a relief if it did happen at midnight, all of us in the lockdown will be cleared of suspicion.'

'That's true, Joe, and it's not a bad idea to see if Frank's right, I'll have a word with the boss. Well, I'd better get off, it's nearly lunchtime and investigating's thirsty business. One of the perks of working in a pub is Vera's lamb stew and a pint of best bitter.'

'On a brighter note,' continued Joe, 'the monks up at the Hall are planning Christmas festivities for the lads and Rosser's gone over to the Army G-20 depot at Burton-on-Trent this morning to collect a couple of turkeys. I shouldn't be telling you this but they're getting the veg and beer on the black market so it sounds like they'll be in for a treat. I'm sure they'll warm to a good old-fashioned traditional Christmas with full bellies and plenty of beer!'

Hopkins laughed. 'I didn't hear a word.'

The two men laughed and shook hands. 'Good luck, lad,' said Joe. 'Let's hope you can clear up this nasty business before Christmas.'

CHAPTER 21

December 1943, Police HQ Newark

As Hopkins was tucking into Vera's delicious lamb stew Inspector Green was entrenched with the chief inspector in his office at Newark Police Station. It was nearly three weeks since the start of the murder investigation and he was feeling under pressure to solve the case. After coming out of retirement when the force was depleted of men due to the call-up, Green had spent most of his time investigating petty crimes and this was his first major inquiry. He was keen to find the culprit but finding it frustrating that he was no further forward than that first day when he was called to Dukes Wood.

'Well, what have you to report? I was hoping you'd have cleared this up before now,' said the chief inspector, with a patronising sneer on his face. He was a large florid-faced man sporting a handlebar moustache, wearing a pristine uniform to underline his status. He liked to assert his authority over his men. He was a vain man full of his own importance, but was intimidated by the keen intellect and popularity of the man he was addressing. Sitting behind his imposing oak desk he looked towards Green who had removed his trench coat and trilby hat to reveal a rumpled pin-stripe brown suit and creased shirt with a frayed collar. He wanted to tell him to smarten himself up but was wary as he knew Inspector Green would react by tendering his resignation. Irrespective of his personal feelings towards the inspector, he knew his reputation for clearing up crimes was well earned and losing him would be counterproductive. The feeling was mutual. Green disliked the chief inspector, he had seen chief inspectors come and go and knew the man sitting in judgement in front of him had only been given the job because he was in the right place at the right time after his predecessor had died unexpectedly from a heart attack.

'So was I,' he replied respectfully, 'but it is more complicated than we first thought. PC Hopkins has been a great help. I didn't think he was the sharpest knife in the drawer when I first met him but he's been a God send with his local knowledge and he has some interesting theories to contribute.'

'Theories are one thing, what we need is hard evidence. What do you know so far?'

'Well, I've just taken a call from Hopkins and he thinks he may have narrowed down the time of the murder to midnight. He's found a witness who heard a gunshot so if it's correct we need to go through all the statements again to check the alibis.'

'I see, well that's something. What about a motive?'

'We have two working theories on the motive. Carmichael seemed to have upset one or two of the locals in the lead-up to the murder so it could be a case of petty jealousy or, because of the secret activities at the oil field, we could be looking at espionage. We are checking all the strangers in the area to see if anyone is suspicious.'

'Is it possible the crime was committed by one of the other roughnecks? Some of those Yanks can be quite hot headed to say the least,' enquired the chief inspector. 'In my opinion, finding the culprit amongst one of his own would be the best result. We don't want the PM to find out that an American worker, who has come over here to support the war effort, was killed by one of the locals. How would that look?' He was getting more and more agitated at the thought that he would be held responsible if the crime wasn't cleared up satisfactorily.

Green supressed a sigh. 'We've considered that but those who were at the darts match stayed together and returned in the lorry that picked them up when the pub closed. Nor is there any evidence of rivalry amongst the Yanks. Mr Carmichael appeared to be a popular member of the team and Mr Noble, the manager, would have told me if it was any different. We aren't ruling anything out though at this stage.'

He continued, 'I've just picked up the ballistics report on the murder weapon. Apparently the bullet came from a German pistol that was used during the last war. The type of pistol used was commonly issued to German Army officers. As such, it may give credence to a possible theory of a German spy in our midst, so we will look a bit closer at the strangers in the village. It's possible, of course, that someone has been in the village longer but until the discussions about opening up the oil field last year this area had no strategic military importance. However, there is another possibility. The pistol could belong to one of the locals, or indeed one of the oil workers who fought in the last war and brought it home as a souvenir. It's a good lead though, and I'll get on to it straight away.'

The two police officers continued their discussion well into the afternoon and the chief inspector reluctantly agreed that although they hadn't yet identified the culprit, the investigation was on track and the inspector was exploring all possibilities.

The chief inspector made it clear though, that he was sceptical about the spy theory and warned Green not to step on any toes by upsetting the Army, who in his opinion were better equipped to sniff out any spies in the area. He was a personal friend of the father-in-law of Captain Blenkinsop and believed the young man was perfectly capable of helping with the enquiry. A sentiment not shared by Inspector Green, but he thought it wise to keep his opinion to himself.

As Green was leaving the police station, he was stopped by the duty sergeant.

'Have you got a mo', sir?' he asked.

'Hello Bert, how's things going? Have you found those sheep rustlers yet? I hear they've been active over the border in Lincolnshire so it sounds like a well-organised operation,' replied Green.

'That's what I wanted to talk to you about if you're not rushing off. I think it's a well-organised operation and the gang are stealing to order. There was a fancy wedding party last Saturday over in Upton and I've been told there was roast lamb on the menu. It's a bit tricky, though, seeing as the father of the bride is a big wig in the Council so we're having to tread lightly. The gang have also been supplying some of the local pubs and restaurants and I've heard on the grapevine that the landlord of the Barleycorn over in Eakring is involved. He's not one to refuse a bit of racketeering if my information is correct. Before taking over the tenancy he and his missus lived up in Newcastle and he was well known for sailing a bit close to the wind. Rumour has it he had to get out before he was caught so did a disappearing act. I'd be obliged if you can keep a look out to see if he's up to his old tricks again. He's got a reputation for getting involved in the black market and if something fishy is going on in the village, my money is on him being involved.'

'Not a problem, mate, the only thing is I might be done for aiding and abetting. I had a delicious lamb stew for lunch yesterday.'

They both laughed. 'Aye well, I'd keep that under your hat,' replied the sergeant.

CHAPTER 22

December 1943

When Hopkins finished for the day, he was in no hurry to go back to his digs so decided to stay on at the pub for a drink by the roaring fire. The only other occupants in the bar were Frank, sitting in the corner reading, and George, who since losing his job at the site, was at a loose end and reluctant to spend much time at home being nagged by his wife who, although still in the dark about his dalliance with the widow at Rose Cottage, was angry that he'd lost a well-paid job and was fed up of his lazy ways. He was nursing a drink and brooding in the corner when Hopkins took over another half pint for him and sat down to have a chat.

'If you've come over here to give me the third degree again you can bogger off and take the beer with you. I've just about had enough of snide remarks. Anybody would think they're all lily white around here but I know better. Quite a few folks are up to no good, even him behind the bar's been up to no good. I know a few things about people round here that they'd like to keep under their hats.'

'Now then,' shouted Jack as he looked up from cleaning the glasses, 'you can pack that in or I'll bar you. There's a war on, you know, and we're all trying to get by the best we can. You know what Churchill says, *"Careless Talk Costs Lives,"* so think on.'

Hopkins ignored the landlord and sat down uninvited.

'I'm just after a quiet drink and a bit of civilised conversation. I'm off duty now and am just as keen as the rest of you for this sad business to be cleared up so we can get back to normal. Let's just change the subject. Have you got anything planned for Christmas Eve, Jack?'

'Not sure the punters are in the mood after what happened following the darts match. We might put on a few sandwiches and if we're lucky some of the Yanks might bring along their fiddles so we can have a bit of a knees up. I've heard they've gone and got a couple of turkeys up at the Hall courtesy of the Army supplies so they'll be in for a treat on Christmas Day. We'll have to make do with rabbit stew again, but our Vera's found a Christmas pudding tucked away and I've asked Arkwright if he can spare some cream. The pudding's been in the cupboard since before the war but if we add a bit of rum to it, I'm sure it'll go down a treat. What about you, Herbert, are you visiting your folks back in Nottingham?'

'I wish. If this murder isn't cleared up in the next few days the inspector won't give me any time off and I'll probably be working on Christmas Day.'

'Well you can't use the snug over Christmas, we'll be closing the bar and I'm not coming down to light fires for you, so you can tell Inspector Green to sling his hook. Having a couple of days off won't hurt. If you've not found the culprit by now, I'm sure he won't be going anywhere. That's assuming it's a man,' said Jack.

Herbert looked at Jack quizzically. 'You don't think a woman would do such a thing, do you?' he asked.

'It wouldn't surprise me. I'll bet George will have to watch his step if his old lady finds out about the widow up at Rose Cottage. You know what they say about a woman scorned, and I bet Mildred's a bit of a fire cracker when she's roused,' laughed Jack.

'You just keep your gob shut, Jack! I wasn't joking about knowing things. After all, Arkwright's farm isn't far from Dukes Wood,' replied George with a knowing smirk on his face.

'Look George,' said Hopkins, 'if you know anything about the sheep stealing, you'd better tell us. The farmer can't afford to lose any more sheep and if you've got any information you need to come clean.'

'He's bluffing. The old bogger's half blind and can't see 10 yards in front of him, let alone over the fields to Arkwright's farm from the widow's bedroom,' said the landlord.

The conversation was interrupted as the door opened. The three land army girls entered, muffled up to keep out the cold.

'Well, good evening ladies,' said Jack as he took down three glasses in anticipation of their order. 'What will it be tonight?'

'We'll have the usual, mine host, if you would be so kind,' said Celia.

'You're in a chirpy mood, young lady.'

'I am. There's only a few days to Christmas and I for one will be well away from here on Christmas Eve. I intend to make the most of my leave in London. I'll be having a gay old time,' she replied, smiling.

Deirdre was still looking out of sorts, and she seemed to have lost weight and her natural sparkle. Although she sat with the others nursing her drink for once she failed to take part in the banter. Edith was trying to include her in the conversation but was failing badly. As if by tacit agreement the conversation in the bar veered away from the murder investigation as they all talked about their plans for the Christmas holidays and local gossip.

'Be careful what you say in front of George,' remarked the landlord after Edith mentioned she had seen the postman spending more time than he should at the farm cottage facing the lower field at Arkwright's farm whilst she was looking for a stray sheep. 'He's been snooping around lately and knows more than he's willing to share with the rest of us. Mum's the word, hey, George.'

George looked up with a sly look on his face. 'You can mock all you like, Jack Harris, but I know things that'll make yur 'air curl.'

Presently Hopkins took his leave, having spent the evening in good company at the pub and for a short time forgetting what was going on in the world outside. It was a crisp cold evening with a bright starlight night and a bomber's moon. Somewhere in the world people were fighting for survival whilst here in this little corner of England the locals were still coming to terms with the violence that had invaded their community. Was it just a domestic crime or part of something bigger? Was it really possible that Carmichael's death had something to do with the war against Germany? Unlikely as it might seem the inspector was following that line of enquiry, which if it was true, could spell danger the closer they got to the truth. Hopkins shuddered at the thought that somewhere in this sleepy village a killer was lurking and one who wouldn't be afraid to strike again if he was in danger of being exposed. Hopkins realised he would need to keep his wits about himself and perhaps he could help the investigation by using his local knowledge about the inhabitants of the village. Unless the perpetrator was one of the Yanks, he had to accept the fact that someone he knew well was harbouring a deadly secret and maybe, he was best placed to uncover what it was. He was still wide awake when he arrived at his digs so he set about making notes about the locals to see if there could be anything in their background that would make them a likely suspect.

First, he decided to eliminate those who had stayed behind in the pub for the lock-in and concentrate on those who had left at closing time. This included Mr Noble and his two right-hand men, Rosser and Walker, who left early, having decided to walk back to the Hall. The rest of the Yanks that had left in the truck stayed together until after midnight in the common room at the Hall so he was pretty sure they all had alibis. They also testified that Noble and his two companions were already relaxing in the common room when they arrived. They all worked at the oilfield and he doubted if they would betray their location to the Germans. After all, if it resulted in the place being bombed, they would surely be killed.

He made a list of the locals who had lived in the area all their lives and a second list of newcomers.

The locals included Billy Clarke, old Joe, George, the vicar who had served the community for the past 25 years, and Farmer

Arkwright whilst the newcomers included Jack, the landlord who had mysteriously been missing from the bar for some time during the lock-in, Blenkinsop, whose activities after leaving the pub had been suspicious, and although the three land army girls had left the farm labourers had stayed behind, and not forgetting Frank and Dorothy at Thistle Cottage. Were they witnesses, as they would have him believe, or in it together? Pleased that he had started on his list of suspects he put away his notebook and decided to discuss his ideas with Inspector Green in the morning.

CHAPTER 23

December 1943

The following morning when Hopkins arrived at the incident room, Inspector Green was hard at work re-reading statements and making notes. He looked up as the constable entered the room.

'Morning Herbert, has it stopped snowing yet? You look perished. I had a hell of a job driving down that back lane this morning, my car was skidding all over the place. If it doesn't stop soon, I could end up snowed in here over Christmas.'

'Well sir, there's a spare room at my digs but my landlady's an awful cook so I can't recommend it. I was hoping to be able to get home for the holidays but even if the investigation is cleared up, I doubt whether there will be any buses running after today. The snow is banking up from the main 617 so it's not looking good. I've been hedging my bets and trying to wangle an invitation to spend the day up at Arkwright's but the farmer hasn't taken notice of any of my subtle hints.'

I don't suppose he understands subtlety, you ought to come straight out with it and ask him. Mind you, I'm sure your landlady is looking forward to spoiling you, even if her cooking leaves a lot to be desired. I've heard you can get a nice leg of lamb on the black market if you know where to look,' laughed the inspector.

'Sir,' said Hopkins, 'I was making a list of people who don't have an alibi for the time of the murder last night but am stumped when it comes to a motive. Carmichael was a bit of a rogue but was well liked and if it had something to do with the war, I can't image why he was targeted.'

'I know, lad,' replied the inspector. 'Sometimes we overthink the motive and end up eliminating the wrong people. Let's stick to the facts. He was either shot when he disturbed someone in the site office who was ransacking the place, or he went there with someone else for whatever reason and after they'd shot him, they ransacked the office to make it look like a break-in. There's also the possibility that someone may have been at the site to steal oil.'

Just then there was a loud knock on the door to the public bar. Jack, who was working behind the counter, shouted out to say they were closed and continued with his work. Another knock came, more insistent this time which prompted the landlord to cross over to open it. 'I told you we're...' he began but stopped short as he recognised George's wife standing on the door step. 'Hello Mildred,' he said, 'is there anything wrong?'

'Is that useless bobby around? I've come to report a missing person,' she said.

'Who's missing then?' enquired Jack.

'My George, he didn't come home last night so he's either laying under one of your tables kalied or fell into a hedge bottom somewhere on the way home.'

'When he left here last night he was as sober as a judge. He said he was going straight home,' replied Jack with a worried look on his face. 'The inspector's in the snug, just knock before you go in, and tell him if he wants to mount a search party for George, I'll be ready in a jiffy.' Hearing the commotion, Vera came into the bar to find out what was happening. Jack took her to one side.

'It looks like George has gone AWOL; make Mildred a cup of tea and keep her here while I pop round to Rose Cottage to see if he's there. I wouldn't be surprised if he's got fed up of her nagging and decided to move in with the lovely widow. He was in a bit of a strange mood last night, as if something was on his mind.'

'Oh Jack, surely not. It's nearly Christmas, he wouldn't do that to Mildred, not at a time like this.'

'Well, I'll go and find out while she's reporting him missing to the inspector. If I find him, I'll drag him back and we can say he was sleeping it off in the outhouse.'

With that, he put on his overcoat and hat and rushed out.

Mildred took out a hanky and dabbed her eyes as she relayed the information to the inspector. George left the house yesterday saying he was going to the pub for a quick pint and hadn't returned. She told the inspector she had gone to bed at her usual time, half expecting George to roll in blind drunk when the pub closed to sleep it off on the settee. When she got up though, he was nowhere to be seen and after seeing the heavy snow outside she began to worry.

Inspector Green ushered the woman into a chair in the incident room and listened to her story with interest. As she was finishing her story, Vera appeared with a cup of tea for her. Mildred thanked her and after being dismissed by the inspector she hovered outside the door to the snug trying to listen into what was being said.

Presently Hopkins led Mildred out, telling her to go home and wait for George to return. 'Don't worry too much, Mrs Saunders, I'm sure we'll find him. He's a tough old bird, I'm sure he's come to no harm,' he assured her as she buttoned up her coat and prepared to leave.

Back in the snug the inspector was looking pensive as Hopkins returned.

'Sir, I'm sure it's nothing but last night in the bar George was bragging about knowing folks' secrets around here. He was in a funny old mood and I got the impression he was warning someone. You don't think he has some information about the murder and was thinking of indulging in a spot of blackmail, do you?'

'What exactly did he say? Did he mention any names?'

'Not specifically, he just said one or two people around here had something to hide when he was riled about the widow in Rose Cottage. I thought he was just showing off and didn't take any notice but he's a crafty one, I wouldn't put it past him to withhold information from the police. When he said it, there was just me and

Jack in the bar but later on those land army girls turned up along with the regulars and they were laughing at something. George thought they were laughing at him so repeated his threat and said he just might upset the apple cart and spill the beans about what people have been up to around here. No one took him seriously though, I don't think.'

'Who else was in the bar?' asked the inspector.

'The usual crowd, Billy and Fred, Frank was in the corner, and Blenkinsop turned up and sat with Celia,' he replied.

Green was stopped from pursing the line of enquiry as Jack came in to report that he'd been to Rose Cottage and there was no sign of George. The widow said she hadn't seen him since the night of the murder and wanted nothing more to do with him.

By now the inspector was getting worried. He was pretty certain there was a connection between the murder and the disappearance of the night watchman; it was too much of a coincidence. He called the police station in Newark and asked Bert, the duty sergeant, to send some officers to form a search party and check the area around Eakring, whilst he and Hopkins went to talk to some of the people who were in the pub the night before.

Their first stop was at Billy Clarke's digs. The school was closed for the Christmas holidays and he had decided to have a lie in after drinking a skinful the night before. When they knocked on the door to the small cottage he had just got out of bed and was reluctant to let them in, demanding to know why they were bothering him. They explained about the missing night watchman and so he relented and opened the door. He said his aunt was visiting an old lady who lived down the lane so they could talk in the living room. The room was sparsely furnished and the meagre fire burning in the hearth barely took the chill out of the air.

'So, what have I got to do with it? I didn't leave until last orders and George had long gone by then. Have you checked on the widow at Rose Cottage?' he asked. The inspector told him that they were following all leads but no one had seen him after he left to go home around 9 o'clock.

'You must be mad if you think I've got old George locked away somewhere. You're welcome to have a look round though, but what on earth would I want with him?' he said when questioned.

'I'm not accusing you or anyone else of doing anything untoward at the moment, we're just doing some routine enquiries and are speaking to everyone who was in the pub last night. Did you hear George say something about people having secrets in the village?' asked the inspector.

'Of course, we all heard him. He was just blowing off steam because someone mentioned him shacking up with the widow at Rose Cottage. He's a nosey old bogger but there's no harm in him. I bet he's fallen into a ditch somewhere. If you give me a mo' I'll get me coat and help you look for him.'

After he left to get changed the inspector looked around the room. Although spotlessly clean the room was shabbily furnished with two threadbare armchairs next to the fireplace and a table with a lace tablecloth under the window. On the mantelpiece next to the clock there was a sepia-toned photograph of a soldier with the insignia of the Sherwood Forester Regiment on his uniform.

'Who is this?' enquired Green as Billy returned to the room.

'That was me dad,' he said. 'He was killed not long after that photo was taken. He was at home because I'd just been born and he managed to wrangle compassionate leave for a few days. He left soon after to go to France and that was it. He was killed at the battle of the Somme so that was the one and only time he got to see me. Me mam never got over the shock, it affected her nerves and she was eventually sent to an asylum and that's when I came here to live with me auntie. She's a funny old stick but her heart's in the right place and she's looked after me as best she could.'

'That's quite a sad story but not unique. There were a lot of widows left after the last war, mind you there's likely to be just as many this time around. At least you've got a photo to remember him by,' said the inspector kindly.

'That and a few possessions they sent back from the front after he was killed. Still, talking about me dad won't help us find old George so we'd better get going,' he said as he buttoned up his coat and pulled on some woollen gloves.

After leaving the cottage the inspector sent Billy to the pub to meet up with the other volunteers being organised by Jack, and the two police officers continued their journey. The next visit was to see old Joe who had nothing to add although he suggested they go up to Kelham Hall to enlist the help of the roughnecks in the search for George. Oil production had stopped due to the heavy snow so they would all be at a loose end and more than willing to help.

Back in the car the inspector debated on where to try next; he was still suspicious of the couple at Thistle Cottage but thought it best to try to get extra help with the search before the light started to fade so they set off for the Hall.

CHAPTER 24

Kelham Hall

It was a slow journey as the snow had begun to drift along the access road to the 617 but on reaching the main road driving became easier. The snow plough had forged a track along the road and they arrived at the Hall by mid-morning. The driveway up to the Hall had also been cleared of snow to make access easier, although it was still snowing and fresh snow was beginning to settle.

Captain Blenkinsop's MG was parked outside the main door next to the Army truck that was used to transport the roughnecks to and from the oil field. The bonnet of the truck was open and a couple of soldiers were peering into the engine, looking puzzled. After parking the police car, the two officers greeted the men and enquired about the problem they appeared to be having.

'The truck was working OK last night when we got back to the Hall,' one of them said, 'but it wouldn't start this morning and Bert has just looked at the engine and it seems the distributor cap has been taken off. It's a mystery why anyone would do that, it's not as if it's any use to anyone. It's been parked well away from the road overnight so I doubt anyone would see it if they were walking past. I can't imagine anyone here doing such a daft thing, even if it were for a joke.'

As they were talking Captain Blenkinsop rushed out of the main door; he was looking agitated and seemed to be in a hurry. Without acknowledging the two police officers he jumped into his car and sped off. Green and Hopkins exchanged a look and went through the door that Blenkinsop had left open in his haste to get away. 'What's up wi' him...?' asked Hopkins.

'...And more importantly what is he doing here today? I thought the Yanks were taking the day off due to the snow so he won't be needed for anything,' replied Green. 'Let's go and find the matron to see if she can spare a room for us to conduct some interviews.'

As they entered, the matron was coming down the stairs carrying a pile of fresh linen. She saw two police officers and approached them to find out why they were there.

'Good morning, officers,' she said as she reached the ground floor. 'To what do we owe the pleasure of a police visit? Is there anything wrong?'

'Good morning, madam,' replied Green, taking off his trilby hat and looking appraisingly at the attractive older woman before him. 'We've just come over from Eakring and would like to speak to some of your residents who were at the Barleycorn last night. One of the regulars has gone missing and we need to find out if anyone saw him after he left the pub, or heard him say where he was going. Would it be possible for us to use one of your rooms to interview some of your residents? I assure you it is just a routine enquiry and we are hoping someone can help us.'

'Oh dear, I'm sorry to hear that. Is it anyone I know?' she enquired.

'It's George Saunders, the night watchman, he left the pub about 9.30pm and didn't arrive home. We're hoping someone may have seen where he went,' replied the inspector.

'That's Mildred's husband, she must be out of her mind with worry. She's a friend of mine form the church, a lovely God-fearing woman. I don't want to speak out of turn but that husband of hers is a bit of a waster. I don't really know why she puts up with him, I wouldn't be surprised if he was up to no good. Do you think I ought to go and keep her company? She must be really upset.'

'That's a grand idea, madam,' replied Green, 'but if you're hoping to get a lift to the village in that Army truck outside, you'll be out of luck. Someone has stolen the distributor cap so it'll be out of action for a while.'

'Well I have got a few things to do this morning so will walk up to the village this afternoon to see Mildred. Let me find you somewhere to sit and if you tell me who you want to speak to, I'll go and round them up for you. I daresay you could both do with a nice cup of tea so I'll rustle up some refreshments for you as well. It's certainly not a day to be out and about in this weather.'

The matron showed the two men into the small writing room; a roaring fire was in the hearth and chairs were strategically placed to make the most of the warm air. As they were removing their outer clothing Mr Noble entered the room.

'Good morning, I understand someone from the village went missing last night. Is there anything we can do to help?'

'It's George, the old night watchman. He hasn't been seen since leaving the pub last night.'

'Oh, I am sorry to hear that. George wasn't the best night watchman but I rather like the old guy. I do hope wherever he is he's managed to find some shelter; it's freezing cold out there. If he's fallen into a ditch he could die of hypothermia. My men are kicking their heels today because the bad weather is holding up production so I'm sure they will only be too happy to mount a search party.'

'That's one of the reasons why we came here, but I understand your truck outside is out of action so I guess your men will have to walk to the village.'

'Yes, I've just been told someone's removed the distributor cap. Heaven knows why. It's not a problem though, most of the men are used to this weather back home. It may be better if they walk to the village anyway, they can keep an eye out for him on the way. I'll go and round them up and we can get started straight away. Every minute counts in a situation like this.'

'Before you go,' said the inspector, 'could you ask if anyone saw George after he left the pub? As far as we know he left just after 9 o'clock and some of your men were in the pub at the time so I just need to see if they noticed anything.'

'I will and if anyone has any information, I'll send them along to see you. I was there with Don and Gene and I think he left quite a while before we did, although I couldn't swear to it. There was no sign of him in the village when we walked home,' replied Noble.

'Did you notice if anyone else left around the same time as George?' asked Green.

'Not really, the bar was pretty full at the time and I was discussing the production schedule with Don. The weather hasn't been kind to us for a few days and we were thinking of ways to make up for our losses.' Noble turned to leave and Green thanked him for the offer of help.

'Sir, don't you want to interview any of the men before they go?' asked Hopkins.

'No, I think the priority here is for them to search the hedgerows in case George has fallen down a ditch. His remarks about secrets seemed to be aimed at the people in the bar before the roughnecks arrived. Whilst we're here I'd like to interview the land girls.'

The door opened and the matron reappeared with a pot of tea and some homemade biscuits. She put the tray down on a table near the fire and proceeded to pour out the drinks. She was a pleasantly plump middle-aged woman, with a pretty face and salt and pepper hair tied back in a bun. She had lived in the village all her life. Her fiancé, a local man who had been in the Sherwood Forester Regiment along with George and old Joe, had been killed during the First World War. She, like many women of the time who had lost their menfolk, had remained a spinster, involving herself in local activities and never straying far from the village. Prior to the war she had worked as a housekeeper at one of the large houses in the area, taking up the post of matron at Kelham Hall when it was requisitioned to billet the land army girls. Despite the fact that she had never married or had children, she was a motherly soul who had become very fond of the girls in her care. Her friendly demeanour had not gone unnoticed by the inspector, who had formed a good impression of the sensible and kindly woman.

She handed the officers a cup of tea each. 'Help yourselves to biscuits. Now who is it you wish to speak to? I can go and fetch them for you,' she asked.

'I understand some of the land army girls who work at Arkwright's farm called in to the Barleycorn on their way home so I'd just like to ask them if they saw or heard anything that might explain why George went missing last night,' replied the inspector.

'That will be Deirdre, Edith and Celia. They are all lovely girls and I'm sure they will be keen to help if they can. I'll go and find them and send them in.' With that, she left the room on a mission to round up the girls. After she left Green sipped his tea and ate his fair share of the biscuits and the two men sat in companionable silence as they waited.

Presently Deirdre entered the room without knocking. 'Did you want to see me? I haven't got a lot of time as I'm getting ready to leave. I'm catching the train home from Nottingham at 2 o'clock so I can't stay long. What's happened, have you found the person who killed James?'

Green ushered her into one of the chairs near the fire and explained the reason for the visit. Deirdre looked shocked but calmed down a little, as if relieved about the turn in the conversation. Since the night of the murder she had lost weight and was looking tired and run down.

'Well when I saw him in the pub, he was sitting with you Herbert so you already know that,' she said. 'He was a miserable old sod, forever moaning at us telling us to pipe down when we were having fun. It's as if he'd forgotten what it's like to be young and was always complaining about the noise.'

'I understand he was saying he knew secrets about people in the village before he left. Have you any idea what he meant? Do you think he was talking about the night when James Carmichael was killed?' asked the inspector.

'How would I know? I left early that night and went straight home. I already told Herbert.' It was true that Hopkins had already interviewed her about the events on the night of the murder but Green, thinking there was a connection between the two events, decided to revisit the statement she'd previously made.

'Thinking back to the night of the murder, I understand Carmichael followed you when you left. Did you have a conversation with him outside?' asked the inspector.

'I did, I told Jimmy I needed to go home early as I wasn't feeling well. He offered to come with me but I had my bike with me so I rode home on my own.'

Hopkins took out his notebook and read out a statement that Brenda Whitaker had made about the events of that night. 'According to a witness who overheard you and Carmichael arguing outside the pub; you said, *"You can't mean that, Jimmy, not now…"* Now perhaps you'd like to explain exactly what really happened that night.'

Deirdre looked stricken and began to cry. 'I didn't have anything to do with his murder, I told you I went straight home. I don't know where Jimmy went after I left.'

'Now then, young lady, if that's true you've got nothing to worry about. Let's start again and tell me what happened that night,' said the inspector.

Deirdre tried to compose herself. 'I thought you were here to ask about George. What's happened to him?'

'We are, but there may be a connection. So just take your time and tell me what you and Carmichael were arguing about on the night of the darts match.'

'You won't say anything to the others, I feel such a fool.' She looked imploringly towards the inspector.

'I assure you, if it has nothing to do with the crime no one else will need to know. PC Hopkins and I will try to keep your name out of it but it may have a bearing on the case. Go ahead, it looks like you've been bottling something up, I can tell it's been playing on your mind. You'll feel better if you get it off your chest.' He gave her a handkerchief to wipe her eyes and asked Hopkins to fetch her a cup for her.

Deirdre began to speak. 'I was really looking forward to meeting Jimmy that night. We'd been courting for a few months and I wanted to ask him to come home with me to Liverpool for Christmas to meet my parents. I thought he loved me as much as I love him but he was being horrible to me during the darts match and was flirting with Brenda. She's a bit flighty and was throwing herself at him all night and he was encouraging her.

'About 10 o'clock I'd had enough, I told him I was going home and wanted to speak to him outside where it was quiet. I said I needed to tell him something.' She dabbed her eyes and continued. 'When we were outside, I asked him if he'd come to Liverpool with me. I'm pregnant, you see, and really thought that Jimmy wanted to marry me and take me back to America with him. I really loved him, you know, and thought he'd be happy but he laughed at me. He said he was just having a bit of fun with me, and...' she hesitated, 'and, he told me he was already married and there was no way he'd take a little tart like me back with him. I wouldn't have gone with him if I'd known. I'm not like Brenda, I really thought he loved me. I feel such a fool, I don't know what me mam and dad will say when I tell them. They were so proud of me when I joined the land army, they've been telling all the neighbours that I'm doing my bit for the war effort. I even told them about Jimmy being a film star and they couldn't believe it, me being courted by a film star. I thought it was too good to be true, and it was.'

'So, after your argument, you rode home on your bike. Did you see where James went? No one saw him go back into the bar,' asked the inspector.

'As a matter of fact, when I looked back, I saw Brenda coming out to talk to him.'

'Your secret's safe with us, but I think you need to confide in someone and I'm sure if you speak to the matron, she will help you,' replied the inspector. 'Now before you go, is there anything you can tell us about last night that may shed a light on the whereabouts of George?'

'Not really, he was there when we arrived, sitting with you, Herbert,' she replied. 'We stood at the bar getting our drinks and went to sit at a table near the window. Edith had to pop out to give her mum a ring from the phone box across the road, and was only outside a few minutes. When she came back in, she was covered with snow and said it was getting worse so we decided to hitch a lift back to the Hall with the guys when the truck came to pick them up at closing time. Captain Blenkinsop came in and sat with Celia for a while but I think he left before George. I think George left after 9 o'clock but I wasn't taking too much notice so can't be certain.'

The inspector thanked her for her information and for telling the truth about the night of the murder.

As she left the room, she turned back. 'Thank you, sir, you won't say anything to the others, will you?'

He reassured her, and said he wouldn't mention anything that didn't have a direct bearing on the murder. He urged her to speak to the matron, and asked her to fetch Celia or Edith for him.

The inspector turned to Hopkins and asked him if he'd taken a statement from Brenda that night.

'I did, and she told me she'd left the bar for a few minutes, and I thought she'd gone to the toilet. She wasn't gone long as she was leading the singing when the darts match finished and was there until the end of the night. I'll have another word with her when we get back to the village but I doubt that she had anything to do with the murder, although she may have noticed where James went after the argument.'

'Good idea, check that out when we've finished here.' There was a knock on the door and Celia entered.

'Hello Celia, we're just following up on the questioning about the murder of Mr Carmichael and George Saunders went missing last night so we're talking to everyone who was in the Barleycorn,' said Hopkins.

'Oh, he was the night watchman up at the wood, wasn't he? When we arrived, he was boasting about knowing secrets in the village but I thought he was just trying to sound important. He left fairly early just after it started to snow quite heavily. We – Deirdre, Edith and I – left at closing time and cadged a lift from the film guys. When we got back Deirdre and I went to the common room for a while but Edith went straight to bed saying she was tired.'

'Thank you, we are also revisiting the statements made by people regarding their movements on the night of the murder. According to your statement you left the pub about 10.30 that night and were about to cycle home when Captain Blenkinsop offered to drive you in his MG. Is that right?' asked the inspector.

'Yes,' she said hesitantly, 'Gerald dropped me off at the main gate and I walked up the driveway arriving home about 10.45. I went straight to bed and heard Edith arrive a bit later. I don't remember the time as I was dozing but just heard her moving around the room as I was dropping off to sleep.'

'It is possible your bicycle was used by the perpetrator of the crime to ride up to Dukes Wood? Did you happen to notice if it had been moved from where you left it when you picked it up in the morning?'

'No, not really. I was in a hurry as I was a little bit late for work.'

'I see, and can I ask how you got back to the village the next morning?' asked the inspector.

'Umm, I suppose I walked,' she replied. 'I can't remember, it's all a bit confusing.' She couldn't meet the inspector's eyes as she spoke.

'What is it you're not telling us?' he said. 'I don't think you're telling us the truth about your movements that night. What is it you've got to hide?'

Celia looked stricken and got up and paced around the room while she decided what to do. 'We had nothing to do with the murder, I promise. Gerald came round this morning to warn me not to say anything,' she confessed.

'Please sit down, and tell me exactly what happened that night. We know you are withholding some information, and if it has nothing to do with the murder up at Dukes Wood you need to tell us so we can eliminate you from our enquiries.'

Celia did as she was told and sat down again. She tried to compose herself before beginning to speak.

'I wanted to tell you the truth from the start but Gerald was against it. He came round again this morning to tell me to keep quiet, he was very persistent, I don't know why. It's not as if we have done anything wrong.'

'OK, go on,' encouraged the inspector.

'Well, when the darts match finished, Gerald and I did leave together and went out the side door. We saw James and Brenda outside; Deirdre had just ridden off on her bicycle towards the footpath, and as we were getting into the MG, I noticed Brenda going back into the pub leaving James outside. He was just standing on his own.'

'What was he doing?' asked Hopkins.

'He was lighting a cigarette and just looking around. He didn't seem in any hurry to go back into the bar and there was no one else around at the time.'

'And what happened then?' said the inspector.

'I don't know why Gerald asked me to lie, he didn't drive me home to the Hall. He'd made arrangements for us to go and stay at a friend of his who's got an apartment in Newark, so we could spend the night together. He came round again this morning to warn me to keep quiet about it. He was quite threatening which was out of character, he said he's worried in case his CO finds out. We had an argument just before you arrived as I told him that I wanted to tell you but he said he'd deny it if I did. I don't know what's got into him, he's been acting strange ever since that night and now says he doesn't want to see me anymore.'

'Are you sure that he was with you all night? Is there any chance he could have sneaked out after you fell asleep?' asked Hopkins, who was still keen to pin the murder on the captain.

'It's possible, I suppose, I am a heavy sleeper and have to admit I fell asleep quite soon after we'd arrived at the flat. I was a bit embarrassed about that at the time. When I woke up the next morning he was just coming in the door, he told me he'd been to the newsagent's. We had breakfast and he drove me straight to work as arranged. I'd taken a bag with my work clothes with me. When I'd finished for the day, I collected my bike from the pub and that's when I heard about the murder.'

'Thank you, there is just one other thing. Why did you lie about hearing Edith arrive home? She must have known you were out all night.'

'I guess she just wanted to help by saying I was in bed asleep. I'd told her where I was and she was sworn to secrecy so things just got out of hand. If you ask Gerald about it and he says I'm lying, I'm not. It's the truth, I can even take you to the apartment. I'm sure his friend will verify that he lent him the keys for the night.'

'Well, you've been very helpful. You shouldn't have lied. Giving a false alibi has hampered our enquiries. I'm sure you'll agree that we need to find the culprit and if George's disappearance has anything to do with the case you may have inadvertently helped our murderer. Remember that if you're ever tempted to lie again, sometimes there are serious consequences,' the inspector said, dismissing her.

'There is something else. I suppose you want to speak to Edith as well?' she asked the inspector.

'We do, so if you'd be kind enough to fetch her, we'll speak to her next.'

'Well, there's a bit of a problem, she's not here.'

'What do you mean?' said Hopkins, looking alarmed.

'Well, last night after she arrived back, she went straight to bed and was asleep when I went up but when I woke up this morning she wasn't there. I thought she'd got up early to go for a walk before breakfast, but she didn't come back. She may have walked down to the village and is helping with the search party. If you ring the pub she may be there. We haven't got work today so there's no reason for her to come back if she's helping out in the village.'

'What time did you notice that she was missing?' asked the inspector.

'I woke up about 8 o'clock and haven't seen her since then.' After she'd left the room the two detectives looked at one another.

'You don't think she's disappeared as well, do you?' asked Hopkins.

'Now then lad, let's not be hasty, she may be in the village as Celia said, although she didn't come into the pub when we were there this morning and we didn't see her when we drove over. I'll give the landlord a quick ring and have a word with him.'

'She could have taken the short-cut through the woods; most people do that to get to the village,' replied Hopkins.

'Pop out and have a word with those two soldiers who are working on the truck out there, they may have seen her leave, and have a look to see if her bike has gone whilst I ring Jack.'

Hopkins rushed out of the room to do as he was bid. He had a bad feeling. Could Edith be caught up in the murder? After all, if Celia didn't return home on the night of the murder Edith didn't have an alibi, but what reason could she have for killing Carmichael? She, by all accounts was courting Arthur from the pub so had nothing to do with the dead roughneck. Would she have killed him because he was cheating on her friend? It seemed a bit far-fetched. Perhaps he was panicking unnecessarily; he told himself not to get carried away as he made his way to the front door to have a word with the soldiers.

CHAPTER 25

December 1943, the Barleycorn

The snow was still falling heavily as Lloyd Noble and his team reached the pub, having trudged through the drifting snow along the footpath in the woods to reach Eakring. They had kept their eyes and ears open for any signs of the old night watchman to no avail. Joe and Jack had set up a command centre in the public bar and had sent out small groups of local men to scour the fields and barns around the village, having sectioned off the area to be searched. It seemed unlikely that George would have wandered off on his own but they weren't ruling out the possibility that he had fallen over and was suffering with concussion, wandering off in a daze, disorientated and alone. The temperature during the night had fallen drastically and unless George had found shelter his chances of survival were slim. The mood amongst the men was sombre and after a quick briefing the roughnecks left the pub to join in the search.

'I know this is a long shot,' said Noble, 'but you don't think he got confused and went into Dukes Wood. If he had fallen and banged his head he may have concussion and be disorientated, thinking he still worked there.'

'We thought about that, Lloyd,' replied Joe, 'so I've already been up to the site. There were a couple of soldiers in the security hut by the entrance and they'd not seen hide nor hair of him. I even thought he might have got through the fence where it was breached on the night of the murder so went to have a look around inside. He was nowhere to be found.'

'I even went and had a word with the widow he's been friendly with but she's seen nowt of him either. She wasn't too complimentary about him so I don't think she's got him hidden away in her cottage,' said Jack. 'It's a rum do. He's a crafty old sod but it's not like him to go walkabout. I hope he's OK, wherever he is.'

'Aye, and it's looking black over Bill's mother's, I reckon there's a storm brewing so if he's out there somewhere we'd better hurry up and find him,' said Joe.

Lloyd looked confused. 'Where does Bill's mother live?' he asked innocently.

Jack and Joe laughed. 'Don't mind him, Mr Noble,' replied Jack. 'Looking black over Bill's mother's is one of the weird sayings folks round here use.'

As the locals were discussing his whereabouts, George was regaining consciousness in a dark and cold room. He felt dazed and ached all over as he lay in the darkness trying to remember where he was and how he got here. He tried to sit up but his hands and feet were tied and for the life of him he couldn't recall what had happened. Gradually as his mind cleared, he remembered saying goodnight to Herbert in the pub about 9.30; he'd promised Mildred he'd get home in time for supper so left the pub to walk home. He didn't want to be in bad books with her again as she could make his life a misery if he wasn't careful. He'd only drunk a couple of pints before leaving the warmth of the public bar to walk down the main street towards his home and he wasn't drunk. By that time, it was snowing heavily and the snow was settling on the pavement, blurring the line of the curb and making it difficult to walk without stumbling. He recalled hearing a car approaching from behind but thought little of it as the throaty engine came to a halt. Although the throb of the engine seemed familiar, he didn't take much notice as it stopped. Then, nothing. That was it, until just now when he woke up. His limbs were stiff and he was in desperate need of a pee but when he tried to get up, he fell back on the hard floor, banging his head. He'd been laying on an old mattress with a musty-smelling blanket covering his legs. The room was dark and the air felt damp.

'Hello!' he shouted. 'Is there anybody there? Help!' His voice echoed around the room as he realised that he was in a cellar; a small shaft of light was seeping through some wooden boards that had been nailed over a high window. For one moment he thought it was the cellar at the Barleycorn but as his eyes adjusted to the darkness, he knew he was mistaken. There were no full barrels of beer, just an old table and a couple of broken chairs. Realising he was helpless he began to shake with fear. What on earth had he got himself into? Why would anyone want to kidnap him? Had he been left here to die?

He strained his ears to see if there was anyone around who could help him but there was just silence.

CHAPTER 26

Kelham Hall

After leaving the two police officers Celia went in search of Deirdre and she found her dragging a heavy suitcase down the main staircase.

'Are you off then?' she asked.

'My train leaves at 2 o'clock so I can't hang about. If I don't get a train today, I won't be able to get home before Christmas. There's nothing I can do to help with the search for George so there's no need for me to hang around here. You know what the old goat's like, I bet he's tucked up somewhere and hasn't realised there's a search party looking for him,' she replied, trying to sound optimistic.

'I know, but I think Edith's missing as well. She wasn't in the room this morning when I woke up and she's not been seen since.'

'She can't be missing, perhaps she went down to the village to see the Arkwrights. She's spending Christmas Day with them so probably wanted to go and help Mrs Arkwright with the preparations. She may be needed to stir that pudding again,' said Deirdre with little conviction.

'I know, you're probably right, but with everything else that's going on around here I can't help but worry. Never mind, you get off, you've been looking forward to seeing your family for weeks. I'll send you a telegram when Edith shows up,' Celia said. 'Merry Christmas, Deirdre. I'll miss you but we'll all be together again in the New Year. Richard's pal Aubrey is driving me down to London tomorrow. It's awfully good of him, he's been such a rock since

Richard was captured.'

'That's because he fancies you, Celia, you ought to give him some encouragement. After all, a squadron leader from a wealthy family isn't a bad catch and if you don't snap him up someone else will.'

Celia laughed. 'I'll think about that, he's not bad to look at either.'

'Well, I wouldn't kick him out of bed,' agreed Deirdre whilst Celia feigned outrage at Deirdre's forwardness, 'and neither would Brenda.'

On impulse Deirdre stepped forward and hugged her friend. 'Goodbye, Celia, give my love to Edith when she turns up. You two have been such good friends to me.'

'And we shall continue to be well after we've won the war. We can still be friends in peacetime and you'll have to come to London so we can celebrate in style. I'm on my way to the village so I'll see you when you get back after Christmas.'

Celia helped Deirdre drag her case to the main door and they peered out looking for the truck. It was snowing heavily and the driveway was becoming obliterated under a thick blanket of snow. The driver had promised to give Deirdre a lift to the station and although they could see the truck shrouded in snow, there was no sign of the driver. A couple of soldiers were clearing a path outside the front door. Deirdre shouted out to ask about the driver; it was cutting it fine and she was keen to get to the station. One of the soldiers approached the door and told her the truck was out of action, the driver had hitched a lift to Newark in search of a new distributor cap.

'You won't be catching a train today anyway,' he said. 'All trains from Nottingham's Victoria station have been cancelled because there's snow on the lines,' he announced cheerfully.

Deidre sighed and sat down on her case in the porch feeling despondent, as Celia left to walk to the village.

Tomorrow would be Christmas Eve and Deirdre was stranded. She suddenly felt all alone and frightened. What was to become of her? There was a stigma attached to being a single mum and she had no money. Carmichael had made it clear that he didn't want anything to do with her the night he died, and even if she knew where his parents lived, she couldn't write to them for help. Her mum was the only one who would understand even though she knew it would break her heart. Her family had been so proud of her when she joined the land army to do her bit for King and Country and now, she had let them down. Going back to Liverpool a single mother would bring shame on her poor but respectable parents.

She had been sitting there for some time lost in her misery, when she heard Billy Clarke's voice. 'Ay-up, gel, what're you doing there? You'll catch your death of cold sitting out here, it's freezing.'

'Oh Billy, me train's been cancelled and I can't get home for Christmas. Edith is missing, and I don't know what to do.' She began to cry.

Billy lifted her up and held her in his arms, stroking her hair. 'I know things haven't worked out as you hoped, but you know I'm here for you, don't you.'

'Oh Billy,' she cried. 'I've been such a fool and you won't want anything to do with me if you knew what I've done.'

'I'm not blind, Deirdre,' he said, 'and it doesn't matter to me what you've done. You know how I feel about you. If you'll let me, I'll look after you.'

'But you don't understand,' she said miserably, 'I'm pregnant. I thought Jimmy loved me but he said I was a tart who should have known how to take care of things. He had no intentions of taking me back to America and said a girl like me probably knows where to get a back-street abortion. He was so cruel to me, I hated him.'

She looked so young and vulnerable. 'Do you want to keep the baby?' he asked.

'I was scared at first but I do, I don't know what to do for the best. I've got no money and my family can't help me with all those mouths to feed. I feel so ashamed.'

'Now look here,' he held her at arm's length, and looked lovingly into her eyes, 'there is a way you can keep the baby. I promise I'll look after both of you if you'll marry me. I know you don't love me but I'll treat you right and in time maybe you'll become fond of me. We get on OK, and I've got a good job so you and the baby will want for nothing,' he said.

Deirdre started to cry again. 'Oh Billy, would you really do that for me?'

'I will, if you'll have me. There's a cottage near the school that we could rent and I'll treat the bairn as if he's my own. I may not show it but I love kids and I know any child of yours will be adorable, just like his mum.'

'Oh, Billy, you are a lovely man and I don't deserve you. You are ten times the man Jimmy was, and I was stupid not to see it. I think it will be easy to fall in love with you and if you really mean it, I'd be honoured to be your wife.'

'That's settled then, I'll go and see Reverend Sykes at St Andrew's and ask him to read the banns so we can get married after Christmas.'

'Billy,' said Deirdre seriously, 'I don't want you to think you're second best. I promise I'll always be a good wife to you. There is one problem though,' she said.

Billy looked alarmed. 'Oh, what's that?'

'You might be having a daughter and not a son, is that a problem?'

'Absolutely not,' he replied, laughing. 'We can just keep trying. After all, I'm used to loads of kids in the school room, having half a dozen at home will be a doddle.'

'Well it looks like I'm snowed in here, so you'll have to help me carry my case back upstairs. After all, now we're engaged Matron won't be on the warpath if I take a man to my bedroom. Seriously though, Billy, you have made me the happiest woman alive today.' She smiled at him and for the first time in the past few weeks she looked happy.

Together they re-entered the Hall and bumped in the matron who was on her way out wearing her hat and coat. She looked at the two young people and noted their beaming smiles.

'You don't look too upset, Deirdre, about cancelling your plans for Christmas, my dear.'

'Oh Matron, Billy has just asked me to marry him. Isn't he wonderful?'

Matron, like the many others in the village, already knew that Billy had feelings for Deirdre and she thought they would make a lovely couple. She embraced Deirdre and gave Billy a stern look. 'Well I expect you to look after our girl and if you think you're going to worm your way into her bedroom on the pretext of carrying her case up the stairs you've got another thing coming, young man. You may be engaged but whilst she under my roof you'll keep your distance until you're legally married.'

Billy smiled and said he wouldn't want it any other way. He was happy to wait for the wedding night and would be calling on Reverend Sykes as soon as he got back to the village. 'And if you're lucky, Matron, you could be a bridesmaid,' he said with a wink at Deirdre which made them giggle.

'I think I'm a bit long in the tooth for that, young man,' she replied, 'but I can think of two young ladies who would be delighted to do the honours.' Turning towards Billy, she asked if there was any news of George.

'No one's seen him since last night and Herbert asked me to come over to see if Edith has turned up,' he replied.

'She hasn't, and her bicycle is still here. Celia walked down to the village a while ago to see what's happening. This is terrible,' said the matron. 'I'm just on my way out to see how Mildred is coping.'

'I passed Celia just now. If we hurry up, we'll be able to catch up with her,' he said. 'You stay here, Deirdre, and I'll phone you as soon as there's some news.' He kissed Deirdre goodbye and told her not to worry about her friend; he was sure she was safe and well somewhere and would turn up before nightfall.

CHAPTER 27

December, Cambridge

The sitting room was expensively, but shabbily furnished with a bay window looking out onto a wide expanse of lawn surrounded by trees and shrubs. The chaise longue was covered in gold brocade that had seen better days and the old-fashioned chairs flanking the grand Victorian fireplace looked worn with plump cushions giving a promise of comfort. On the occasional table a pile of books was stacked precariously as if thrown together randomly as the contents of each book had been digested and discarded by the owner. Potted plants were scattered around the room and a large specimen of a mother-in-law's tongue partly obscured the view of the extensive garden lit now by the weak morning sunlight. The snow was lighter here but with a darkened sky there was an ever-present threat of more to come.

Edith was pacing the room, preoccupied and barely noticing the faded opulence of the country home where she had spent the night after fleeing from the village with her companions. What had she done? Why had she allowed herself to become so attached to the cast of characters in Eakring she had called friends over the past few months? Her loyalty had been severely tested but now there was no going back; her options were limited as the life she had made for herself had been completely compromised.

At first it had been easy and exciting, she had been flattered by the attention of her brilliant tutor who had cleverly manipulated her and taken advantage of her background. Growing up with an emotionally inhibited mother, she had been ignorant of her origins and her life in Germany with her extended family before the Great War.

On her mother's death in 1924, clearing out the attic at their smart London townhouse, she inadvertently stumbled on the secrets that had been so carefully and deliberately kept from her. Having been led to believe she had no living relatives and with a mother who was a successful scientist, revered by colleagues but devoid of friends, she grew up lonely and emotionally retarded, suspicious of anyone who tried to break down the barriers she had erected to protect herself from rejection. School friends were not welcomed or encouraged to visit the house where they lived and she spent her days immersing herself in books and trying to gain her mother's approval by becoming a brilliant student, able to follow in her mother's footsteps.

The evidence of a different world filled with love and laughter, if the sepia-toned photographs were to be believed, was far removed from the life she had endured in post-war Britain. As a scientist, her mother devoted her life to finding cures for childhood diseases, working in the laboratory at the Royal Free Hospital, avoiding friendships offered and the admiring advances of men who circulated in her orbit. She supressed any motherly instincts she may have had, and was dismissive of her daughter's need for nurturing. The photographs showed a different story and glimpses of what life could have been, a young woman smiling broadly and gazing into the eyes of her husband, a proud man wearing the insignia of a German officer. They made a handsome couple and Edith saw herself in the Army officer's handsome face; she had his blond hair and crooked smile. Searching through the metal trunk found in the loft, Edith also found a bundle of letters that told the sad story of her mother's life.

Her mother, Prudence Jones, was a high flyer. The daughter of a doctor and his wife from Cheltenham, she had excelled at her studies and qualified as a medical scientist at a time when women were only just beginning to forge inroads into a man's world. She had met her future husband whilst on a research trip to Germany and settled down in a home in the Potsdam area of Berlin. Hans Schneider was the only son of a retired diplomat and his wife, and when he took Prudence to live at his ancestral country estate, she had been welcomed into the family with open arms. Edith was born prior to the outbreak of the Great War, into a warm and loving family, and the family lived happily together before the war clouds began to gather.

Hidden in the trunk she was shocked to find her birth certificate in the name of Erika Schneider. When war clouds were gathering in Europe, Hans took the heart-breaking decision to send his wife back to England to sit out the war and wait for them to be reunited. Sadly, it was not to be, Hans was killed during the battle of the Somme and Prudence spent the rest of her life mourning his passing. When Edith discovered her mother's sad story she decided to return to the country of her birth and in 1925, nine months after the death of her mother, she rang the bell on the door of her grandmother's home in Potsdam. The door was opened by a frail white-haired lady who looked at her curiously when Edith said, *'Ich bin deine Enkelin.'* The elderly lady's eye lit up and she welcomed home the child she had last seen before the Great War had torn her family apart. A granddaughter who she thought had been lost to her forever.

'Good morning, my dear.' Marcus entered the room, disturbing Edith's reminiscences and bringing her back into present. 'I trust you slept well. I'm sorry my housekeeper couldn't be here to attend to your needs but I thought it prudent to give her some time off to spend with her sister over Christmas.' He was carrying a tea tray with a pot of freshly brewed tea together with toast and homemade marmalade. Edith cleared the books from the table to make room for the tray and smiled her thanks.

'Will Frederick be joining us?' she asked, noting only two cups on the tray.

'Unfortunately, he left early this morning to make the arrangements as I'm sure you want to leave the country as soon as possible. He'll be back later today and with luck we'll soon be on our way. In a few days you'll be back with your grandmother in time to celebrate the new year.'

Edith was torn. She desperately wanted to see her grandmother but so much had happened since the beginning of the war and her loyalties were divided. Stories she had heard about Hitler and the atrocities committed by the Nazis had coloured her view of the Third Reich and shaken her beliefs. Her grandmother was getting on in years and she hadn't had any contact since the beginning of the war. She shuddered at the thought that she may have died, and then what? Re-establishing a life in a country she barely knew would be difficult and she only had Marcus' word that she would be accepted without suspicion. The information she carried was her salvation but handing over the intelligence about the oilfield would be a death sentence for the friends she had made. Thinking about her friends, she remembered George.

'How's George?' she asked. 'Frederick must have hit him hard; he didn't come round at all in the car. I do hope he hasn't suffered any permanent damage. Is he comfortable? I know you have to keep him hidden until we are able to escape but I am worried about him.'

'He's fine, don't worry. As you say, we are only keeping him captive until after we've left for the continent and then I'll contact the authorities to let them know where he is.'

Changing the subject, Marcus turned his attention to the tea tray. 'Now, how do you like your tea, my dear?' he enquired, signalling the conversation about George was over.

After breakfast Edith decided to take a walk around the garden for some fresh air. The snow had started to fall again and her feet left prints in the snow as she explored the extensive grounds surrounding the country house. She walked along the driveway to the main gate and found it to be locked, a precaution she had been told was to keep out prying eyes, but she shuddered to think that it was perhaps to keep her in. Peering through the railings, she scanned the area for signs of life. There were no other houses in the vicinity and the small country road skirting the perimeter of the property, was deserted. She felt a stab of fear. Could she trust Marcus and Frederick? She had no idea where she was and her fate was entirely in their hands. Retracing her steps to the house, she tried to push her concerns to the back of her mind.

Hidden in the lane opposite, a car was parked just beyond her view; someone was watching the house.

CHAPTER 28

December, Eakring

By late afternoon the light had begun to fade and still with no sign of George or Edith, Inspector Green thanked the volunteers and dismissed them for the day. The police officers from Newark were in the village doing a house-to-house search and asking if anyone had seen anything suspicious the night before. They searched outbuildings and barns for signs of life, and questioned neighbours in case George had taken shelter somewhere for the night. Green didn't hold out much hope of getting any useful leads but felt it was important that the police were seen to be doing something to reassure the local community. He was sitting with Hopkins in the snug when Jack brought them a fresh pot of tea.

'That bloke from Thistle Cottage is in the bar asking to see you. Shall I send him in?' he enquired.

'You might as well, and bring in another cup if he's walked from the cottage, I dare say he'll be gasping for a cuppa,' replied the inspector.

Frank Stevenson entered the room unravelling the scarf tied around his neck. 'It's nice and warm in here,' he observed as he began unbuttoning his overcoat.

'It's a bitter day to be out and about, Frank,' said the inspector kindly. 'Is there anything we can help you with?'

'I wasn't sure whether to come as it might not be significant but Dorothy said I should. I left the pub about 8.30 last night, as you know, Herbert. As I walked home a car passed me heading towards the village; I didn't think anything of it at the time but Dorothy thought it might be important. It was driving quite fast even though it was snowing and the road was getting icy.'

'I'm glad you came to tell us. Did you see the make of the car?'

'Well that's just it,' he went on, 'I think it was a Riley, it looked like that car those two teachers came in during the summer. I could be mistaken, I'm not that knowledgeable about cars but it was an unusual car.'

'That's interesting,' said the inspector, turning to Hopkins. 'Did the Army chaps on duty at the site see anything around that time?'

Hopkins studied his notebook. 'Corporal Brandon mentioned something, he said they heard a car sometime between 8 and 9pm but didn't see it as they were checking the area around the site office at the time.'

When Jack brought in the extra tea cup for Frank, the inspector asked him what he knew about the two academics.

'We've got their details in the visitors' book. I'll go and fish them out for you,' he replied.

The inspector thanked Frank for coming forward with information and after he left, the two police officers speculated on the possibility of the two academics having anything to do with the crimes that had been committed in the village since the summer.

'There is a possibility that Frank coming forward with this information is a red herring to throw us off the scent,' said Hopkins.

'That's true, but if he really did see a car it would explain why there's no sightings of George or Edith since last night. George could have been picked up, and that would explain why there's been no sight of him all day. But what's the connection?'

Jack returned with the visitors' book and handed it to the inspector who made a note of the two visitors' home addresses. He also had some useful information about the car they drove.

'It was a Riley Kestral big four,' said Jack, 'quite an unusual car and it caused quite a stir in the village. I asked them about it and they said it was first registered on the day before the war broke out. It was a beauty, quite a sleek design and was one of the first cars off the production line after Lord Nuffield took over the Riley car factory, in Coventry. According to the older one, who was the owner, he got it for a good price last year after it had been stored in a garage gathering dust. The previous owner wasn't able to get petrol for it so couldn't use it very much. We laughed about it as it was in such good condition for its age.'

Green thanked him and Jack left the snug to prepare for the lunchtime opening.

'What if George was blackmailing Frank? He was shouting about knowing secrets and Frank was in the bar at the time. I don't think he was taking much notice though, as he had his nose a book as usual and he left soon after I'd sat down. The story about the car belonging to those blokes who came over in the summer could be a way to put the blame on them. Frank could have waited outside for George to leave and tackled him then,' said Hopkins.

'It's one explanation but where is George now? I don't think he'd come here with a cock and bull story; it's drawing attention to himself. Anyway, I've done some digging into Frank Stevenson's background and his story checks out. He was in the Sherwood Foresters during the last war and was injured when the Germans attacked his unit using mustard gas. As a result, it damaged his lungs and he's had a weak chest ever since. He moved to Radford in Nottingham when he got a job in the offices at the Raleigh factory after his demob. He contracted TB about 18 months ago and was an inpatient at the sanatorium for over a year. After being discharged he and Dorothy moved to the village, that would be a few months ago now. They keep themselves to themselves but I don't think with his war record that he's a German spy,' replied the inspector. 'On the other hand, he could have acquired the gun and brought it back with him as a souvenir after he was demobbed and made up the story about hearing the gunshot the night of the murder to deflect suspicion. He is a key witness, and it may just be a coincidence that he has also been able to give us a vital clue to the disappearance of George last night.'

'So, I guess his sighting of a car is a useful clue. If it was being driven by those toffs, they may have a contact in the village who has been working with them. It's hard to imagine who it would be, I doubt whether any of the locals are Nazi sympathisers and that leaves one of the Yanks or another newcomer.'

The inspector nodded in agreement. 'I asked the duty sergeant to look into the background of the land army girls and he should be getting back to me with the information today. There's also been one or two itinerate labourers on the farms but they haven't hung around long. We also have to think about the weapon used to kill Carmichael. We know it was a pistol widely used by the German Army during the Great War. It could have been smuggled back into the country by one of our lot who kept it as a souvenir so we can't necessarily rule out one of the locals.'

'There is also another clue we seem to have overlooked,' said Hopkins. 'When we searched the hole in the fence where the bicycle tire tracks were found there was a piece of green wool caught on the barbed wire. It might not be significant but it's likely to have come off a green jumper. It's the same colour as the land army girls' jumpers, and I've seen Billy Clarke wearing a similar coloured jumper as well.'

'I know it's difficult to imagine Billy caught up in this but we have to consider all possibilities. Spies are only successful when they are integrated into the community and no one suspects what they're up to. He told us his father was killed in the last war and he's got some of his dad's possessions. Let's just imagine that when Clarke Senior came home on leave that last time, he brought back a pistol as a souvenir. And what's the story behind him not joining up along with the rest of the lads from the village? It's not as if teaching is a reserved occupation.'

'He did try to join the navy when war broke out but he failed the medical. He had rheumatic fever as a child and it has weakened his heart.'

'Is there any link with the fellows from Cambridge? We know he went to university, where did he do his training to become a teacher? Was it at Cambridge by any chance? Perhaps you can check that out, Herbert,' asked the inspector. 'If anything we need to rule him out.'

Herbert agreed to make some enquiries just as Vera came into the room without knocking.

'There's a telephone call for you, Inspector, he said it was urgent,' she said.

CHAPTER 29

Cambridge

George was feeling cold and frightened. How long had he been laying in this stinking cellar? He knew it was still daytime as light from outside was seeping through the slats on the window. He looked around the room in the dim light, it was about 12 feet square with a metal bucket in the corner. He was lying on an old mattress with a rough Army blanket to give him some warmth and protection against the cold wind that blew through the cracks of the window. Wooden slats had been nailed to the outside of the window frame so it was impossible for him to escape. There was a flight of stone steps leading up to a heavy wooden door, but with his arms and legs tied he found it impossible to climb up and even if he did, he knew the door was locked and bolted so it was doubtful if he could escape. Things like this only happen in books; he must have stumbled into something with his big mouth.

Presently he heard a key being turned as the door at the top of the cellar steps opened and footsteps descended into the room. A light was switched on, hurting his eyes with the instant glare, as Marcus came into view.

'What do you want with me? Where am I? I've done nowt, just let me go and I won't say anything,' he cried, a note of desperation creeping into his voice.

'You can't be trusted, that's why you're here. You tried to blackmail us and we can't let you get away with that. If we let you go now, you'd go running to the police as you should have done in the first place, instead of trying to blackmail us. Now, I'm afraid it's too late.'

'I don't even know who you are, I didn't blackmail anyone,' he cried. In his addled brain he wondered what this man who was keeping him prisoner had to do with Edith. He was only trying to make a few bob; he thought Edith might have been responsible for killing Carmichael but he wasn't bothered about going to the police. He never liked the bloke, and thought he'd got his comeuppance.

Marcus laid a tray on the floor containing a cup of tea and a sandwich. 'I'm going to untie your feet so you can move around and use the bucket if you need to relieve yourself. If you behave yourself, your ordeal will soon be over and we'll let you go but if you try to escape, I'm afraid I'll have to shoot you. I'm not a cruel man, I'll leave the light on for you. Don't make any noise. You're well away from the road so you might as well save your breath.'

With that, he left the room and George picked up the cup of tea with shaking hands, hoping it would warm him up a little and help him to work out what to do.

Upstairs Edith was in the kitchen preparing lunch. Frederick had returned after making their travel arrangements and Marcus had promised her that they would be on their way the next day.

'Perhaps we should call you by your real name now, Erika,' said Marcus. 'In a few days' time you'll be starting your new life. The boat leaves Hull tomorrow afternoon and we'll be met in Belgium and smuggled over the border into Germany the next day. It may take a few days to reach Berlin but the plan is for you to be with your grandmother by the new year. Our contact over there will be able to relieve you of the information you copied at the oil field and once they know the times and dates when the cargo is to be transported, they will be able to mount an attack to stop the supplies reaching their destination. Destroying the oil rigs will put a stop to the whole operation.'

Edith looked concerned. 'The oil field is so near the village and the explosion will wipe out everything for miles around, killing the civilian population.'

'Collateral damage, my dear, what's the loss of a few local yokels in the great scheme of things?' said Marcus. 'The American roughnecks are a threat and need to be stopped from using their expertise to rebuild the oil rigs so we need to eliminate them, and the handful of locals caught up in the attack won't be much of a loss.'

'Millions of people are killed during war time, Erika,' Frederick added. 'If cutting off the oil supplies to the allies is successful it will shorten the war and guarantee success to the Nazis.'

'Well said,' agreed Marcus.

Edith felt uncomfortable, realising the extent of her treachery and the threat it posed to her friends in the village. It was easy to talk about collateral damage but these were people she knew, her friends: Celia and Deirdre, the Arkwrights and Arthur's parents, even grumpy old Joe. People who were going about their business trying to get by and defend their way of life. They weren't the aggressors but ordinary people caught up in the fight for freedom. She remembered the kindness and friendship offered to her by those people who in a few short months had come to mean so much to her. Could she really betray that friendship? Was it too late?

Marcus and Frederick shared a look. Was Edith becoming a liability?

'I think you should let me have the information you're carrying; I'll lock it away in my safe overnight. It pays to be cautious,' said Marcus.

Edith reluctantly agreed and said she'd fetch the film after lunch.

'Splendid,' replied Marcus, 'and what have you rustled up for us to eat?'

'There was some ham in the pantry so I thought I could boil some potatoes and vegetables. It won't take me long,' she replied.

'While Erika is busy in the kitchen, Frederick, I'd like to have a quick word with you in my study. Just to double check the arrangements.'

Edith left the two men and returned to the kitchen to carry on with the lunch preparations.

CHAPTER 30

December, Eakring

Hopkins was tucking into the sandwiches prepared by Vera when Inspector Green returned to the snug after finishing his phone call.

'Well I think we can rightly assume that young Edith hasn't been abducted. That was HQ on the line, they've done a bit of digging into her background and that young lady was not an innocent bystander. We need to find her to get the full story but it's likely she was the local contact we've been looking for.'

'I can hardly believe that, sir,' said Hopkins. 'Surely they're mistaken.'

'No mistake, lad,' continued the inspector. 'Her real name is Erika Schneider, the daughter of a German Army officer and his English wife. They changed her name to Edith at the outbreak of the Great War when her mother brought her home to live. Jones is her mother's maiden name. Her father was killed in the war and Edith went to live in Germany for a time with her grandmother after her mother died in 1924. She returned in 1935 to go to Cambridge University and after graduation got a job at the Home Office. She speaks German fluently and was transferred to the War Office on the recommendation of her university tutor, Professor Marcus Johnson.'

'Isn't that the name of one of those blokes who came to stay at the Barleycorn in the summer?'

'The very same, Herbert,' replied the inspector. 'So, you see, I think we've uncovered the spy in the camp, or should I say village, and found the link between Edith and the two visitors from Cambridge. Now all we need to do is find out where they have gone.'

CHAPTER 31

November 1943, Dukes Wood

Carmichael watched as Deirdre rode off on her bike, feeling guilty for leading her on; it seemed a laugh at the time pretending to be a film star and she was a sweet kid. He was sorry about the predicament she was now in and he resolved to see her tomorrow to apologise for his behaviour, he didn't mean to be so cruel. She had taken him by surprise with the news of her pregnancy. He would be going home to his wife in the spring and couldn't do anything for Deirdre except offer her some money he'd been saving to help her out.

'What are you doing out here all alone, handsome?' Carmichael turned to see Brenda in the doorway. 'The match has just finished and we're going to have a sing-song. Are you coming back in?'

'I'll be back in a minute, Brenda, start without me. You know I'm tone deaf,' he replied. Brenda laughed and returned to the bar leaving Carmichael alone with his thoughts.

A few moments later Edith left the pub and rode off on her bicycle. He stood looking up at the stars, so far away from home. He wasn't in the mood for joining in the communal singing; it seemed a bit callous after what Deirdre had told him and he needed to think things through so he decided to walk back to the Hall. The others would be staying for a lock-in and not leaving any time soon and he needed time to think. The route took him along the footpath skirting the perimeter of Dukes Wood. It was a clear night with a light breeze and warm for the time of year, so pleasant enough for walking.

As he entered the footpath, he saw a bicycle propped up in the hedgerow. Frowning, he looked around to see if someone had fallen off but instead of a body lying on the ground, he noticed a hole in the fence big enough for gaining entrance to the site of the oil field. Without thinking of possible danger, he decided to follow the pathway into the site to see what the intruder was doing at that time of night. George would be in the hut near the gate so he could alert him if the intruder was up to no good. He assumed it to be kids being curious and he could send them on their way with a flea in their ears.

The site office was situated 100 yards from the fence separated by a heavily wooded area that kept it hidden from the main road and the night watchman's hut. When Carmichael neared the office, he noticed a torch light bouncing off the walls and the door had been forced open. He could hear someone moving around inside, and still thinking it to be local kids he decided to give them a scare and pushed the door open noisily to confront the miscreants.

The last thing he saw was a bright light as the torch sought out his face framed in the doorway.

CHAPTER 32

23rd December, Cambridge

After lunch Edith offered to do the washing up and said she would collect the plate from George in the cellar. Marcus, thinking it could do no harm, thanked her and said it would give him and Frederick a chance to discuss some business arrangements. He suggested that Edith may like to have a lie down in the afternoon after she finished in the kitchen. They had a long journey ahead of them and she needed to conserve her energy.

She left the two men and crossed the hall to unlocked the cellar door. 'Take care,' Marcus shouted after her, 'I know he's tied up but he may try something so keep your wits about you.'

George was sitting hunched up on the mattress looking tired and dishevelled; he had the blanket draped around his shoulders to keep out the cold and when Edith descended the steps a look of pure hatred crossed his face.

'You traitor,' he said. 'I hope you're proud of yourself. After we'd welcomed you into the village, this is how you repay our kindness. I hope they get you and them poncey blokes. Stringing up's too good for you.'

'I'm sorry, George, I wish things could have been different. You shouldn't have threatened me. What else could I do?'

'I didn't know you were mixed up in all this. I just thought you and Jimmy had gone into the site office for a bit of hanky-panky. How was I to know you're a German spy? Still, I guess this time tomorrow you'll be miles away and what's to become of me?'

'How do you know all this?' she asked.

'You think I was still unconscious in the car but I wasn't, I overheard everything that was said. You're a fool if you think those two toffs are going to look after you, they'll probably throw you overboard once you get out to sea.'

'No, you're wrong. They're patriots fighting for Germany in their own way. Not everyone carries a gun. I'm going home to my family, that's where my loyalties lie. I didn't start this war and I'm sorry about the lads who are being killed every day, but it's not just the allies who are suffering. How do you think I feel when people are laughing about the bombing of innocent people in Germany? I pray every night that my grandmother is being kept safe; she lives near Berlin and the allies have been bombing the area night after night. She's elderly and there's no one to look after her, she needs me.'

'Well good luck to you, I hope you can live with yourself. Once the Germans get their hands on the information you've stolen, they'll bomb the village and all of those people who thought you were a friend, will be killed. You'll have their blood on your hands. I hope you're proud of yourself and your warped loyalties,' said George.

'You're wrong, they'll only target the oil field to cut off the supply of crude oil. In the end it will shorten the war and save thousands of lives. Don't you see? The longer this war goes on more and more lives will be lost on both sides.'

'Aye, and I'm the King of England. They've used you and you're just as expendable as me, lass. You won't get to set foot in Germany. The bottom of the ocean is where you'll end up.'

With that threat ringing in her ears, Edith fled from the cellar and locked the door. On her way to the kitchen she passed the study where she overheard Marcus and Frederick talking. Quietly she stopped to listen.

'Has she given you the documents yet?' asked Frederick.

'Not yet, she's going to fish them out this afternoon and once they are safely stored away, we can act,' replied Marcus.

'I'll be glad when all this is over and we can get back to normal. You promised to drive me over to my uncle's house before Christmas and it's cutting it a bit fine.'

'Frederick, my dear boy, you worry too much. A few more hours and this will all be over. My contact will be here shortly to take care of the pair of them and then we can carry on as if nothing happened. If she had been more careful in the first place we wouldn't be in this predicament. No one saw us in the village so we're in the clear but we can't risk the authorities picking her up, she knows too much. As I said before, it's collateral damage. It's a shame, she's a nice kid but she got us into this and I can't trust her to brazen it out. Once we've taken care of our little problem we can get back to normal and continue with our work.'

Edith had heard enough. She quickly crossed the hallway and went back to the kitchen to finish her chores and to think about her options. She knew now she had to get away before whoever they were waiting for turned up. She had been a fool, and she realised George was right, they never had any intentions of helping her to escape to Germany. She was a liability to the organisation and the two Dons were going to go back to the university after the Christmas holidays and carry on as if nothing happened. Neither did it bode well for George; he knew too much and would be killed along with her. They were both loose ends that needed to be tied up. Her mind was racing. Could she leave the house and alert the authorities or should she fetch George from the cellar to escape with her? The first thing she needed to do was to collect the documents from her room and—

A hand touched her shoulder which made her jump and cry out.

'Oh, my dear,' said Marcus, 'I'm sorry I startled you. Are you alright?'

'Yes,' she replied. 'I'm sorry, I was miles away just thinking about my grandmother. She'll be so pleased to see me. I was just wondering if there's a village shop near here where I could go and buy a present for her. I don't want to turn up over Christmas empty handed. I've got some money on me, which won't be any use after tomorrow so I thought I could spend it on a scarf or something for her. What do you think?'

'What a splendid idea. Unfortunately, the shops are all closed around here, Thursday is their half day and tomorrow is Christmas Eve so perhaps we can find a shop open on our way to the coast. Now, why don't you pop up to your room and get those documents for me? I'll keep them safe until we leave.'

'Of course,' replied Edith, trying to act naturally. 'I'll just go up now. Won't be long.' She left the kitchen and ran lightly up the stairs.

In her room she took out the roll of film she had used to photograph the documents in the site office. Carefully taking it out of the casing, she exposed the negatives before rewinding and returning the film to the canister. Whatever happened to her, the Nazis wouldn't receive the damaging information about the secret activities at the oil field in Eakring. It was the least she could do to try and repair some of the damage she had done to her friends in the village. Time was running out for her, but she needed to do something to help George.

'Here's the film, Marcus,' she said, returning to the drawing room where the two men were still talking. 'I have to admit I'm relieved to pass it on.'

'Thank you, my dear, I'll store it in a safe place and our contacts will be really pleased with your work. It's a pity your cover has been blown, I had high hopes for you. Still, not all is lost, I'll personally recommend you to my opposite number in Berlin. They will be happy to have someone with your talents helping the war effort.' Edith tried to smile but was feeling agitated.

'I think I'll go out for some fresh air before having a lie down. Do you want to join me for a walk around the garden, Frederick?' she asked.

'No thank you, Edith, I have some work to do this afternoon and the snow is getting thicker out there. I don't want to catch a cold.' As he smiled, she recognised a malicious look in his eye. She felt like a spider caught in a web of deceit. What a fool she had been to trust these two self-satisfied monsters.

'It's cold outside, are you sure you want to go out? You'll need to wrap up warm, my dear,' said Marcus.

After she left the house Frederick turned to Marcus. 'Is it wise to let her go out on her own?'

'Of course, dear boy, the grounds are quite secure and the gate is locked, so even if she wanted to escape, I doubt whether she could. It's best to keep her on side, that way she won't cause any problems.'

'But she could attract someone's attention, if she goes to the gate,' said Frederick.

Marcus laughed. 'But why would she? She's burned her bridges and it won't be long before the authorities are on to her. After all, my dear boy, she's the one who's been spying, and there's no real links to us. You and I, my friend, are in the clear, we can go back to the dreaming spires in the new year no worse for wear after our adventure. This house is secluded, it's a few miles away from the relative civilisation in Great Wilbraham and I doubt if any of the locals would venture this far on a day like today. Relax, in a few hours our problem will be well and truly over. Rest assured I'll be able to drive you over to your uncle's house first thing tomorrow morning.'

Outside, Edith wandered around the lawn, stopping to admire the shrubbery and covertly checking to see if either of the two men were watching her from the house. The extensive grounds led down to a stream that meandered through the estate. If she followed the stream to the boundary, perhaps she could reach the road. Then what? She knew in a few hours' time someone would be arriving to take her and George away to dispose of their bodies. If only she could get a message to the police. She knew her fate was sealed the moment she raised the gun in panic. Even if she escaped from the clutches of Marcus and his organisation of so-called merry men, the British police would track her down and she'd be executed as a spy.

Escaping to Germany was a pipe dream; even if she made it to Berlin she didn't know if her grandmother was still alive. Either way, her life was over but she could try and do something for George, but what?

It was late afternoon and the light was beginning to fade. Before returning to the house she decided to walk along to the bottom of the driveway to see if it was possible for her and George to climb over the wall. Being acutely aware though that Frederick was watching her from the drawing room, and not wanting to arouse his suspicion, she gave up the idea and went straight back in. Little did she know that she was passing up a chance of rescue; the local police were gathering outside.

CHAPTER 33

Eakring

Edith Jones graduated from Cambridge in 1938 where one of her tutors was Professor Johnson. She was known as a serious student who hadn't mixed with fellow students or taken part in the lively social life enjoyed by the undergraduates. After graduation she had been recruited by the Civil Service, working in Whitehall, but resigned in the spring of 1943 to join the land army. On checking with the university, Green found out that both Dons lived in rooms in the grounds during term time, although both had left at the end of term for the Christmas break. The Dean of the Faculty, who was keen to help but unaware of the implication that a spy ring may be operating under his nose, told the police that Marcus had a country house in the area but he wasn't able to furnish them with an address. Frederick had told colleagues he was going to stay with an uncle somewhere in the West Midlands but hadn't shared any further details. Neither of the men had close friends in the faculty. Marcus was a respected member of staff but not particularly liked and Frederick was his protégé who didn't mix with people his own age.

Green was processing the information when Hopkins joined him in the incident room.

'What about the car?' asked Hopkins. 'Can't we trace the address through the car registration?'

'Not as easy as you would think, Herbert, when there's thousands of cars the same make and model. It will probably take us weeks to find it that way.'

'I don't think so, sir,' he replied with a smile on his face. 'Jack told me the car was unusual. It was manufactured just before the war started when production came to a halt. There was only 20 of them built by then so perhaps we can check with the makers to find out the registration numbers of each one and get owner's details from the Ministry of Transport.'

'Good thinking, Herbert, get on to it whilst I talk to the chief inspector to see if we can get the cooperation of the local boys in Cambridge. We need to get a move on and drive down there today, I'm sure that's where they've taken Edith and if we're lucky George may still be alive.'

An hour later they were on their way; the weather conditions had improved which made driving easier. Hopkins, having checked with the Ministry of Transport had managed to trace Johnson's home address to a village east of Cambridge called Great Wilbraham. They had agreed to meet a team of officers from the Cambridge constabulary in the village pub and Green had high hopes of being able to make an arrest before nightfall.

The village of Great Wilbraham lies six miles east of Cambridge, partly bounded to the south-west by the Fleam dyke and further north separated from Fulbourn and Little Wilbraham by two brooks meeting at its north-west corner. Arriving in the village the two officers pulled up outside the local pub where they had arranged to meet Sergeant Collins from the Cambridge constabulary. He was easy to spot as soon as they walked into the bar; he was a large man with thinning hair and a handlebar moustache. He stood propping up the bar with a pint of bitter in his hand when the two officers entered. He offered to buy them a pint which Green refused on behalf of them both and they settled for cups of tea. The three men retired to a table near the window where they could speak in private.

'Before you begin,' said Collins, 'just to let you know, I've sent a couple of plain-clothes men to watch the gateway to the manor house and they'll report any signs of movements. We've established that the place is occupied at the moment and I've had a word with Mrs Foster, the housekeeper. She's staying with her sister in the village for Christmas after she was given this week off.'

'Did she say when Johnson arrived at the house?' asked Hopkins.

'She did, apparently he phoned her the night before last saying he'd be coming down to stay the next day and she was to stock up with some provisions for him. He told her he'd only be staying for a couple of days before going back to Cambridge for Christmas.'

'That ties in with what's been happening in Eakring,' said Green. 'I'm afraid I can't tell you too much at the moment because of "official secrets" but we suspect that he is holding someone hostage so we need to act quickly. What do you know about the owner?'

Sergeant Collins took out his notebook and began to read. 'Marcus Johnson is the only son of the previous owner and his wife Sir Aubrey and Lady Cecilia Johnson. Sir Aubrey was born and brought up at the manor and at one time the family owned quite a lot of land in the area, renting out farm land to local farmers. Their son Marcus was a brilliant scholar by all accounts but fell out with his parents at the start of the Great War. Sir Aubrey wanted him to join his old regiment but he refused to fight, becoming a conscientious objector, which didn't go down too well with the old man. Apparently, Sir Aubrey was a bit of a gambler and over the years had to sell parcels of land to pay off his debts so on his death the only thing left to leave to his son was the manor house which is, by all accounts, a bit of a white elephant. There's no money for the upkeep and Marcus only has his salary from the university to live on. Rumour has it that he tried to sell the house just before the war but there were no takers. He's a bit arrogant and unpopular in the village so we don't see him around much at all and Mrs Foster is employed to air the beds and gets the place ready for him when he comes to stay, which isn't very often.'

'Has anyone from the village seen him since he arrived?'

'No, but as you can see there's not many houses around here and only the pub and post office and he doesn't frequent either. He keeps himself to himself and rarely has visitors. When you've finished your tea, I'll take you over there, you'll be able to park your car on the main road out of sight whilst we have a look around and decide how you want to proceed. We've called the local Army unit who are sending over some backup just in case we need help to apprehend the suspects.'

The house was just visible from the road along a winding driveway that was overgrown and neglected since the death of Sir Aubrey. Marcus had dismissed the gardener and full-time housekeeper with the intention of selling the property, but without success, and the gardens had become neglected. Green and Hopkins approached on foot having left their car out of sight 100 yards away from the entrance. The two PCs who had been on duty watching the house reported seeing a young lady walking in the garden earlier in the afternoon; she was slim, about 5'6" tall with blonde hair, fitting the description of Edith Jones. They said she had approached the gate and appeared to be looking for something or someone before returning to the house. They had kept out of sight so no one up at the house was aware of the police activity.

By now it was late afternoon and the light was beginning to fade. Sergeant Collins had borrowed a set of keys to the property from Mrs Foster, and although she had been reluctant to relinquish them, she agreed after being warned that failure to assist the police with their enquiries could result in prosecution.

'We could just walk up to the main door and ask to speak to Professor Johnson. He may think the gate had been left open by mistake,' suggested Hopkins whilst they were discussing how to approach the property.

'They may be armed, and on the lookout, so let's wait until its dark and go in together, taking them by surprise. The troops from the local barracks will be here by then,' suggested Collins.

'That sounds like a good idea,' replied Green, 'we could do with getting closer to see what's happening inside the house until the backup arrives. Hopkins and I will go into the grounds and skirt around the building. We'll leave the gate unlocked so you can come in as soon as the others arrive.'

Hopkins didn't look too pleased with the suggestion but couldn't argue with a senior officer so reluctantly followed his boss across the road and into the grounds. There were trees flanking the driveway giving them adequate cover but as they neared the buildings the ground opened up.

'It looks like this is the nearest we can get to the house,' said Green as the two men crouched down in the undergrowth. 'Can you see in the window? There's a light on in the room but I can't see anyone from this angle.'

Hopkins strained to see through the window, and thought he saw someone sitting in an armchair facing the fireplace. It was a winged chair with a high back that obscured the sitter so it was difficult to tell who it was. Another man entered the room carrying a tray which he put down on the table under the window. Hopkins recognised him as Frederick, one of the two visitors to the village. He was looking out into the garden as he poured out the tea so Hopkins shrank back into the bracken, hoping in the twilight his movements couldn't be seem from the house. Crawling back to where Green was hiding, he reported the sighting he had had of the two men. 'It looks like they're having afternoon tea. I haven't seen the girl at all and there's no sign of George. You don't think we've got this all wrong and they haven't got anything to do with the murder and kidnapping.'

'I think it's too much of a coincidence to think they're not involved. Remember, their car was seen the other night in the village when the girl went missing. She must be in that house somewhere. Maybe she's not mixed up with the crimes; she could have recognised her tutor in the summer and at the time accepted their story of a walking holiday. It could have been much later when she suspected they had something to do with the murder and agreed to meet them the other night to talk to them. She may have been kidnapped as well as George.' Even as he presented the explanation Green couldn't believe she was entirely innocent and if she was in the house she could be armed and dangerous.

Hopkins saw the door into the drawing room open as Edith entered the room. 'Look, she's there,' he said, moving forward to get a better view. Just then she appeared at the window and looked straight at where the two men were hiding.

'Has she seen you?' asked Green who was beginning to feel alarmed and unsure of their next move.

'I don't think so, it doesn't look as if she's alerted the other two.'

CHAPTER 34

The Manor House, Great Wilbraham

'Thanks, Old Boy.' Marcus accepted the cup of tea offered by Frederick as he sat by the fire.

Frederick was beginning to getting impatient. 'Shouldn't they be here by now? You said they'd be along in this afternoon and it's 4 o'clock already. You don't think something's gone wrong?'

'Of course not, they won't want to draw attention to themselves so will probably wait until after dark. I'll go down and unlock the gates when I've drunk my tea. There's no need to panic, no one knows about this place.'

Just then Edith entered the room. 'Ah, tea, that's good of you Frederick. I was just going to make some.'

'Come and join us. Frederick is getting impatient to be off on our journey. Did you have a good rest, my dear?'

'I did, thank you Marcus. Do you want me to take a cup down to George?'

'Later perhaps. Come and sit by the fire, it's a draughty old house, and so difficult to keep warm.'

Whilst in her room Edith had been thinking of ways to escape without raising suspicion. On passing the front door in the hallway she noticed that Marcus had locked it and taken out the key. Was his suspicion already aroused? Had she said something to alert him to the fact that she had overheard their conversation earlier in the day?

'Penny for them?'

'Pardon?' She jumped as Marcus cut into her thoughts. 'I'm sorry,

I guess I'm a bit on edge. Can you just tell me the arrangements again? I know someone is picking us up to take us to the coast. Have you chartered a boat?'

'Don't worry, we've had contingency plans in place for some time now. We can trust those who are working with us with our lives, I can assure you,' said Marcus.

His smile made her think of a Cheshire cat and she felt like a mouse who had been caught in his trap.

'When we arrive in Berlin, will I still see you both?'

'Frederick and I will be working at the university in Berlin; we have both secured teaching posts although I doubt whether the head of the faculty there will be taking up references,' he laughed, 'and once we're settled I'm sure we will be able to find you an administrative role.'

She moved to the window, and commented that the snow had stopped, making it easier for the journey ahead. Looking towards the driveway she thought she saw a movement in the wooded area at the top of the drive. Was there someone there, she wondered? Not wanting to arouse the suspicion of her two companions she scanned the grounds for signs of life in the hope that someone was out there. She would prefer to take her chances with the British authorities than to end up in the bottom of the ocean. She also wanted to help George; after all, it was her fault he had become mixed up in all of this.

CHAPTER 35

Great Walbraham

When the Army backup team arrived at the manor house, the officer in charge approached Sergeant Collins and the two men shook hands.

'What's happening?' he asked. 'We were told you needed backup and my men are armed and ready. I take it this is the house; can we access the grounds?'

'We've unlocked the main gate and two police officers are inside checking on movements inside the house.' Collins acquainted the officer with the details and ended with information about the likely inhabitants. 'We're not sure if the night watchman is being kept prisoner in the house and although the young lady could be in cahoots with the two men there's a possibility she also being held against her will.'

'Righty ho, I'll brief my men and we'll spread out around the grounds in case anyone tries to escape. Do you know if they are armed?'

'Not for certain but it's likely. One, or all three of them were involved in a murder a few weeks ago, so they may try and shoot their way out. After all, if as suspected, they've been involved in espionage as well as murder, they'll be facing the gallows so they've really got nothing to lose.'

On that the officer briefed his men and one by one they entered the grounds to stake out the house. The officer also entered the grounds to link up with the two policemen to inform them that his men were in place.

'Excuse me if I don't shake hands, gentlemen,' he said as he drew near, 'my men are surrounding the house waiting for orders. How do you want us to play this? The sergeant has given me a quick briefing and I understand you would prefer to take the occupants in the house alive. If they are armed though we may have to open fire.'

'I understand,' Green replied. 'At the moment we're not sure if the girl is involved or a hostage. From what we've seen so far, she's been walking around the garden and at the moment is taking tea with the others in the drawing room. We need to question her; she's a suspect in a murder enquiry and could be dangerous.'

Suddenly the main door opened and Marcus Johnson appeared wearing a long black overcoat and hat with a woollen scarf wound around his neck. He proceeded to walk down the driveway towards the gate. As he reached the end of the drive two soldiers stepped out of the woods pointing guns at him. As Green approached he heard Johnson speak.

'What's the meaning of this?' He sounded outraged. 'This is private property and you are trespassing. Get out immediately before I call the police.'

From behind him Green spoke. 'We are the police. Professor Johnson, we meet at last. I'm arresting you on suspicion of aiding and abetting in a murder, and on suspicion of abduction.' And turning to Collins, 'Would you be kind enough to take him into custody, Sergeant?'

'With pleasure,' the sergeant replied, taking Marcus by the arm and ushering him towards the Black Maria standing by on the road. Marcus, realising his options for evading arrest were limited decided to go without a struggle, believing he could plead ignorance and divert the blame onto Edith and Frederick. Turning to Inspector Green, he asked if he could have a word before being taken into custody.

'Thank God you've arrived, the man you want is inside the house, he's hoodwinked me along with a number of colleagues at the university. He's threatened to hurt the girl inside the house if I don't co-operate. I was sent to open the gate and if I'm not back in the house shortly he will kill her. He's a dangerous man.'

The inspector believed him to be bluffing. 'Take him away, Sergeant.'

Hopkins having witnessed the arrest, and still unsure of Edith's involvement approached the inspector to ask for instructions.

'Just a moment, Sergeant,' said Green, turning to Marcus. 'Would you mind removing your coat, hat and gloves, sir?'

'As you have just pointed out, they will be expecting you to return and I wouldn't want to put you in danger so PC Hopkins will return in your place.'

Realising he had no choice but to comply he handed over the garments to Herbert who reluctantly put them on over his uniform as Green pressed a service revolver into his hand.

'Pull the hat down over your eyes and walk up to the main door,' instructed Green. 'The other two are still in the drawing room. Once inside leave the door open so we can follow you inside. If we approach from the other side there won't be any danger of being seen from the window at the front.'

Hopkins was worried; his aim in life was to have a quiet life and steer clear of danger. Being a local bobby had served him well so far and he didn't sign up to this, but the excitement got the better of him and he willing played his part in the operation. On entering the house, he stamped his feet in the hallway to announce the return.

'Is there any sign of them?' shouted Frederick from the drawing room.

'No,' replied Hopkins, who hoped his voice sounded like the professor's. Two armed soldiers quietly followed him through the door. The drawing room was on the left with the door slightly ajar, and from his vantage point he could see Frederick sitting in the armchair next to the fire. Edith was standing by the window observing the covert activity in the garden. She picked up the tea tray to return it to the kitchen and as she entered the hallway she came face to face with Herbert, who, having removed the coat stood with a gun pointing at her. On seeing him she dropped the tea tray and quietly raised her hands in submission.

'What on earth is happening?' said Frederick, hearing the commotion. He followed her out of the room to be confronted by the soldiers who were also pointing their guns in his direction.

'Edith Jones and Frederick Weber, you are both under arrest for the murder of James Carmichael and the abduction of George Saunders,' said Hopkins. Frederick frantically looked around to make an escape and ran down the hallway into the kitchen and out by the back door, only to be stopped in his tracks by Sergeant Collins who was guarding the rear of the building.

An hour later, the three spies were safely locked up in Cambridge Police Station and George was nursing a cup of tea at the Cambridge Royal Infirmary where he had been taken for a check-up after his rescue.

CHAPTER 36

Christmas Eve 1943, Eakring

Celia and Deirdre were drinking gin and tonic in the bar of the Barleycorn. Vera, behind the bar for once, was serving the few customers who had gathered to see if there was any news of George or Edith. After the police officers left in a hurry the previous day the locals were curious to know what was happening. Speculation was rife about the murder of James and the recent turn of events and they were all eager to find out what had been happening in the village under their noses.

'You don't think Edith's caught up in all this? Surely, we would have suspected something. We've been so close the last few months,' said Celia to her friend as they sipped their drinks.

'I don't know, Celia,' she replied. 'What do we know about her? She's never spoken about her family, not like us two. I bet you know the names of all my brothers and sisters, where me dad works and even who me mam's favourite film star is. But Edith has never said anything about her family.'

'That's true, and you know all about Richard, and his mate Aubrey from the base who came over to comfort me when he went missing. We only know Edith has a mother because she kept disappearing to ring her, but she hardly ever received any letters except the ones from Arthur.'

'What time is Aubrey picking you up? I'll really miss you over Christmas. I was so looking forward to going home but Billy's invited me to join him and his aunt for dinner tomorrow which'll be nice. It won't be the same though. Christmas Day at home is always good fun, the blokes go to the pub whilst Mam cooks the dinner. Every year she tells them to get home by 2 o'clock and every year they roll in an hour late and by that time the girls have started on the sherry and Mam's always a bit drunk when they arrive. We miss my two brothers who joined up together and every year we raise a toast to pray they'll come home safe and be with us the next year.'

Celia hugged her friend. 'I'll be back for New Year's Eve, and we can have a party. With luck, this business with Edith will be sorted out and she'll be back.'

The door to the door opened and a handsome Flying Officer entered, smiling at Celia. 'Hello old girl, the matron up at the Hall said I'd find you in here. Don't tell me you've started celebrating already?'

Celia laughed. 'Oh Aubrey, you're early. We had to work this morning and called in for a quick one on our way home. Deirdre missed her train home yesterday, so she's stranded here for the duration; I thought a G&T would cheer her up.'

'I'll buy you both another one for the road then, and then we can go and collect your case.'

As he approached the bar, Deirdre commented, 'He's quite a catch, Celia, you want to snap him up before Brenda arrives. You know how fond she is of men in uniform.'

The phone in the bar rang and Jack emerged from the cellar to answer it, and after a few minutes he made an announcement to the regulars.

'That was Herbert on the phone, folks, George's been found safe and well,' to which they all cheered. 'But it looks as if our Edith has been up to no good, she's been arrested along with those two toffs who were staying here in the summer.'

Aubrey returned with the drinks looking puzzled and asked the girls what had been happening in the village. They filled him in with the news as far as they knew and Deirdre promised to ring Celia when she found out more.

Jack poured himself a pint and went over to join Joe and Lloyd Noble who was sitting in the corner. 'Have you two heard anything?'

Joe took a swig of his pint. 'We've not been told anything officially yet, I guess we'll have to wait for Herbert to get back. I'd be surprised if Edith has anything to do with the murder, I mean why would she? George was hinting that he knew something the other day in here when she was around but so was half the village.'

'Let's hope they've solved the mystery now and we can get back to normal. The men have been unsettled since the murder and it's affecting morale. It was a hard blow when Herman died. It's a dangerous job and the men accept that but murder is another matter,' Noble said.

CHAPTER 37

Christmas Eve, Cambridge Police Station

Edith sat in the holding cell at the Cambridge police station with her head in her hands; she was feeling ashamed and confused. Over the last few days, she had betrayed her friends and trusted two men who were planning to kill her to cover up their own actions. She didn't mean to kill James, and was shocked at her own behaviour, regretting the part she had played in the espionage. Resolving to do whatever she could to assist the authorities in tracing the other people involved in the spy ring, she was resigned to her own fate and prepared to accept the ultimate punishment. Since killing James she had hardly slept and found it increasingly difficult to carry on the subterfuge. She knew her carefree existence had gone forever. She had spent the night in the cell on an uncomfortable mattress and was unable to eat the breakfast they had provided.

The cell door opened and a uniformed officer escorted her to the interview room where Inspector Green and a distinguished-looking man wearing a pin-striped suit were waiting.

'Good morning, Miss Jones. I am Inspector Green from the Nottinghamshire Police Force and the gentleman next to me is Mr Brown from the War Office who will be observing the interview. You have been detained on suspicion of the murder of James Carmichael on the 5th December. I would like to ask you about your movements on that night. We know you were present at the darts match in the Barleycorn public house and left at closing time around 10.30pm. Could you tell me about your movements for the rest of that night?'

Edith looked tired and withdrawn. 'I would like to make a statement. I never meant to kill anyone.' She took out a handkerchief and blew her nose.

'Go on,' encouraged Green.

'My father was German and he was killed during the Great War, but I only found out about him and my German family after my mother died in 1924. I found my birth certificate amongst some papers when I was clearing out her flat. She had kept the truth from me all those years., I discovered that I was born in Germany and my birth name was Erika Schneider. I also realised I had a grandmother, my father's mother, still living in Potsdam near Berlin so I decided to visit her. She was so pleased to see me, she told me that I'd lived with her for the first three years of my life and begged my mother to leave me with her when she returned to England just before war broke out. After my father died, she thought she would never see me again.

'Whilst in Germany visiting my grandmother, I saw first-hand the devastation caused and the stringent measures imposed by the allies that decimated their economy. Hitler was seen as the saviour of Germany by the time I left in 1935 to study at university in Cambridge. I believe because of my background Marcus thought I'd be a willing recruit to his organisation. I know I wasn't the only undergraduate he groomed but he was careful to keep the identity of the others secret. I only knew about Frederick because he became my intermediary after I'd graduated. He felt it would raise less suspicion if I was to report to him rather than directly to Marcus.

'After graduation I applied for the Civil Service. Marcus gave me a good reference and I secured a post at the War Office, as a secretary to the Chairman of the Oil Control Board and that's when I learned about the operation in Dukes Wood. I reported back to Frederick and it was his idea for me to join the land army so I could keep an eye on the production.

'Things changed when I arrived in the village and began to make friends. I realised I didn't want to carry on and told Frederick I wanted out. That was when Marcus and Frederick turned up in the summer. I was shocked to see them. They threatened to expose me if I didn't find the information they wanted. I had to carry on but kept telling them the work was behind schedule and the production was being held up. I thought if I could send false reports saying the oil production was a failure, they would stop harassing me. I was a fly caught up in their spider's web and they said if I found out when the oil was going to be transported, they wouldn't ask me to do anything else. I suppose I was being naïve, but I believed them.

'After leaving the pub that night, I cycled along the footpath and stopped to get into the oil field, leaving my bike hidden in the hedgerow. Everyone was still in the pub as Jack was having a lock-in so I thought no one would be about and I could break into the site office and be back at home before anyone else left the pub. We all knew George was a lazy old sod and wouldn't bother to check the site once he got settled in his hut. As far as the locals were concerned the American crew were making a Hollywood film, which delighted the girls and made the local lads jealous. I thought it would be easy to break into the office, take some photographs of the schedules, and get them off my back. Anyway, when I'd reached the office, I was able to gain access easily. The door was locked but a window had been left open. As I was taking the photos, I heard a noise outside; someone was there and I started to panic. It all happened so quickly. I had taken my father's revolver with me, I don't know why but thought if I fired it in the air, it would scare them off and I could escape. But he came through the door and I hit him. I wasn't aiming it at him, you have to believe that. I was so scared; I just ran off and rode back to the hall. There was no one there when I got it so went straight to bed. When I found out the next day who I'd killed I felt so guilty. I knew if I was caught, I'd be executed so the next day I called Frederick and he said they would make arrangements for me to get back to Germany and to do nothing until the investigation died down.'

Green looked at his companion who asked if they could have a word in private. They left Edith alone in the room and he asked the sergeant to get her a cup of tea.

The man in the pin-striped suit was J.C. Masterman, an Oxford historian recruited by MI5 to chair the Twenty Committee with the responsibility for recruiting double agents. He had listened to Edith's confession with interest and spoke to Green in confidence.

'Inspector, I know this is unconventional but I think we could use that young lady in our organisation. I know she was carrying a weapon but I don't think she meant to kill anyone. We've also seized the roll of film she used to photograph the schedules and she deliberately exposed the negatives so no vital information would be passed to the other side. We've interrogated Johnson and Weber and they have refused to give us the names of their contacts. They, of course, will be prosecuted and punished accordingly, but with training Edith, or should I say Erika, could become an asset and help us expose the higher up operatives in the Cambridge spy ring.'

'But can you trust her?'

'I think so, I believe she was telling the truth in there. We can say she escaped in the confusion last night and I will take her to London to brief her. Alternatively, we could say she was a witness and has been put into witness protection for her own safety.'

Inspector Green agreed with Masterman's assessment of the situation and was relieved that Edith would escape the gallows. She had made a mistake and seemed to be truly sorry about her actions.

An hour later Green and Hopkins were back on the road to Eakring, and Hopkins was brought up to date with the events of the day.

'Sir, what are we going to tell the locals when we get back to the village? You know what a nosey lot they are.'

'I'll think of something, let's just pick up George from the hospital and get back to the pub to close down the incident room.'

CHAPTER 38

Christmas Eve, MI5 HQ London

'Would you like another cup of tea before we start?' enquired Masterman kindly.

'No thank you,' replied Edith. 'I don't think drinking tea will make me feel any better at the moment.'

'Quite, well let's get started. You do realise you are in serious trouble, young lady. Your two companions are busy declaring their innocence, blaming one another and intimating that you are the mastermind behind the spy ring at Cambridge.'

'What! That's not true. I'll admit my involvement but Marcus is the one who recruited me and has the links to Germany.'

'But without proof we only have your word against theirs. Perhaps you can start at the beginning and if you tell us all you can about the underground activities at Cambridge, it will go in your favour.'

Edith put her head in her hands and began to cry. Eventually she wiped her eyes and began to talk. 'I wish I'd never met them,' she said with raw emotion. 'I started my course in Cambridge in 1935, I was a little older than the other undergraduates as I'd been living in Germany with my grandmother. Hitler was gaining power at the time and *Großmutter* was concerned about the threat of another war. She wasn't a fan of the Third Reich and used to call Hitler a fanatical "jumped-up corporal" whose followers were a danger to the stability of the country. I witnessed first-hand the destruction in the country after the defeat they suffered following the Great War. Food was still scarce when I arrived in '25 and there was so much poverty and suffering in the country. People were starving and angry about the restrictions that had been placed on them by the allies. Hitler took advantage of the demoralised population and promised them salvation. He brainwashed ordinary Germans into thinking they were the *"superior race"* who needed to fight for their rightful place in the world. I think my *großmutter* was worried that I too was becoming brainwashed and that's why she encouraged me to return to England to continue my education.

'At university I enrolled on a subsidiary course for political science and Professor Johnson was my tutor. He seemed interested in my background and we often discussed my experiences living in Germany and the restrictions placed on the country by the allies. I guess I was flattered; being older than my contemporaries I didn't have many friends and Marcus seemed to value my opinions. It was just before I was completing my finals that he asked me to join his organisation. I'd heard rumours about it from other undergraduates but no one knew for sure if it really existed and, if it did, who were the key players. Most of the students thought it was fantasy but I now know he was grooming me with his attentions, and once I'd agreed there was no going back.'

Masterton listened with interest; he had heard it all before. Well-educated young people being groomed to join spy rings and before they realised the implications they had been sucked in, and, whenever the organisation was threatened, thrown to the wolves to save their own skins. He realised she was telling the truth in a straightforward narrative. She wasn't making excuses for her behaviour and seemed resigned to her fate.

'I have a proposition for you, Edith,' he said. 'You have vital information that can be used by the British Intelligence Services. If you agree to co-operate with us, we can overlook any crimes you may have committed. We found the roll of film you were carrying and I'm assuming it was you who exposed the negatives to render it useless. Am I correct?'

'Yes, I don't know why I didn't destroy it earlier, but they were expecting me to pass it on to them. I was frightened and felt so conflicted. I wanted so badly to go back to Berlin to see my *großmutter* and believed it when they told me they had found an escape route. I didn't mean to kill James that night, I just panicked when he came into the office and fired the gun in the air to frighten him off. I thought if he ran out, I could follow him out and disappear in the woods.'

'The forensic evidence at the scene backs up your story. If prosecuted you would be able to plead manslaughter but it would still lead to a lengthy sentence. What I'm offering you is immunity from prosecution if you work with us to uncover the other people involved in the Cambridge spy ring, not just the "cannon fodder" like yourself but those higher up in the organisation so we can close it down before it does lasting damage to our country. You don't have to answer straight away, think it through and we'll talk again later.' With that, he left the room and Edith to her thoughts.

CHAPTER 39

Christmas Eve 1943, Eakring

The bar at the Barleycorn started to fill up in the early evening on Christmas Eve. Word had spread throughout the village during the afternoon that the murder had been solved and curious locals were gathering to find out the latest news about the arrests.

Billy picked up Deirdre from the Hall and together they walked to the village making plans for their wedding. He had wasted no time, calling at the vicarage to see Reverend Sykes in the afternoon to set a date for the nuptials in January. The banns were to be read the first Sunday after Christmas for three consecutive weeks, and Billy joked that she couldn't back out now or he'd have her for breach of promise. Deirdre laughed and she had no plans for that now she had got her claws into him. She had already phoned her dad's local pub in Liverpool to speak to him to let him know she wouldn't be home for Christmas and to pass on her news. She knew they would be confused about the identity of her fiancé but would understand when she had the chance to relay the whole story.

At the bar Jack was preparing for a busy night when Vera came through from the kitchen with plates of sandwiches for their customers. 'I'm expecting quite a crowd tonight,' he told her. 'You know what they're like around here, they'll be coming in in droves to catch up on the latest gossip.'

'It may be just gossip to that lot but what will people think of us? If it's true that Edith's involved in the murder up at the Wood, they may think we've also had something to do with it,' she said with a worried frown on her face.

'Don't be daft, old gel, just because she's been out with our Arthur a few times they won't think we're involved. Anyway, it's good for business. If it continues like this much longer, we'll be able to retire to Mablethorpe on the profits before the wars over,' he replied, laughing.

The door opened to admit more arrivals, amongst them Frank and Dorothy from Thistle Cottage. Dorothy looked around nervously; it was the first time she had been into the pub and wasn't sure what to expect. Deirdre caught her eye and waved her over to sit with them.

'Come and sit over here, Mrs Stevenson,' she called, 'there's some spare seats and I could do with some female company. Both of me mates have gone and left me to the mercies of this lot,' she laughed.

Dorothy looked relieved to have been invited over and sat down next to Deirdre whilst Frank ordered the drinks. The two women started to get to know one another better. Since the news of the arrests any suspicions about the Stevensons was forgotten and Deirdre was keen to find out what they knew about the night of the murder. Living so close to Dukes Wood they were in a prime position to watch the comings and goings. That night the two women began forging a lasting friendship.

A little later some of the Yanks walked to the pub, bringing along their musical instruments ready to entertain the audience. They gathered next to the fireplace and began tuning up ready for the sing-song and were pleased when Jack sent over a free drink for the musicians. The atmosphere in the village had improved as people stopped suspecting one another, relieved that the culprits had been uncovered and it put an end to the speculations that had circulated over the past few weeks. Some of them, like the Arkwrights and Deirdre, still felt that Edith had been caught up in the drama by mistake and would be back with them in the new year.

By 9 o'clock the public bar was full and people were mingling and chatting easily with one another. The Yanks had been accepted by the locals as over the past few months friendships had been formed and consolidated as they got to know one another. The monks at Kelham Hall were busy preparing a good old-fashioned traditional English Christmas, one they hoped their American visitors would remember with fondness despite the circumstances that had brought them to this sleepy English village. The roughnecks, following the example of their leader, Noble, remained respectful when at the Hall but were happy to let their hair down when visiting the local hostelry and enjoy the hospitality of the landlord and his wife.

It had been a long and difficult year and it remained important for the Yanks to stick to their cover story, although by tacit agreement between them and the locals, some of whom suspected the real reason for their presence in the village, no questions were asked or answered. The oil production on the site was a great success and crude oil was transported in the middle of the night, with convoys skirting around the village to avert suspicion from the locals and cause least disruption to village life. Christmas had brought a brief respite and everyone was determined to enjoy their evening. The music started up and the spontaneous musicians played a selection of country music songs and rousing wartime favourites and as the evening came to a close Deirdre whispered in Billy's ear, 'I will never forget this night. A few days ago I was convinced my life was over and you came to my rescue.'

Just as Jack was ringing the bell to call for last orders, the door opened, blasting in a flurry of snow along with Hopkins and Green with George bringing up the rear. Their entrance heralded a round of cheers from the assembled regulars. 'Three pints please, Jack,' said Green. 'We've had a long journey, and I'm just about spitting feathers.'

Jack, mindful of his licence and the close shave he had earlier in the year, replied, 'I'm sorry, gents, I wish I could oblige but I've just called time and by law I'm not allowed to serve you, I could lose me licence.'

'Don't be silly, man,' replied Green. 'It's not the first time there's been a lock-in and it is Christmas Eve. I'm sure Constable Hopkins will be able to turn a blind eye.'

CHAPTER 40

1991, Dukes Wood

Deirdre and Billy sat together in the snug bar at the Barleycorn. Their daughter, Celia, who was waiting for their drinks order at the bar, looked fondly over towards her parents as she chatted to the landlord. Deirdre was still a pretty woman with snow-white hair swept up in a messy bun. Her blue eyes, turned milky with age, sparkled as she talked animatedly about the imminent arrival of the Yanks. It was obvious to anyone who saw them together that they were a devoted couple; married now for nearly 50 years, they never tired of each other's company and Deirdre had come to love and respect her kind and lovable husband. Retired now from the local school where he had been the headmaster for the last 10 years of his working life, Billy had watched local kids grow up to become parents themselves, and more recently grandparents.

After the war ended Deirdre stayed on at Arkwright's farm to help with the bookkeeping for their eldest son, George, who took over the tenancy and built up the business following his demob from the Army. She was an active member of the Eakring Women's Guild and was instrumental in the provision of the refreshments at the Church Hall, baking cakes for the visitors who were coming to the village to see the unveiling of the 7 ft bronze oil patch warrior statue in Dukes Wood.

Celia, their daughter, was tall and slim, with blonde hair and blue eyes and people often remarked that she took after her father Billy, which gave both of them such pleasure. Although her parents told her of her origins and the events leading up to her birth, she had no desire to seek out her birth father's roots in the USA. Billy was her dad and he had always been there to love and protect her; he was there to share her success when she graduated from the Bishop Grosseteste Teacher Training College in nearby Lincoln and followed in his footsteps to become a teacher, working in a challenging school in a deprived area of Nottingham. She was curious to meet the roughnecks who were on their way to the village but had no desire to hurt the feelings of the only father she knew and loved.

'I wish Celia and Edith could be here today,' said Deirdre. 'We never did find out what happened to Edith after she was arrested. I wonder if she's still alive today and living in Germany.'

'If she is, old love, she'll be over by 80 now. She was a lot older than you, my spring chicken,' replied Billy, fondly reaching out to comfort his wife. She was also thinking of her friend Celia who had died a few years ago, succumbing to breast cancer. After the war she had married Aubrey in a lavish ceremony. Deirdre still remembered how beautiful she had looked on her wedding day, walking down the aisle on her father's arm, with her brother Richard, who had survived the deprivations of the prison camp, acting as his friend's best man. She smiled at the memory of how welcoming Celia's mother was when she met Deirdre. The war had certainly broken down the class barriers, the girl from the slums of Liverpool mixing with high society in London and being warmly accepted as an equal by Celia's parents, Lord and Lady Fenwick. Their friendship had survived the war years, and when time allowed, they met up to reminisce about the years they spent working together during the war. When Deirdre gave birth to her daughter in 1944, she named her after Celia and asked her old friend to be her Godmother. A role she relished and, unable to have children of her own, she had doted on the child.

Life in the village had changed little over the years. Old Joe died not long after the war, after refusing Noble's offer of a job in America. Jack and Vera never got to own the select hotel of Vera's dreams but stayed on at the pub until they retired. Their son Arthur married a local girl after the war and moved to Nottingham.

The gang from Nottingham responsible for the sheep stealing were caught by Herbert later in the war, although Jack's involvement in receiving stolen goods was brushed under the carpet. After all, half the village had sampled the lamb that Vera had cooked on special occasions so they could all have been convicted of aiding and abetting.

After the arrest and conviction of the two Dons from Cambridge for treason, Inspector Green was promoted and retired as the war came to an end. He moved to Skegness with his wife Sarah, the matron from Kelham Hall. Herbert was also promoted and ended up as the Custody Sergeant at the Newark Police Station, still seeking out a quiet life.

Village life continued at its own pace and old-timers spent many nights in the public bar at the Barleycorn, exaggerating the part they played in the secret activities in Dukes Wood. The oil field was finally decommissioned in 1966 but the story of the Roughnecks of Sherwood lived on and now people were gathering for the reunion between the Yanks and locals who formed a lasting bond.

The door opened and a man entered the bar and scanned the room seeking out a friendly face, and he was accompanied by a tall, elegant woman in her early 60s. When the man saw Billy and Deirdre sitting in the corner, he crossed the room to say hello. Billy looked up from his pint and smiled broadly.

'Well bogger me, if it ain't Herbert Hopkins,' he said, standing to shake hands with the new arrival.

'Hello Billy, how are you? Long time, no see,' replied Hopkins.

Deirdre, who also recognised Herbert jumped up to give him a hug. 'Hello, what a lovely surprise. I heard you'd moved away to the big city.'

Herbert laughed. 'Only back to Nottingham. Let me introduce you to me wife,' he said, turning to his companion. 'This is Val.'

Val was an attractive woman with an infectious smile. She quickly made friends with Deirdre by asking her about Herbert's time as the village bobby. She had never been to Eakring before so insisted her husband treat her to a guided tour of the village before returning to Nottingham after the ceremony.

As they were all renewing their acquaintances and welcoming old friends to the village, a coach drew up outside the bar and 14 surviving oil workers from the USA trooped inside, laughing and greeting the welcome committee. The reunion was tinged with regret. Lloyd Noble had died in 1950; the charismatic leader whose vision and determination had led the volunteers from Oklahoma on a secret mission that quite possibly turned the tide of the war and contributed to the ultimate success of the allies, was absent along with many others who had quietly left when their year-long mission was over. Those who returned were determined to drink to the health of their comrades and the friendships formed in those dark days.

Later in the afternoon the party decamped to Dukes Wood. The oil rigs were long gone but not the memories. When the unveiling ceremony of the oil patch warrior ended and the revellers returned to the village to continue the celebrations, Deirdre stayed behind. She'd asked Billy to go with the others as she wanted a few moments alone with her memories.

As twilight began to darken the sky Deirdre stood alone thinking about her absent friends.

'Penny for them.' A voice from behind broke into her thoughts. She turned around to see a smartly dressed elderly lady resting on a walking stick.

'Hello Edith, I was hoping you'd come.' The two friends separated by the years smiled at one another.

Edith stepped forward with difficulty to get a better view of the statue.

'I wasn't sure what sort of welcome I'd get so I kept out of sight until the others left. I wanted to try and explain many times but I guess I'm a coward. I never meant to hurt anyone.'

'Water under the bridge, my friend. Celia and I often spoke about you. She's dead now, she had breast cancer and fought so hard right up until the end but it wasn't to be. She's at rest now.'

'Did she marry that dashing airman, what was his name?'

'Aubrey, and yes she did. They couldn't have children but she doted on my daughter. She was over the moon when I named her Celia Edith in honour of the two best friends a girl could ever have. Billy and I married just after... well, no need to dwell on the past. What about you, did you make it to Germany?'

Edith laughed. 'No. I never did. I stayed in London. I shouldn't be telling you this, but you have a right to know. I went to work for MI5. I found out my grandmother had been killed early in the war. She was half Jewish and the Nazis seized her property and sent her to Auschwitz in 1939. The "spy master" who recruited me knew all along but kept it from me. In the end I never gave away any secrets. I've tried to make amends for my behaviour over the years. I have so many wonderful memories of my time here. Living with you and Celia up at the Hall was the happiest time of my life. I was so ashamed of myself but things had gone too far and I couldn't escape. I was glad when we were caught and quite prepared for whatever punishment was due to me. The inspector offered me a lifeline and I was grateful to accept it. In the end I realised where my loyalties lie.'

'Inspector Green married our matron just after the war. They asked Celia and I to be bridesmaids. We were so pleased for her, and she looked lovely on the day.'

'So, it was a happy ending for her. It was a long hard war for everyone and she did so much for us when we lived at Kelham,' said Edith.

'It feels like another world now. I've been happy with Billy; I remember you telling me he was the one for me. He came to my rescue, you know, I was pregnant with James' child, and Billy promised to look after us both, and he has. I've been lucky, he's been a good husband and father to Celia.'

'I'm glad. I thought about writing to you after the war but I had no idea how to find you. I didn't mean to kill James; it was an accident, you know. I panicked and thought if I fired the gun in the air, he would run away, but it ricocheted off the wall. All these years there hasn't been a day go by when I've not been consumed by guilt. Not for him, he was already married and leading you on, but for you as I knew how much you loved him.'

Deirdre walked over towards her long-lost friend and gave her a hug.

'Are you coming back to the pub for a drink for old time's sake?' she asked.

'I don't think so, he was one of them and I guess they'll be mourning his passing today. He wasn't a bad man, a bit on the wild side but he didn't deserve that fate. My son is parked at the entrance and I need to get back home. It's been lovely seeing you again, Deirdre, please don't think too badly of me. I know it's no consolation for what I've done but I have truly regretted my actions and tried to make up for them ever since. Goodbye, my dear friend.'

Deirdre watched her old friend walk slowing and painfully down the overgrown driveway to the waiting car.

THE END

EPILOGUE

Dukes Wood Oil Field

In May 1991, the Noble Drilling Corporation funded the return of 14 surviving oilmen to the dedication of a 7ft bronze oil patch warrior statue in Sherwood Forest. The statue was placed in the grounds of England's Dukes Wood Oil Museum on land donated by British Petroleum. The statue was later moved and now stands in the grounds of Rufford Abbey.

The English Project contract was complete in March 1944 and by the end of the war more than 3.5 million barrels of crude oil had been pumped out of the ground from England's 'unsinkable tanker' oilfields.

Of the 42 volunteers who came to Britain from America to undertake this contract, all returned with the sad exception of 29-year-old Herman Douthit, who died in a tragic accident when he fell 55 feet from a derrick platform. He is buried at the American military cemetery in Cambridge, England. The only civilian buried at the cemetery, at Plot C, Row S. Grave 2.

ABOUT THE AUTHOR

Linda has had a keen interest in social history since studying for her MA in Modern Social History at University. She is fascinated by the way historical events impact on the lives of ordinary people and enjoys using the backdrop of real-life events into her fiction writing.

She lives in Nottingham with her husband Geoff and elderly cat, Plato.

Printed in Great Britain
by Amazon

18781883R00139